A NEW DOCTOR AT ORCHARD COTTAGE HOSPITAL

LIZZIE LANE

Boldwood

First published in Great Britain in 2024 by Boldwood Books Ltd.

Copyright © Lizzie Lane, 2024

Cover Design by Colin Thomas

Cover Photography: Alamy

The moral right of Lizzie Lane to be identified as the author of this work has been asserted in accordance with the Copyright, Designs and Patents Act 1988.

Every effort has been made to obtain the necessary permissions with reference to copyright material, both illustrative and quoted. We apologise for any omissions in this respect and will be pleased to make the appropriate acknowledgements in any future edition.

A CIP catalogue record for this book is available from the British Library.

Paperback ISBN 978-1-80483-426-8

Large Print ISBN 978-1-80483-425-1

Hardback ISBN 978-1-80483-427-5

Ebook ISBN 978-1-80483-424-4

Kindle ISBN 978-1-80483-422-0

Audio CD ISBN 978-1-80483-432-9

MP3 CD ISBN 978-1-80483-431-2

Digital audio download ISBN 978-1-80483-430-5

Boldwood Books Ltd
23 Bowerdean Street
London SW6 3TN
www.boldwoodbooks.com

PROLOGUE
ALL SAINTS WORKHOUSE, WHITECHAPEL, LONDON

March 1900

The workhouse was clean enough but cold and stark. Six babies wearing labels stating date of birth, girl or boy, lay on a double mattress. Each was swaddled in the old-fashioned way, a blanket preventing unnecessary movement. Only their crumpled faces showed and they were quite silent, eyes closed and oblivious or even uncaring of the world they'd entered.

Mr Timms, the workhouse manager, was polite but wary of Miss Brakespeare, the formidable-looking woman he'd brought into the baby unit. A blue-stocking type, he thought, unfeminine and with a strong disposition. Not exactly upper crust but of independent means. Such women were a world away from workhouse inmates. Such women had little deference for either his gender or his position which made him nervous.

He waved a plump hand as a fishmonger might over the latest catch of the day.

'There you are, Miss Brakespeare,' he said. He wore his

humility like a Sunday coat – for show only and put away on week-days. 'Just six. Isn't that right, Matron?'

The matron was a wide woman with a swarthy complexion. She wore a dark blue uniform that set her apart from lesser staff who wore grey.

Matron had been forewarned of this visit and was ready to comply with whatever transpired.

'Yes, Mr Timms. Just six today for madam to choose from provided the right paperwork has been signed.'

The cigarette at the corner of her mouth jiggled as she spoke.

Isabelle Brakespeare – Izzy to her friends – regarded the smoking woman with contempt. 'Everything has been signed that needed to be signed.' Her tone of voice and general demeanour discouraged challenge.

She glided around the mattress platform looking at the living detritus of the failed lives of young girls without the means to support their unfortunate offspring.

'Which one is Mary Baker's baby?'

The two workhouse officials exchanged looks. They hadn't expected her to select a specific name and thus a specific baby.

'Well? Which one is it? Speak up.'

A baby responded to the sound of her voice and for a moment she anticipated its eyes opening and being as blue as the ones Mary Baker had flashed at the wrong man without realising what the consequences would be.

Mr Timms hovered by the door whilst the workhouse matron picked up the small bundle that had stirred whilst the rest slept on.

'This is her,' she said after glancing at the label. 'Baby Baker.'

Miss Isabelle Brakespeare, a thirty-five-year-old spinster of sound means and good pedigree had made her decision when she'd found out where Mary had ended up pregnant and alone. A cold feeling coursed through her but not once did she reconsider what she was about to do. Adopt a baby girl. Mary Baker's baby who would become her baby and replace the one that had been taken away from her, the one the family pretended had never existed.

This child would be encouraged to be as independent as she was. She would make her strong, teach her to fear no one and to be whatever she wanted to be. Izzy's greatest desire had been to be a doctor. Perhaps this baby could be encouraged to follow that path, not that she would push. But she would support her in any path she wanted to take. She owed it to her, to herself and to the baby's mother.

Barely out of childhood, her dreams had been cruelly destroyed by a member of her own family and she'd been the one blamed, the strong-minded coquettish one who climbed trees like a boy and rode horses like a man and was the apple of her father's eye – too much so as it worked out. He'd blamed her for what had happened, but over time she'd hardened to the accusations, hardened to the heartache he'd imposed on her – and on others.

'Lovely little thing,' said the matron dragging Isabelle's thoughts back to the present. 'Being an orphan she doesn't have a Christian name. But there, I expect you'd like to name her yourself.'

'Her name will be Frances Isabelle Brakespeare.' She pointed a rigid finger at the ledger lying open on the matron's desk beside a packet of Wills' Woodbines. 'Write it down. Now.'

A nervous-looking Mr Timms did as he was ordered.

After both baby and guardian had departed, Matron and Mr Timms shared a self-satisfied moment smoking cigarettes and sipping neat gin.

Mr Timms blew a pall of cigarette smoke towards where only

five babies now slept quietly until their next feed and a little tincture of laudanum – 'baby comfort' as they called it.

'You told her the baby was an orphan. I thought the mother
said she'd be back for her baby,' said an amused Mr Timms.

Matron pursed her lips and sent a cloud of smoke over the
sleeping babies. 'They all say that. But they never do.'

1

LONDON – FEBRUARY 1930

For what must have been the tenth, twelfth or even twentieth time, Frances Brakespeare sat in the familiar front room at number twenty-six Ambrose Villas in Carwell Street, where she'd grown up a happy child, rereading the letter from a firm of solicitors, Messrs Kendrick, Meredith and Flint.

Dear Miss Brakespeare...

Frances winced and muttered to herself. 'Doctor. I'm a doctor. Is it too much to ask you to address me properly?'

Likely the man who had written this letter wasn't ignorant of the fact. As solicitor to Miss Isabelle Frances Brakespeare, the woman who had fetched her from a workhouse and brought her up, he must have known. But that was the way it was. There were less than two-thousand female doctors. Men were and always had been in the ascendant.

Having regained her composure she went on reading.

Relating to the recent death of Miss Isabelle Frances Brakespeare and having had communication with the family, we are
obliged to give you notice to quit the property at twenty-six
Ambrose Villas by the end of January this year, 1930. As has
already been outlined to you by Miss Isabelle's sister, Mrs Beatrice Trinder, the property was owned by their father and only
bequeathed to Miss Isabelle for her lifetime. Consequently,
ownership of the property now reverts to the immediate family,
that is, blood relatives. I understand that although you carry the
name Brakespeare it was given you by Miss Isabelle Brakespeare when she adopted you. However, the terms of the will of
Mr Forsythe Brakespeare clearly stipulate *that residence of
Twenty-six Carwell Street was only granted for the period of his
daughter's life. Therefore...*

Frances laid her aching head against the backrest of the chair
and closed her eyes. No matter how often she read the legal
terminology there was no getting around the fact that she was
homeless. There was a short-term facility available at the hospital
but restricted to male doctors only. Not that she wanted to stay.
Not without Miss Izzy, the woman who had balked at being
called aunt. As a child, Frances had had difficulty calling her
Isabelle so they'd settled on her calling her Miss Izzy, which had
rolled easily off and around the child's tongue. Later it had short-
ened to Izzy.

Never had she queried the identity of her natural mother. Izzy
had contented her with the explanation that she'd gone along to
the workhouse and chosen her above all others. It was enough to
feel privileged and chosen from several abandoned babies and
thus strive to prove herself worthy, to want to be whatever her
benefactress wanted her to be.

A vision of Izzy vibrant and alive lit up in Frances's head.

'I am a woman but will not be restricted by accepted form. I'm too young and wild to be called Auntie – by anyone!'

Frances smiled as she looked around the room at the gaily coloured cushions, the copper art deco picture rail running around the wall just below ceiling height, the manicured wood mimicking an Elizabethan past but modern and of a style that was fast coming into its own.

Memories have seeped into these walls, she thought as her eyes swept the room but stalled on the collection of silver-framed photographs ranged along the top of the piano, their shiny outlines reflected in its ebony black wood.

Pride of place was a frame containing photographs of Frances at various ages, including one taken on the day she'd finally graduated as a doctor.

Commendable, she thought. Izzy had said it was commendable that eight years after the end of the war she'd passed her final exam. The war had first been viewed as an aid to her getting into medical school. The killing fields of northern France were crying out for nurses and doctors, neither of which she was trained for back then. Young as she was, barely eighteen in 1917, she'd been taken on by the Voluntary Aid Detachment. Yes, it was bound to help her get entry into medical school with a view to becoming a doctor. Perhaps aware of her ward's yearning to prove herself and fall in with the future she'd planned for her, Izzy hadn't considered that Frances would be surrounded by handsome men in uniform, that she might indeed fall in love with one – which is exactly what had happened.

After meeting Ralph, the idea of becoming a wife and mother as opposed to a doctor took root. When she found out, Izzy was furious.

'You would throw all your hard work away for the sake of a man?' Izzy had been beside herself, at first only in letters but also when Frances had come home on leave and attempted to explain how she felt, that her emotions had kidnapped her heart and that Ralph was the love of her life.

'And we're getting married once the war is over.' She was being brave saying it but knew she was head over heels in love. Suddenly becoming a doctor didn't matter so much.

Izzy showed her hostility by not writing, or not speaking on the rare occasions when Frances did come home.

Brooding silences also led to deep thoughts, for instance Frances suddenly became aware that men rarely crossed the threshold of the house in Carwell Street. It had been a house of women, Miss Izzy's friends, some of whom she'd met back in the days when women were fighting for the right to vote.

'Don't be taken in by the sweet words of men only out for their own ends. Be the woman you were meant to be not the one they want you to be.'

Her warnings made no difference to Frances. Her mind was made up.

Amid war Frances found herself feeling happier than she'd ever felt in her life. She and Ralph made love in summer fields of dried corn and drank sweet red wine from unlabelled bottles. Love blinded them to the distant sound of guns, too far away to worry them, but consistent, ever present.

Despite the war they held on to what they had, talking of the future, how many children they would have, where they would live, what kind of house and how many roses they'd grow in the garden.

She was on duty the night when the news came. Even now she couldn't quite recollect who told her and how she'd reacted. A sense of numbness had set in and although life went on around her she participated in it in the stiff mechanical way like something made of clockwork, wound up and gradually winding down.

Working through it without feeling. Without caring about what was happening around her.

It happened just two months before the war was over. She'd not written to tell Izzy but on arrival back home found she didn't need to. Izzy saw the look on her face and promptly enveloped her in loving arms, sweet words of comfort whispered against her hair.

Izzy's stiffness had softened. She had become her confidante, her shoulder to cry on, a willing listener as she'd poured out her heart. Patiently and kindly she'd allowed her to grieve, but in time had renewed her efforts to get Frances into medical school.

'You know what war is about. You've done more than stroke a fevered brow. The time has come to be serious about medicine.'

Izzy held tea parties where sherry and French wines were provided for women who smoked and drank more moderately than gentlemen but not without enthusiasm.

Whilst war had raged these same women had wound bandages, served in hospitals and factories and knitted hundreds of socks and mittens and were now attired in flowered fabrics that floated around their newly exposed ankles. They chattered and laughed just as they always had yet somehow, perhaps because they were older, or wiser in the ways of war and deprivation, their joy sounded more brittle than it once had.

Deborah Goldman, Izzy's closest friend, confided that it had always been Izzy's dearest wish to become a doctor. 'But it was not to be,' she'd said sadly. 'Things happened. Family things. Dark things.'

Frances detected a shudder.

'I don't know much about her family. I've never been introduced to them.'

'Forget I mentioned them,' said Deborah with a dismissive wave of her hand and looking regretful that she'd mentioned it at all. 'It's all in the past.'

In the absence of the love of her life Frances resumed fulfilling the future Izzy craved for her, throwing herself into studying and gaining the very best marks she could – sometimes beating the top men in her year – because in the absence of Ralph it was medicine that mattered. Still she was marked down. Other 'lady' doctors reported the same treatment.

Tucking Ralph's photograph beneath her arm, she took it upstairs with her to bed, set it on the bedside table and gave the cold glass a kiss before she turned in.

The bed felt colder than she'd ever known it. Her toes wriggled in an effort to keep warm and the letter from the solicitor for Izzy's family weighed heavily on her mind.

For a while she lay awake staring into the darkness until finally she threw back the bedclothes and went downstairs. A hot water bottle would settle her toes and hopefully her jumbled thoughts would follow.

Before heading back through the house and up the stairs she paused outside the study where Miss Izzy used to entertain her female friends over shots of sherry and French cigarettes, the smell of those days lingering in the air. The past and present collided in the quiet shadows of the room where women had debated the issues of the day with the same confidence as some women would wear a new hat.

Gathered, they had presented a formidable force to the world. Would they be the same now without Miss Isabelle Brakespeare?

Papers had been cleared out from the top portion of the roll top desk, an American beast of a thing that Izzy insisted had once belonged to President Theodore Roosevelt.

'He used to shoot bears,' she'd declared and sounded as though she was considering doing the same herself.

The papers had been cleared out by Izzy's sister, Mrs Beatrice Trinder, presumably taken to the solicitors acting for the estate –

not that Beatrice had told her so. In fact she'd hardly acknowl-edged her at all but blown into the house, brushing Frances aside except to ask where Izzy had kept her legal documents. Disdain was written all over her face. How dare her sister be the woman she'd been. How dare she take a lower-class creature from the workhouse and raise her to be a proxy version of herself.

When Frances had remarked that the lower drawers contained mainly books and political pamphlets Beatrice had favoured her with a scowl and declared that such things were the prerogative of unnatural women and should be burned. Beatrice was easy to dislike.

Now, in the middle of the night and on a whim to preserve Miss Izzy's memory, if only in a small way, she dragged open each of the bottom drawers. There were pamphlets, books and diaries from years back and no time to sort through them now. But she couldn't throw them away. In time she would go through them but for now she bundled them into a carpet bag of green and blue birds, snapped the clasp shut and put it with the rest of her things – for onwards transit to her new home – wherever that might be.

2

Getting behind the steering wheel of her little Austin Seven was reassuringly familiar, part of her past – a present given her by Izzy when she'd passed her finals and could call herself a doctor.

'A doctor needs a car. I insist.'

She smiled at the memory of how they'd both laughed when Frances had christened the car Molly after the matron on the men's ward, who could be nice as pie one minute and as contrary as you like the next.

Like my life, she thought, her spirits dampened as the prospect of finding somewhere to live took her thoughts by the scruff of the neck.

She consoled herself that she still had a position at the hospital. It didn't pay well and every time a better position came up she was not the one chosen for promotion. So far she'd accepted the situation with resignation. After all, male doctors had families to provide for. But times had changed, and convinced she would remain a spinster, her hunger to succeed had intensified, plus she now needed funds to pay rent for accommodation. This job was all she had, that and her car. Finding somewhere else to live was achievable – so long as she had a steady income – although Deborah had offered her a room on a temporary basis.

As the grey stone facade of St Aldelm's Hospital came into view, she pushed her concerns to the back of her mind took a deep breath and made her way into the entrance hall and along the oak-panelled corridors to the doctors' common room. The doctors had their own cloakroom adjacent to the common room, which had the air of a gentlemen's club, with its masculine chairs, polished wooden floor and tobacco ash spilling out from ceramic ashtrays.

There were two other women doctors at the hospital. One of them had won a prize for medicine and was therefore deemed a great asset, so unassailable by the male establishment and had her own facility close to the laboratories. The other was engaged and would shortly leave to get married, having already given notice. The shared 'lady doctors' dressing facility had been requisitioned for other purposes.

'Golf clubs,' Edwina, the doctor who was leaving to get married, had said. 'Senior staff only.'

They'd made promises to keep in touch. Edwina was moving to Portsmouth with her new husband, a naval officer.

'Do write,' said Edwina.

'Of course I will.'

It left Frances obliged to share a cloakroom with the nursing fraternity. Not that she minded. Their bright smiles and chatter about sweethearts, family and what they'd seen at the pictures last night brightened her day. On occasion, she'd accepted their invitation to accompany them on a night out – though only when they didn't have a date with a young man who just might drag them away from nursing and up the aisle.

'I went out with Doctor Oliver last night,' one of the nurses confided. Suddenly realising she shouldn't have said it, she slapped a hand over her mouth. Nurses were not supposed to fraternise with doctors or anyone else on the hospital staff. 'You won't tell will you,' she implored.

'I'd sooner be boiled in oil than betray your confidence,' Frances reassured her.

'You're a good egg, Doctor Brakespeare. Not snooty at all. Just like one of us.'

Leaving the cheery atmosphere behind her, she made her way to the doctors' common room with gut-wrenching apprehension. A doctor smoking a cigarette nodded a silent greeting. Another ducked down behind his newspaper and the third looked her up and down as if he could see through her clothes. *Nothing unusual there*, she thought. He did the same to every female member of staff.

Behind her, a porter tipped the contents of the overfull ashtrays into a metal bin, wiped them clean and put them back where they belonged.

Once that was done, he threw open the windows to let in the fresh air. The shouts of street sellers and costermongers bawled inwards, along with the drift of muslin curtain. She found the smell preferable to the pungent stench of spent tobacco.

Before the porter left, she asked softly, and out of the earshot of everyone else, after the health of his wife.

'Much better,' he assured her. 'I can afford to get her a few treats since I got this job – thanks to you, Doctor. I'll always be grateful for what you did.'

She waved away his thanks. He'd been a young man with a family when she'd come across him being set upon by a couple of equally young men of good family pushing him around. She'd intervened and after giving them a piece of her mind helped him home. He'd sought her out when he'd lost his job and asked if he could mow the lawn or cut the hedges – if she had a garden that is. With Izzy's help, she'd done better than that. When the vacancy had arisen for a porter, she'd put his name forward and he'd got the job.

Her eyes scoured the doctors' rota pinned onto the back of the door in disbelief. The only slot she had for that day was in the infection unit, assisting a doctor who did not deserve to be promoted above her but knew there was nothing she could say or do about it. The dice were loaded in favour of men. 'One day,' she muttered to herself. 'One day.'

Steeling herself to the task, she headed for the infection unit, gritting her teeth and asking herself just how long she could put up with being overlooked. Having seen infection at proximity in the East End of London, she donned a mask before entering the ward.

Doctor Richard Mardon was in the company of a coterie of third-year students who were hanging on his every word.

His eyes narrowed and his jaw clenched when he saw her approaching wearing a face mask. His superior gaze swept from her to the enthralled students in their white coats with their slicked back hair and air of male supremacy. A contemptuous smile twisted his mouth.

'This is the infection unit, not the operating theatre, Doctor Brakespeare. Were you thinking to remove someone's growth, sew up a gut or amputate a leg?'

His sarcasm brought a tinkling of nervous laughter from the students.

Half her face was hidden by the mask so he couldn't see that her look of contempt matched his.

'TB has no respect for members of the medical profession.'

'This is not a facility for the severely at-risk consumptives, Doctor.'

She couldn't hold it back. 'A little germ goes a long way, as you would know if you'd seen it close up as I have.'

'Ah! Fighting talk. Doctor Brakespeare's claim to fame is having served on the Western Front. With the Voluntary Aid Detachment. Not as a doctor, of course. That would have been too difficult – for a woman.'

'How would you know, Doctor Mardon? You, who were safely at home pleading a bad chest. And here you are in the infection unit. You need to be more careful.'

The tinkling laughter faded and Doctor Mardon's angry expression was a sight to behold.

'Get out of my sight, woman. Your presence is no longer required.'

Boiling with indignation she was already marching from the ward, his words ringing at her back.

Tearing off her mask, she headed to where a few of her nursing friends were making tea. On seeing her angry expression, they didn't hesitate to press a cup into her hands.

'Doctor Mardon being nasty again?'

'I can usually cope with it, but what with everything else...'

She didn't elaborate on her loss and impending homelessness but did express how she was feeling.

'I feel I could do with something stronger,' she said grimly.

'Not taking any sugar might help,' said Olive Haines, a girl from up north who had a cheery face and wide hips. The sugar tongs paused above the basin.

'Two,' said Frances. 'No. Make it three.'

Nurse Haines looked concerned. 'Did you give him a piece of your mind?'

Frances sipped at her tea. She knew very well that she'd insulted Doctor Mardon. Men did not like reminding that they'd not served their country even this long after the war.

'One could say that I served him the white feather – in a manner of speaking – and in front of a group of juniors.'

Nurse Haines pulled a face. 'Oh dear. He'll want an apology.'

Frances exchanged a knowing look with Nurse Haines and the others.

'You and I both know what that could mean. Called into his office and forced to eat humble pie before I'm allowed back on the wards.'

'And more,' added one of the younger nurses. 'That man can't keep his hands to himself at times.'

Frances shook her head. 'Certainly not when he's got you alone. I will not allow that to happen. I'd leave rather than say I'm sorry.'

'Let's hope it doesn't come to that.' Nurse Haines shook her head. 'I don't know how you as a doctor put up with it.'

'Because I have to,' returned Frances. The London Free Hospital was open-minded about female doctors but they were in the minority. St Aldelm's, founded by some old Etonian surgeon who'd prided himself on quick amputations and a tot of rum to relieve the pain, did so only begrudgingly.

The day wore on. No request arrived ordering her back to the infection unit but she did manage to fit in one or two emergencies on the geriatric wards and another in the maternity ward where her expertise and careful handling of the mother was most appreciated.

Senior medical staff ignored her. Those doctors on the same level as her pretended to be otherwise engaged with bits of paper or the need to attend to an urgent telephone call. Did they know something she didn't? Had word gone round that she'd upset a senior doctor and that he'd complained to his superiors, one of whom happened to be his uncle?

Frances, you're burning bridges at a rate of knots, she said to herself.

At a loose end, she headed for the hospital library, looking for the most modern books on various aspects of medicine, although many of them were already out of date. Medicine was marching on faster than books could be printed but it was down to physicians to keep up which was exactly what she intended doing.

When she tired of textbooks, she perused a newspaper someone had left behind. Her attention veered away from articles about what was happening in government, the country at large and politics in Whitehall. The classifieds drew her attention. Houses for rent. Would she be able to afford a house? Somehow she doubted it. Her attention travelled on to flats for rent and from there to rooms. The latter were the most affordable. Thankfully a salary of two hundred and fifty pounds a year would stretch to that. She consoled herself that at some point future promotion might enable her to live in something more spacious. For now she would make do though that of course depended on her keeping her position at St Aldelm's.

If only she'd held her tongue. Concern about her future weighed heavy.

A room. Look for a room.

She ran her finger down each column in the classifieds until she found it, straying into a column with the title 'Professional Positions'.

Butlers, housekeepers, managers and secretaries were listed and still her finger kept travelling despite reminding herself that it was a room she needed not a new position – at least she hoped that was the case. Not that she was really concentrating on a position. A room! Not a job.

But then her finger stopped as her eyes took in a bolder advertisement.

Resident Doctor required.
  Orchard Cottage Hospital, Norton Dene, Somerset.

Duties to be wide ranging. Accommodation supplied. A basic stipend of three hundred and fifty guineas is payable. Individual consultation fees for panel and private consultations are at the incumbent's discretion.

Apply by letter to the Management Committee, Orchard Cottage Hospital, Norton Dene, Somerset.

'Doctor Brakespeare.'

Taking Frances by surprise, Nurse Haines poked her head around the door.

'Nurse Haines. You surprised me.'

She folded the newspaper into four and stuffed it into her pocket.

'I was just reading an ancient tome on herbal cures. Not something I know much about.'

Nurse Olive Haines sidled around the door as though reluctant to be there at all.

'I've been looking for you.' She looked worried.

'Well you've found me. Sorry,' Frances added on realising that she'd sounded brusque. 'I was deeply intrigued by the Knights of St. John and their use of larkspur for all manner of cures.'

'Doctor Bennani asks if you could meet him in the bursar's office right away.'

Her stomach churned with nervous anticipation. 'Did he say why?'

Doctor Bennani administered to the hospital committee including Doctor Mardon. He didn't have his own office and, surrounded by accounts ledgers and piles of paper, the bursar rarely gave up his patch unless for a good reason.

Olive shook her head. 'I'm only the messenger. He told me nothing but did look nervous.'

'Oh well,' exclaimed Frances blithely, sounding as though she wasn't in the least bit worried when in fact a knot of tension had tightened her stomach. 'Fine. I do hope he's got some of that wonderful coffee with him. Nobody makes coffee so dark and rich as he does.'

Doctor Renard Bennani hailed from Paris. His Moroccan father had run a successful restaurant-come-nightclub where the wine had flowed, the food had come sizzling from the kitchen whilst a host of nubile young women had high-kicked up on a dimly lit stage. His mother had been in the chorus line but had helped manage the restaurant and showgirls once they had a family. Frances suspected that she was the only person to whom he'd imparted this interesting and rather colourful information.

It had always surprised her that, with his background, he had entered the field of medicine. When she'd asked him the reason, he had merely shrugged, said it was in the blood and that the Moors of southern Spain had carried out operations long before Christian Europe.

Apprehensive as to why she'd been summoned, she breezed into the bursar's office presently requisitioned by Doctor Bennani, her apprehension intensifying when she failed to detect the smell of coffee.

She jokingly asked him if she was being promoted or sacked.

He didn't respond and kept his eyes averted – a bad sign if ever there was one.

'There's been a complaint.' His tone of voice was subdued but to her ears had worrying undercurrents.

'Ah. Doctor Mardon, I presume.'

'He demands an apology.'

'I see. In person? In his office?'

She kept her voice even whilst seething inside.

Still with eyes averted Renard replied that was the case.

Her jaw stiffened as she gritted her teeth.

'And if I don't?'

Renard cleared his throat and shuffled a few papers. His gaze remained downcast as he haltingly proclaimed, 'Then the hospital will have no alternative but to relieve you of your position here.'

Frances froze. She felt almost as numb as she had when Ralph had been killed but less so. Nothing could compare with losing him.

Suddenly he looked up at her, pleading in his liquid brown eyes.

'Frances. We are friends. I implore you apologise. It's not worth throwing away your career over this.'

'I can go to another hospital.'

'It might not be as simple as that. His family is powerful. He has contacts in a lot of London hospitals.'

'It doesn't have to be in London. I can go to another city, another town. A country practice if I must.'

He shook his head. 'Reconsider, Frances. You're throwing a lot away.'

The thought of grovelling to Doctor Mardon was too much to bear. How to make Renard understand that? How to make any man understand that?

'So, I go in there, apologise and let him have his way as he's done with other women who were forced to eat humble pie. Would you give in to that kind of pressure, Renard? Would any man?'

Renard reddened. 'I don't know...'

'No. You're not a woman. But I get the impression from your expression that you do know what I'm talking about. You've heard the rumours or the shared sniggers between male doctors. I can see it on your face. But that's it. You men stick together. It's only women and they'll soon get over it. Well, I won't get over it because

I won't let it happen in the first place. I will not apologise. I will not eat humble pie, Doctor.'

The man she'd thought of as a friend looked down at his hands, his lips moving in a chewing fashion as he fought to tread that middle path between a friend and a colleague.

'I'm very aggrieved to give you such devastating news.'

Frances exploded. 'Aggrieved! Damn it, Renard, I'm the one aggrieved.'

He coughed in a light and nervous way as if a fishbone was stuck in his throat.

Feeling her face draining of colour, Frances knew that nothing she could say would make any difference.

'I won't apologise. Not on his terms. How long before I have to leave?'

Renard sucked in his bottom lip, his teeth biting in.

'Immediately.'

He maintained downcast eyes, his head bent awkwardly, hands fiddling with a pen.

She looked at his dark skin and chocolate brown eyes that she'd always thought kindly, understanding. His hair was smooth as satin and black as night. It occurred to her that he'd been handed this poisoned chalice for a reason. They were both in a minority at the hospital. She was a woman. He was a man, but a foreign one, not just French but North African.

He looked up suddenly and said with hand-wringing apology, 'I'm sorry, Frances. I'm so sorry.'

* * *

Sorry. He wasn't the only one who had the chance to say that before she left. The porter for whom she'd secured a job helped her carry a few things out to the car. Olive Haines and several other nurses came out to say goodbye.

'It's not right,' said a humble student nurse, who shook her head and went on to say she just didn't understand. 'You've always been friendly to us. Not many of the other doctors are – unless they're after something,' she added with a dark frown.

Frances embraced each of them. 'Nurses are the backbone of this hospital, just as they were back in the war. I was only a VAD, but I admired nurses then and I still do. Take care of yourselves and bear me in mind if ever you need someone to dance at your wedding.'

Tears stung her eyes as she drove away and it was a while before she regained self-control.

The London traffic was heavy and a fully laden coal lorry had broken down in the vicinity of Westminster Abbey. The ancient building towered over people, pavements and traffic. Outside the arched entrance, a queue of women wearing black and laden with poppy wreaths queued to go in. They were war widows, women who'd lost their loved ones and were now waiting to pay their respects at the tomb of the Unknown Warrior to those whose last resting place was unknown.

Like Ralph. No more than a memory. What would life have been like if he'd lived?

That evening, the house hollow with silence, she sat thinking about what to do next. There was no Ralph, no Izzy and the little savings she had wouldn't last long without a regular income.

London and everything about it was now empty of warmth, laughter and purpose. Perhaps she would go elsewhere.

Gripping Ralph's photo with both hands, she asked him what she should do. 'Without you and medicine I feel as if the fates are scattering me to the winds.'

Rain and wind chose that moment to whip dry leaves and twigs against the window. Was it the weather or Ralph urging her onwards? She felt tearful but wouldn't give in. Izzy had told her never to give in. Ralph, when she really considered it, would have said the same.

The newspaper she'd stuffed into her pocket was still folded into four lying on the sofa beside her. She glanced at it briefly, thought to discard it then changed her mind and added it to the box containing Izzy's personal possessions. They would all go together to pastures new – wherever that might be.

3

Deborah Goldman, Izzy's best friend, came round to help pack the items she was taking with her, barely enough to fill two tea chests and one suitcase.

'I've been dismissed,' Frances said to her before she'd hardly had the chance to enter the narrow hallway.

Deborah's thick dark eyebrows rose in disbelieving arches. 'Dismissed. Why?'

Frances outlined what had happened.

Deborah tossed her head and flung what was supposed to be carefully packed on top of everything already in the tea chest.

'Men. They disgust me. They've always disgusted me. Izzy wasn't keen on them either. If you only knew...'

She didn't elaborate further but lit up and fiercely inhaled then exhaled the smoke from a French cigarette, its smell sweet like chocolate.

'I could have killed him,' Frances said through gritted teeth.

Deborah, her hair shorn to ear level, laughed.

'Ah. It's not yet April the first, so I take it you're not joking. Anyway, I thought you liked the French Moroccan doctor.'

'I'm serious.'

'I must point out, my dear, that it was hardly likely to have been Doctor Bennani's fault. It sounds to me as though he was merely the mouthpiece instructed by the powers that be. Anyway, the Hippocratic Oath forbids you to murder anyone.'

'I'm willing to make an exception,' Frances said with a grimace that she couldn't prevent bordering on a smile. Deborah was good at lifting one's spirits.

'Let's face the basics. If you don't get hanged for doing it, you'll be without an income.'

Frances didn't need reminding. 'I will get another appointment somewhere.'

'Of course, dear. Something will turn up. Oh gosh! Mr Micawber used to say that didn't he?'

Frances puffed a sigh of indignation. 'This is not a book by Charles Dickens. It's real life.'

Deborah, dressed in a purple velvet coat over a pale mauve dress, dramatically outlandish enough to turn heads, patted her shingled hair. 'I've known many of Mr Micawber's type. They exist all right. Chin up, darling. You'll get something. You just see if you don't.'

'I may have blotted my copybook as far as London is concerned.'

'Has it occurred to you to look at hospitals outside London? At other cities, even small towns?'

'I'm not sure I want to leave London.'

Deborah sighed and put out her cigarette. 'Fate may have decreed otherwise.'

Mention of fate lending a hand turned Frances's thoughts to the night before when she'd asked Ralph's opinion and heard the windblown leaves rattle against the window.

'Yes, yes, yes,' she exclaimed shaking it all from her head. 'In the meantime I suppose we'd better get out of here before the Gorgon comes to throw us out.'

Deborah laughed. 'Wasn't the Gorgon a staring monster with hair of writhing snakes?'

'Not at all like Izzy. That's all you need to know.'

'Indeed I get the picture. Now come on. Hermione and I are looking forward to having you stay.'

'It's very good of you two to take me in.'

Deborah waved a hand in a dismissive manner.

'We can cope. Anyway, I'm sure you'll get a new position quicker than you think. Just don't aim too high.'

Her comment jolted Frances back from what felt like a deep dark well.

'Because I'm a woman.'

Deborah's expression turned serious. 'That was the whole point of what we were fighting for – me, Izzy and the rest. Now come on. Hermione is making us lunch and she hates to leave things to get cold.'

Despite Deborah's attempts to assure her that she and Hermione would welcome her staying, she knew the two women – who shared the same bed – were settled in their own little world. She had no wish to impose on their generosity for too long.

'It's very kind of you both.'

'Nonsense. Oh look,' said Deborah, dipping into a tea chest into which Frances had tipped the contents of the bottom two drawers of the bureau. 'I gave Izzy this journal as a welcome home present.'

'Had she been on holiday?'

'No, darling. It was a welcome home present for you. Some-where she could record progress from the time she brought you home as a baby.'

Deborah did not notice how stunned Frances looked.

'She kept a record of my life?'

The smile on Deborah's face was diminished. 'Yes. She did. You didn't know?'

Wordlessly, Frances reached for the journal.

Deborah stood watching her. 'She cared for you a lot. As you grew, she wrote down every little thing from eating your first egg yolk to taking your first step.'

Frances nodded slowly as her fingers caressed the leather-bound book and flicked through the pages of neat, rounded writing. Izzy couldn't spell very well but she wrote beautifully. She'd often joked that she could never be a doctor because she couldn't spell English so Latin medical terms were out of the question. Frances had always thought there was something more to it than that. Something had prevented her from pursuing a career as a doctor. Izzy was always flippant about it.

'I was the daughter she never had,' she said, her voice full of sadness.

'And a thorn in the side of her family.'

Frances could not quite comprehend the look that flashed in eyes possessing the limpid quality of a newborn fawn, innocent yet at the same time guarded.

Deborah picked up the folded newspaper that Frances had taken from her pocket and thrown into the tea chest. Her expression changed as she read the first page then found her way to the advert from the Somerset town Frances had never heard of.

'Judging by the fact that this page was torn from the newspaper this insertion aroused your interest.'

'Yes.'

Deborah tilted her head, looking even more like a forest fawn querying the goings on around it.

'It's a nice town.'

'You know it,' Frances asked, surprised.

'Ah, yes.' Deborah acquired a faraway look. 'At least someone who lives there. The lady of the manor, no less. She used to be a suffragette. One of our most respected members.'

'It's just a cottage hospital. I'm not sure it's for me. They're usually quite old fashioned.'

'Well there you are! Bring it up to date. It might be calling out for someone like you.'

The prospect of practising medicine in a country hospital had not quite appealed until Deborah had mentioned someone there who had known Izzy, who had been part of a women's movement that had changed the status quo forever. She liked the thought of that.

'I'm intrigued.'

'And we've just about finished packing,' said Deborah as she sent two more books tumbling into a tea chest.

Frances gazed around the living room where colourful walls blended with copper ornamentation and furniture in the much-admired Charles Rennie Mackintosh and William Morris style. Flowered wallpaper in shades of blue, peach and pale green swirled over the walls. The chairs on which Izzy and her friends gathered and talked of a future where the goal of a female was not marriage but given the choice they could choose a career if that was what they wanted.

'You'll be fine with us.'

'For a while though I have no intention of outstaying my welcome. I respect your privacy and your lifestyle.'

Deborah had the decency to blush.

'I know you won't want to stay forever...'

Frances took hold of Deborah's upper arms and laughed. 'Of course I don't and for good reason. Your world belongs to you and

Hermione. I've yet to find mine. If Ralph had lived...' Her words faded.

Deborah looked at her sadly. 'I'm sorry.'

Frances shrugged. 'I often think of what might have been, but there's no going back. Only forwards.'

*　*　*

In the privacy of her bedroom, Frances spoke to the handsome face looking out at her from within the confines of the silver picture frame. By night, the sepia-tinted photograph sat on her bedside table. By day, he'd travelled in her battered old medicine bag to the hospital – when she'd had a job there, that is. Now he was at home and so was she, in her bedroom, where she imagined him speaking to her, encouraging her to follow her dream just as Izzy had done.

Closing her eyes, she was with him again in those rare periods when they'd snatched stolen moments whilst the war continued in the distance.

What she'd seen in France had also stayed in her mind, the tragedy of the situation, the unfettered carnage between two armies.

Behind her closed eyelids, Frances saw again row upon row of beds. Vats of pinkish water in which bandages were laundered ready for reuse. She remembered singing to a soldier who was no more than a boy. He asked her to sing a lullaby like his mother used to sing and she did so until he slipped away.

The experience had left her numb and the fact that a wounded soldier nearby had remarked on her kindness didn't sink in. Once it had broken through her sorrowing thoughts, she had merely shrugged and responded that it was nothing.

'A few minutes of my time for a soul about to enter heaven.'

She couldn't recall what else was said only that the man who'd spoken sounded deeply touched.

Old memories and a beckoning future collided in her mind. Why not apply to this cottage hospital in the middle of nowhere? Anyway what did she have to lose?

4

THE ORCHARD COTTAGE HOSPITAL, NORTON DENE, SOMERSET

It was early evening and the ward at Orchard Cottage Hospital in the town of Norton Dene smelt of motorbike grease and oil-soaked leather. The source of the smell, Doctor Walker, straightened and made an unsuccessful attempt to disentangle his stethoscope from the loosened chin straps of his leather motorcycle helmet. He'd never used to wear his leathers into the hospital, but he'd become a bit absent-minded of late.

Nurse Lucy Daniels, a coquettish, pretty girl with a slim figure and dancing eyes, and Sister Edith Harrison, her senior, stiffened with apprehension as they waited for the old doctor's verdict. In his younger days, it might have been accurate. Nowadays, it was more than a little hit-or-miss necessitating the nursing staff keeping a weather eye on him. It was the one time, thought Lucy, that Sister Edith Harrison treated her as an equal. The rest of the time she was somewhat aloof.

'This man has an infectious disease. Keep him in isolation,' proclaimed Doctor Walker.

Sister Edith's jaw tightened, a sure sign that she knew he was wrong. 'Yes, Doctor.'

There was disingenuity in her tone, not that he noticed. The pattern during the past year was for him to tender his diagnosis and for one of the nursing staff to iron out the wrinkles.

The patient, Archibald Snell, tried to say something, but a series of coughs intervened and phlegm was spit and dribbled into the bowl Lucy held for him close to his mouth.

Assuming that his job was over, Doctor Walker proceeded to fasten the straps of his leather motorcycle helmet. Glass goggles were pulled down over his eyes.

Sister Harrison pointed out the obvious. 'You won't want your goggles just yet, Doctor. Your motorbike's outside, down at the bottom of the steps. You might take a tumble if you're wearing your goggles.'

Realisation flattening his features, he shoved the goggles back up again. 'Ah, yes, yes, yes.'

He didn't wave or say goodbye but marched out of the ward on bowed legs towards bright daylight beyond the hospital entrance.

As the sound of the motorcycle roared into life, Lucy looked at Sister Harrison and dropped her voice. 'Does Mr Snell really have to go into a room by himself?'

'Doctor Walker's orders.'

'But he's not got an infectious disease – has he?'

Lucy Daniels had been a nurse long enough to know that Mr Snell, a miner like her father had been, was not suffering from an infectious disease. Thanks to the coal – the black gold of many places in the British Isles and elsewhere – his lungs had been destroyed by years of breathing in the gritty black dust. She'd seen quarrymen suffering from lung problems too, problems that were suffered but never cured.

Sister Harrison ordered the patient to open his mouth so she could check his temperature.

Mr Snell tried to speak and by doing so sent the thermometer jiggling. 'I don't want to be in a room by meself,' he finally spluttered.

Edith was not the warmest nursing sister ever to grace a ward, but she did take pride in getting things right and putting the patient first.

She exchanged a look with Nurse Daniels insinuating that she was indeed countermanding Doctor Walker's instructions.

'You can stay on this ward if you wish.'

Mouth clutched around the thermometer, Mr Snell grunted his acquiescence and nodded his head.

Ah, thought Lucy. Edie Harrison has left the decision to Mr Snell. The nursing staff could not be blamed if Doctor Walker ever noticed that his instructions had been countermanded – which was unlikely. Nowadays he lived in a fog of half-forgotten skills and sketchy memories.

Sister Harrison squinted at the thermometer reading, gave it a good shake and popped it back into the receptacle above Mr Snell's bed. 'Fluff up Mr Snell's pillows, Nurse Daniels. Make him comfortable.'

Left alone with the patient, Lucy pummelled the pillows whilst reassuring Mr Snell that all would be well and he could stay in the bed and ward he was already in.

'Glad to...' His chest heaved as he caught his breath before another bout of coughing took it away again. '...'Ear it...'

Lucy helped him sit up. 'There. You can see everything that's going on in the ward and there's a lovely view out of the window. How many hospitals have got that?'

He almost choked on a response as Lucy mentally answered her own question.

She'd done her training in Stoke Park Hospital on the outskirts of Bristol, a large old Victorian place where the corridors were long and echoed with the footsteps of doctors, nurses and relatives of the patients. They'd also echoed with those of her sister, Nancy. There were two years between them, but both had opted to become nurses. Their mother had had a lot to do with it. Mavis Daniels had been adamant that they would do better than her in life and not restrict themselves to being a wife and mother – unless they really wanted that.

'Your life is not set in stone. The world's changed. A woman's lot isn't just to get married, become a mother and be housebound. She can be anything she wants if she puts her mind to it. Just look at what them suffragettes did, getting women the right to vote.'

Both had taken her words to heart, although Nancy had fallen for and married her childhood sweetheart, Ned Skittings. Normally, it was form for a nurse to leave the profession once married. Luckily, the cottage hospital was small and nurses craving further training and a career preferred to find it in the big infirmaries in the city, not in a little place like Norton Dene.

The impetus to following their mother's well-intentioned advice was when she'd contracted a lingering disease. They'd been readily accepted onto a nursing course at the same hospital and, after qualifying, talked of what they should do next. As it worked out, their mother's condition had worsened and she'd needed them to look after her. Fortunately, Orchard Cottage Hospital and the old doctor had been agreeable to having them work part-time. Once their mother had passed, they continued to work part-time, earning extra money serving in a shop in the high street or cleaning for the doctor, or anyone else who needed it.

Back then, although it was only a few years ago, old Doctor Walker's mental capacity had been a little less muddled than it was now. Even though they were only part-time, he'd welcomed their commitment and it was thanks to him that Nancy had been kept on once she was married. Not that he would remember his belief that the people of the town should be involved in the running of the hospital even if it meant them dividing the hours between them.

'Being one big family is to be encouraged,' he was fond of proclaiming. 'And Norton Dene is a big happy family.'

Seeing as he'd been the most senior doctor in the town and consultant to the cottage hospital for years, the management committee – a collection of local notaries – had let him have his way. That same committee were now letting him go. Not that he seemed to mind, in fact his mind was often elsewhere. His pride and joy was his Douglas motorcycle which he boasted about ad infinitum and with great enthusiasm. 'It's got a top speed of twenty miles an hour and I can travel for at least fifty miles before needing to stop for petrol.'

Sister Harrison took off the little round hat she wore that tied beneath the chin. The other nurses wore squares of starched linen that floated behind them when they dashed through the ward.

Sister Harrison, her cloak firmly fastened around her shoulders, came in to check that there was nothing outstanding before she left for home where she lived with her invalid mother.

Out of respect for her seniority, Nurse Lucy Daniels got to her feet.

'All quiet on the western front, is it?' asked Sister Harrison.

Lucy winced at the question, referring as it did to a time when things were certainly not quiet on the western front – if one was referring to France and the Great War, that is.

'Everything is in order, Sister.'

Never did Lucy address her senior nursing colleague by her first name. Edith Harrison was a stickler for protocol and status was important to her.

She lingered, her chin held high and her eyes narrowed. 'Hopefully all will be peace and quiet until the morning.'

'Yes, Sister.'

'And you won't fall asleep.'

'No, Sister. I'll have the kettle on at seven in the morning when Nancy gets here.'

Nurse Harrison's eyes narrowed. 'I trust she'll be here on time. She hasn't been of late.'

Lucy immediately sprang to her sister's defence. 'The baby is teething. She and Ned didn't get much sleep...'

'And that, Nurse Daniels, is why most nurses leave the profession once they are married.' She tutted disapprovingly. 'I fear Doctor Walker made the wrong decision. If I'd been in charge, it wouldn't have happened. The new doctor may be more disciplined on that front. I certainly hope he is.'

'She'll take over from me at seven in the morning,' Lucy informed her. 'Her mother-in-law Mrs Skittings will look after the baby.'

'I trust it is so,' exclaimed Sister Harrison in her usual superior style.

With a swirl of her cloak, she was gone.

Once Sister Harrison had left, Lucy put the kettle on. The nightshift could be long and tiring – not so much because of something happening but generally out of boredom. If she had a book to read, she could cope and tonight she had a romance by her favourite author, Barbara Cartland. A romance could take her to another place, where princes bowed down to serving girls and countesses fell in love with gypsy rovers.

Setting tea and book on the small desk at the end of the ward, Lucy prepared herself to check on each of her patients. If an emergency arose, her instructions were to get a message to Sister Harrison, who had been adamant that she should not contact Doctor Walker.

'We don't want him and his motorbike out in the dark or we'll be having another patient in here.'

In summer, sunset burnt the ward walls with an orange glow. At this time of year the light was muted seeing as winter was only reluctantly ebbing into spring.

There were only three patients in the men's ward and four in the women's ward. The landlord or landlady of the Hat and Feather would bring in the evening meals for the patients. Mrs Skittings had once run the hospital kitchen with a staff of two assistants, but the management had decided it was too costly. Jim and Audrey Faulkland had stepped into the breach – the food strictly controlled to that suitable for sick people: semolina, tripe cooked in milk and chicken broth containing diced chicken and little else.

Twilight turned into night. Lucy sat at the little desk snuggled into a tight alcove – the abode for the duty nurse.

The structure of the cottage hospital benefitted the patients of local general practitioners who needed to be hospitalised but not in need of an operation – most of which were done at the city infirmary. It was then up to the local doctors whether they officiated themselves or paid a stipend to the resident doctor which was mostly what happened. Of late, due to Doctor Walker's advancing years, the local GPs had been obliged to travel from their surgeries to tend to their patients.

Having had several complaints from a few general practitioners, the management committee had finally bit the bullet and gently but firmly suggested to the old doctor that the time had come for him to hand the reins to someone younger.

The dense darkness of the hours after midnight faded into a grey dawn. Clouds scudded across the lightening sky and a slight drizzle began to fall.

Lucy glanced at the ward clock, a monstrous thing of black Roman numerals and hands that jolted with each movement. Ten minutes past seven. Nancy was late again. Thank goodness Sister

Harrison wouldn't appear until eight o'clock when she knew her neighbour would be awake and available to pop into her mother to make sure she was all right.

Mrs Adelaide Harrison, Edith's mother, was a bit of a tartar. No matter how many patients were in the hospital or what the emergency, the old lady regarded herself in greater need of her daughter's care than anyone else.

As the clock struck seven fifteen, Nancy came dashing in, shaking the rain from her cloak. 'Sorry I'm late. My little darling kept us awake most of the night. Luckily, Ned's mother went out picking bits and pieces for her concoctions this morning. She reckoned she could hear Polly from the woods at the back of the house. Everything quiet here,' she added hopefully not admitting that her baby's fretfulness had drained her.

Lucy pronounced that it was. 'And I've left the sluice room spotless.'

Nancy smirked. 'Pans too?'

'Find out for yourself. I'm off to my bed.'

She scooped off her butterfly headdress of crisply starched linen and hung it on a hook. Every two or three days when there were too many creases to overlook, she took it home to be laundered and starched.

Home was a two-bedroom cottage she shared with her Aunt Rose Daniels, her father's sister. Her room, which as a child she'd shared with her sister, was tucked under the eaves. Now she had it to herself. Her parents had once slept in the larger bedroom, but both had passed on. Their father had survived the war but died in the flu epidemic that had followed. Their mother had been the woman who assisted at the births of those too poor to pay for a midwife. She'd also laid out the deceased, leaving little for the funeral director to do except carry away and bury the late departed in hallowed ground. Her own death had come as something of a surprise. She'd gone to bed the night before complaining of a headache. In the morning, the life she'd boldly embraced had gone from her body. Aunt Rose had moved in within the month. It was never quite clear how she made her money, but she paid her way. She also drank. She told everyone that it was tea, but the sisters, and others besides, knew it was sweet cider laced with a spot of gin.

Nancy was tucking the last of her coppery locks behind her ears and inside a hairnet before pulling her headdress into place. Whilst she was doing this, her darker-complexioned sister went through the current state of each patient. When she got to the medical notes for Fred Snell, she sighed and said that he was as well as could be expected then went on to expand on the details.

'Doctor Walker suggested that what he's got is contagious and he'd be best placed in a separate room. Thankfully, Sister Harrison ignored his diagnosis. Poor Mr Snell. Everyone knows that it's the coal dust killing him. And do you know what? He examined the poor man without taking off his motorcycle clothes. Sister Harrison was not amused.'

'Can't say I blame her.'

'Me neither.'

The two sisters fell silent as one straightened her uniform and the other pulled her cloak around her shoulders, readying herself to head for home.

'The new doctor can't come soon enough,' said Nancy.

Lucy grinned and her eyes sparkled. 'Let's hope he's young and handsome.'

'And doesn't smell of oil,' Nancy added with a laugh.

5

ORCHARD MANOR

Lady Araminta Compton-Dixon, chairman of Orchard Cottage Hospital Trust and local magistrate was perusing correspondence and accounts passed to her by Oliver Nielsen. Being the local branch bank manager, he had access to the Compton-Dixon balance sheets with reference to the estates, mines, quarries and assets that had been held by the family for generations. He also acted as secretary to the hospital management committee and because of all these appointments viewed himself as a close confidant of the family.

'In fact you could say that I *am* family,' he was fond of saying to his wife and anyone else he wished to impress.

Unbeknown to him, his wife only appeared to be listening, her mind on her knitting, which at present was a pretty little matinee coat for a baby she didn't have. Once finished it would be placed alongside the bootees, bonnets, caps and cardigans she'd knitted over the years. No child had ever been born to her and Oliver and she doubted one ever would. Oliver had never shown much interest in the physical side of their marriage. Like the Compton-Dixon family she was an acquaintance who he could boast about.

'My wife is one of the Marmaduke family of Upper Stanton.'

Nobody was sure of the whereabouts of Upper Stanton and Oliver didn't enlighten them. The name had a certain status about it and that was enough for him.

Here in late February he was sitting opposite her ladyship with his shoulders back, spine as stiff as a curtain rail. His hands however were restless, continually swiping at the front crease of his trouser leg, brushing at the flecks of dandruff that speckled his dark tweed jacket, the one reserved for days on the golf course. His collar was high and of the old-fashioned high-necked type that was fixed with metal studs and thus dug uncomfortably into his fleshy neck.

Her ladyship took her time perusing the nest of papers he'd presented, even though she knew he was aching to get into his plus fours and off to the golf course. However, his first duty was to her ladyship whose late husband had expressed an interest in golf, another strong link between him and the family. That too was something he thought stood him in good stead.

Not being a man of great insight, he had no idea that her ladyship's opinion of golf was far from his own – and that of her late husband. She found it all quite ridiculous, hitting a small ball around a golf course with an iron rod. As for the clothes golfers wore. Plus fours! If ever there was a more absurd name for an absurd garment that ended at the knees – with a pair of disgustingly checked socks coupled with a pair of spiked brogues that couldn't possibly do any good to the grass – then she didn't know what it might be.

'Everything seems in order,' she said at last, rubbing at the bridge of her nose, where her wire-rimmed spectacles had left their mark. 'Now. Have all the committee read the application letter for Doctor Walker's replacement?'

The bank manager fussily opened his file and set the letter

from Frances Brakespeare flat in front of him plus a copy of the letter he'd sent in response inviting her for an interview. 'Yes indeed. We think Doctor Brakespeare very suitable and have no hesitation in suggesting we ask him for a final interview just to round things off.'

'She, Mr Nielsen. Doctor Frances Brakespeare is a woman and I for one have already made up my mind. She will be coming for an interview. I think she's the breath of fresh air The Orchard needs.'

Mr Nielsen's jaw dropped. The surprised look on his face amused her. It was a joy to see his pomposity punctured.

'Female?' He shook his head, which irritated Araminta because it seemed he was not taking her seriously.

'No, no, no.' He flattened the letter again and stabbed a finger at the name of the signatory. Doctor Frances Brakespeare. 'With all due respect, your ladyship, I think you are mistaken... Doctor Brakespeare – Doctor Francis Brakespeare...'

She cut across his condescending tone. 'Doctor *Frances* Brakespeare.' She fixed him with a look capable of curdling milk. 'I am not so senile, Mr Nielsen, to have forgotten that Frances in the female version is spelt with an "e", whereas in the male version – as referenced to St Francis of Assisi, for instance – it is spelt with an "i". The spelling here is the female version.'

Nielsen's pink face reddened. 'A woman?' He prided himself on his public-school education which he regarded had given him a greater intelligence than most. Her ladyship's statement had certainly punctured that belief.

Nobody liked being taken for a fool but to her mind he deserved it.

She'd been right to suspect that Nielsen and the other members of the committee would misconstrue – with one exception. The vicar had noticed. It was the vicar who had pointed it out to her.

'Say nothing. Let's see if the rest of them have noticed.'

Although a man of God the Reverend Gregory Sampson had an impish sense of humour. He readily promised not to say anything.

Her reserved expression hid the satisfaction she felt inside. Her steady gaze flickered between him and the letter he'd handed back to her, which, although she knew what it said, she read again with barely suppressed glee.

'Yes. We will invite her for a final interview.'

'A final interview,' Oliver remarked with surprise. 'Did I miss the first one?'

'We can regard her letter of application as the first interview – written rather than face to face. The committee had no objections to anything in her application so we can regard that will suffice.'

Oliver Nielsen's inclination to protest faded when she eyed him with such unblinking intensity. Not all men had his attitude to the brave new world women were making for themselves but Norton Dene was somewhat sheltered from the new world emerging following the war which had come to an end twelve years before. It would take it some time to catch up.

'Her credentials are exemplary. I will write today and ask her to come for an interview.'

Mr Nielsen's jaw hung like a carp drowned in fresh air.

'Now,' she said, turning her attention to the cost of pit props, ponies and other capital items that a well-run mine, farm or quarry couldn't possibly do without. 'The costs for this year seem to have gone down compared to last year.'

'So says the report from Mr Grainger.'

Araminta fixed her bank manager with a steely-eyed glare. 'I do hope his economies are not at the cost of safety. I will not have employees' lives put in danger purely to increase profit. If there should be a lapse in safety then I will seriously consider terminating their lease.'

Looking relieved to change the subject, Mr Nielsen turned his attention back to the files he'd brought from the bank and tried to sound light-hearted.

'My day-to-day running of a quarry is confined to finance and banking, not the drilling and blasting.'

His smile was apologetically condescending and not reciprocated.

Lady Araminta pursed her lips. Grainger and Son was the name on the board at the quarry entrance but they were not the owners. The rights were leased from the estate of Lord Albert Compton-Dixon, which was overseen by her, his widow. Unlike many marriages of double-barrelled names, his lordship had been born a Dixon, his wife a Compton. When he'd proposed, she had stipulated that she would marry him if their names were joined together, and only if their neighbouring lands – of which hers were the greater – would also be joined.

Araminta placed her wire-rimmed glasses back on her nose and carried on with the job in hand. 'Now for my charitable works. There looks to be a goodly sum in the Orchard Cottage Hospital charity trust.'

The bank manager nodded his agreement. When he'd first taken over management of family matters, he'd expected that as a man he would guide and undoubtedly have the last say in everything. Things hadn't turned out that way. Lady Araminta had a shrewd head on her shoulders and strong views. He didn't tell her what to do. She told him.

However, he tried to give advice on this occasion. 'There is, indeed, your ladyship, and I was going to suggest to you that you might like to invest in bonds or suchlike which attract excellent interest...'

'No!' Her response was sharp. The pen she threw down onto the desk rolled along the blotting pad, scattering ink in its wake. 'The extra money will be used for charitable purposes. I can't say to the deserving poor, "Oh dear. I'm sorry. I can't give you enough to buy shoes for your children or set up a communal laundry just yet, my money is tied up making even more money!" Certainly not! Besides which, what would I spend it on? I have all I need.'

'It was just a suggestion...'

She fixed him with a look of accusation that diminished him to feeling half the size in the large carver chair he was sitting in. 'Do you know how many twelve-year-olds are working in the mines?'

Feeling even smaller and in need of saying something she might approve of, Nielsen shook his head and attempted what he considered a justifiable remark.

'It's terrible, just terrible. The parents should be ashamed of themselves. Boys of that age should be at school.'

The look she gave him was enough to turn cream sour.

'It's not the parents' fault! They're taken out of school at twelve years old because the parents have no choice.' Her voice was strident and made him want to clap his hands over his ears. Instead he had to defer to her superior status and eat humble pie.

'Of course. Of course,' he responded with abject humility. 'You know more about family matters than I, your ladyship.'

She sensed he'd wanted to add 'because you're a woman' and only just stopped himself.

On arrival, she'd offered him a measure of whisky. His glass was empty now and he looked in severe need of a refill. His eyes wandered over to the tantalus – a solid oak affair containing three cut-glass decanters. Three silver labels hanging on slender chains proclaimed the contents: whisky, brandy, rum.

She ignored his furtive glance. His florid features and rotund physique evidenced, in her opinion, that he drank too much anyway.

Her eyes searched for the time on the gold timepiece pinned to her right breast. It was nearing ten o'clock in the morning. Soon, her son, Devlin, would shake off the sleeping draught from the night before when he'd begged her to give him something that would blot out his dreams. She hadn't refused him.

She slammed the portfolio of papers firmly shut. 'I think we've finished here. I've other things to do.'

There was swift acceptance to her pronouncement.

'So do I,' said Mr Nielsen, speedily gathering paperwork as he got to his feet.

Guessing his plans, she regarded him sidelong. 'It looks like being a fine day.'

'Indeed.'

'A fine day for a round of golf?'

'Yes. Hopefully I might get a round in,' he said without a trace of guilt that he should by rights be at the bank. 'Though it's duty first before pleasure as regards your business matters, my lady, which is why I agreed to meet you at breakfast time.'

Araminta doubted he'd do anything much except have a long, and likely liquid, lunch before dragging his clubs around the Orchard Park Golf Course. It was only a small course created by her late husband. There had been approaches for a larger conurbation, one that would take in most of the land surrounding the hospital – even the hospital itself. She'd resisted the temptation – not that there was much of one. She hated golf. Loved the hospital. It linked her with people and for that she was extremely grateful. Many women of her class never got to know the ordinary folk – the servants that waited on them, the shopkeepers in the high street, the children who ran laughing and shouting on their way to school. She was glad that her path in life had taken her into contact with ordinary working folk. Through knowing them she'd gained a wider perspective of the world and for that she was glad.

After he'd gone, Araminta sat in the same chair staring at the study door steeling herself for the most heart-wrenching moment of her day when her world would become less ordered and infinitely more stressful. Still, it had to be faced.

Gathering up all her strength, she left the study and stepped out into the oak-panelled hallway where ornate plasterwork dripped like icicles above her head.

The roots of Orchard Manor had been put down before the reign of Henry the Eighth. Back then, it had been an abbey, a place of prayer and promises, all the things that had given order to people's lives at that time.

With the dissolution of the monasteries, the abbey had been bequeathed to one of the king's retainers, Master of the Garderobe no less. Keeper of the toilet! Araminta still found the pomposity of such status amusing. Descendants of the man had squandered away much of the family wealth in the early eighteenth century, which was when it passed to one of her ancestors, a lady who was good at playing cards and marrying rich husbands. Some regarded that ancestor and her exploits as scandalous. Araminta was not of the same mind. In fact she was quite proud of those women in her family – men too for that matter – who had kicked over the traces and gave not a fig for convention. Strong women with a wider view of the world.

Taking a deep breath, she noiselessly made her way across the hall to the passageway that led to her son's suite of rooms. On the outside she showed no sign of apprehension though inside her stomach churned and her heart palpitated to such an extent it felt as though it was pumping its way out of her body.

As if on cue a loud keening rose like long sharp nails scraping over glass and barrelled along the ground-floor corridor that led to her son's suite of rooms.

The self-control she'd displayed when dealing with Oliver Nielsen shattered to smithereens and her stout heart felt as though it would surely burst.

Grimes, the valet, whose duty was to look after her son, appeared at the end of the corridor leading to the south wing and the suite of rooms in which her son had resided since coming home blinded and haunted by a war that was meant to end all wars.

He gave a little bow of his head before reporting. 'Captain Devlin is awake, your ladyship.'

Her head felt as heavy as her heart when she nodded and said softly and sadly, 'So I hear.'

By the time she was inside the door of her son's room he was sitting on the side of the bed, still in his pyjamas, arms folded, head hanging forward.

Grimes was standing beside him, a plum-coloured quilted garment hanging from his arm.

'Your dressing gown, sir.'

The young man sitting on the side of the bed, Devlin, her beloved son, had fallen silent and appeared not to have heard what had been said.

She indicated that Grimes pass her the velvet dressing gown, settled herself on the bed beside her son and suggested she help him.

Putting on a brave smile, she asked if he had slept well.

Her son, his hair as silky as her own, did not raise his head to meet her eyes.

He took a deep breath before replying, and when he did, the hollow sadness in his voice gave her pain.

'Well enough. It's the in-between that's the worst.'

The after-effect of the sleeping draught had left his pupils dilated, though glassy in their unseeing. She tried to keep smiling, not to wince as her eyes met his.

'I don't think I know what that means.'

'Of course you know,' he snapped. 'It's the time between deep sleep and waking up. It's where the past lives.'

'Ah, yes. I know what you mean now, my darling.' And all the time her heart quaked.

He shrugged the dressing gown off his shoulders. 'I think I will get dressed now.'

Grimes bowed slightly from the waist. 'Of course, sir.'

His sightless eyes and dilated pupils followed the direction of his valet's voice.

'I think I will have a bath first.'

'Very good, sir.'

Araminta got to her feet. 'Then I suppose I'd better leave you. I'll bring you breakfast up if you like.'

'No need to tire your legs, Mother. Grimes can get it for me. Not that I'm hungry at this moment in time.'

'Lunch then.'

'No. I don't think so.'

'Dinner?'

'Yes. Tonight. With port afterwards. I think I would enjoy dining tonight. Do we have company this evening?'

'Not this evening. Though it would have been nice to hear you and your friends laughing and joking like you used to.' She stopped herself saying more. She shouldn't have said that much but her craving for better times sometimes caused old memories to burst out uninvited.

'That was a long time ago. They're all gone now.'

'Not all of them.'

His mother braced herself to say something that she had tried before. About Grace.

'Grace sent a letter. I could read it to you if you like.'

'No.'

'Darling, she really wants to see you again...'

'But I can't see her. Let's be honest, Mother, Grace was never short of admirers. She must be married by now. And with children. Why would she want to bother with me.' His tone was bitter which was nothing new. The early promise of youth had been destroyed.

'She can still be a friend. There's nothing wrong in that.'

His mother always did the best she could to encourage him to take a positive view. Grace was just one of her weapons, though goodness, no matter how often she'd mentioned his ex-fiancée he'd never responded.

Devlin laughed in a way that mocked himself and dug deeper into sadness. 'I wanted her as my wife, not a friend.'

'There are others who would—'

'Stop it, Mother. No woman would have me now. I can't waltz around the ballroom, play cards with them or... anything. I'm no longer of their world.'

Once darkness had fallen and she was alone without charge of the estate, the hospital or anything for which she showed great strength and purpose, she stared out of her bedroom window with tears streaming down her face. One son. Why had God chosen to strike him down in the flower of his youth? Reminding herself that he had come back alive when others had lost their loved ones went only some way to easing the painful ache. No matter what it took she would continue to do whatever she could to make things better. Her deepest prayer was that he would return from that dreadful battle that still raged in his mind. She would continue to do what she could. She would continue to hope.

6

Daffodils dared to dance in the breeze and feeble sunshine was doing its best to break through and say a final goodbye to the winter.

Arm in arm, mother and son walked around the garden where the paths were flat and straight and his stick prodded grass verges that he'd known as a child. Back then he'd chattered and laughed, talked about serious things but also the fun things. Nowadays the only time she could get him to speak depended on her instigation though even to her own ears the subject matter sounded mundane focused as it was on what was going on in the town and never mentioning The Great War.

'We've selected a replacement for Doctor Walker. A very fine replacement who will do the job extremely well.'

'Does he ride a motorcycle?'

'Thank the Lord, no, though I am sure eyebrows will be raised. I've invited her for an interview although I've already decided that she's the one.'

'Her! Ah. Now I understand why I hear such girlish glee in

your voice. Once a suffragette, always a suffragette.' He sounded amused.

'You sound gleeful too.'

'I'm imagining the raised eyebrows of old duffers and snooty matriarchs alike.'

Araminta smiled to herself as the brittle coating of her heart melted due to her son sounding genuinely happy for once and it encouraged her to go on in the same vein. Anything to hear him sounding happy.

'Doctor Brakespeare will need somewhere to live when she takes up her post. I have decided the vicarage coach house, long abandoned by both coachman, coach and horses would suit very well. I've asked the vicar if he could get it cleaned up.'

'Were there no other applicants?'

'None I felt were suitable.'

Devlin smiled. His mother was indomitable and convinced that her way was always the right way. At times it made her seem domineering and hard, but she would listen when a good case for changing her mind was put to her. In this case he doubted anyone could object. Her decision was a halfway house between common sense and her own drive for having more women in responsible positions.

'You're smiling. Do you think me wrong?'

'The proof of the pudding is in the eating.'

'And I made the pudding.'

'You did indeed. You made the decision without the aid of the committee.'

She spread her hands as though the outcome was bound to be a foregone conclusion – which, of course, it was if his mother had anything to do with it.

'Everyone approved her letter of application and her qualifications are second to none. A letter inviting her was composed and signed by Mr Nielsen. Nobody raised an objection and we wanted...'

'You wanted...'

'The matter resolved expediently. She will do very well.'

'I can hear the humour in your voice and must admit to some surprise. Norton Dene is a bit old-fashioned and so's the committee. Traditionalists to the tips of their brogues – or hobnail boots for that matter. I doubt any of them have met a female doctor in their life. How will you get away with it?'

His mother's laughter rippled with what some might interpret as triumphalist. 'They misread the letter. Her name's Doctor Frances Brakespeare. Frances with an "e"...'

Devlin threw back his head and laughed, the sound music to her ears.

'Mother, you're incorrigible.'

'Nonsense. They had eyes to see...' She stopped herself from continuing. Sightlessness was a topic of conversation she steered clear of.

Devlin appeared not to notice her reference to his condition and patted her hand. 'Mother, your machinations leave me breathless.'

'That's what your father used to say,' she chuckled. 'He said he loved machinations.'

'And he loved you too.'

'Yes.' He couldn't see her sad smile. She so wanted him to enjoy the same deep and lasting love that she'd experienced, hence her pushing for him to see Grace though as he said she might very well be married. It was all such a shame. They'd seemed so well suited, but there, she thought to herself, you can take a horse to water but you can't make it drink.

* * *

At four in the afternoon, the Reverend Gregory Sampson came for tea, which today was being served in the drawing room. Grimes showed him in and Araminta followed, having first changed into a tea gown. The tradition of changing for tea as practised in the late years of the nineteenth and early years of the twentieth century was becoming a little old-fashioned, but any gay young thing would have been envious of the sprigged muslin frock she wore, cut to fit a figure that had not spread too much and could accommodate the latest fashion for fabrics and styles that clung to slender curves.

Tall, blond and having looks that emboldened the racing heart of her youth, the vicar was standing in front of the window, his lean athletic figure silhouetted against the pale light of an encroaching evening. His clothes were black, of course, except for the slash of the white dog collar at his throat. Hat in hand, he turned at her approach, a captivating smile brightening his tanned face, his eyes cornflower blue.

'Good afternoon, your ladyship.' He nodded at the garden. 'Even at this time of year it's a lovely view.'

'I think so. Do sit down.'

Before sitting down, Gregory noted that she also had an unobstructed view of her son, who had got someone to bring out his wind-up gramophone onto the terrace. His back was towards them, head held slightly to one side, listening to what sounded to the vicar's untuned ears as Bach.

First on the agenda over cucumber sandwiches and shortbread was accommodation for the new doctor.

'Is everything in hand?' she asked. Her tone gave him the impression she would be very put out if it was not. Lady Araminta was a kindly person who didn't suffer fools gladly and admired capability in others that matched her own.

'My housekeeper engaged Bertha, your housekeeper, to give

her a hand and the Daniels sisters mucked in too. They've cleaned and polished every nook and cranny. The spiders and mice were seen exiting at great pace. They did seem a bit surprised – the girls not the mice – when I suggested placing a vase of flowers in the living room and bedroom. I didn't enlighten them that we have ourselves a female doctor.'

Araminta chuckled over her late afternoon shot of whisky. 'I'm glad you didn't. I want the town to be surprised. As for engaging a housekeeper, I believe someone part-time would suffice.'

'I agree. I've asked the Daniels sisters – Miss Lucy Daniels and Mrs Nancy Skittings. They're only working part-time at the hospital at present.'

'Good. The sooner she's installed and comfortable, the better.'

Gregory Sampson, scratched at his cheek in a querulous manner. 'Don't think I'm in any way a doubting Thomas, but... Are you absolutely sure she will meet the mark and you can swing the committee?'

'I know a good egg when I see one. If I decide it is so, then the committee will fall into place – if they know what's good for them!'

Gregory smiled over the rim of his teacup. 'You forget that I'm a member of the committee. Do you think I am likely to be swayed by her suitability for the position?'

'I have certainly not forgotten you are a member of the committee! You and I are of like mind. Sensible.' The vicar grinned. 'Broad-minded, if you will,' said Araminta instantly regaining her self-control.

'I was never a suffragette,' he said with an amused smile.

'You were a supporter.'

'I've made it my mainstay in life never to cross a strong woman. A wise man does not. She's not married is she?'

Araminta shook her head in a curt manner that helped her keep an emotionless expression.

'I understand she was engaged at one time. Her fiancé died in the last year of the war. One of the unidentified.'

Pale as it was, the light falling through the window caught the gleam of his hair. More noticeably it also picked out the sudden strained look in his eyes as he nodded in mute understanding.

Araminta saw the look but wasn't sure of its provenance. She was aware that the vicar had fought in the war and at its end, sickened and disgusted by it all, he'd joined the ministry. Unlike her son he had come back unscathed – at least physically. But who knows what was going on beneath the surface. Who could know what he'd seen and endured and what scars and secrets were left buried in his mind.

She felt him studying her in the same way that she did him, trying to read what wasn't being voiced.

'Suffice to say that I have great confidence that I am doing the right thing.'

'Was she recommended by someone you know?'

'It wouldn't make any difference. Her qualifications speak louder than words.'

Thinking he might have hit a raw nerve, Gregory smiled to himself. Although he was relatively new at St Michael's, he'd learned early on that her ladyship was a strong woman of shrewd judgement. Like anyone else, she must have secrets and a network of old acquaintances to whom she could refer if need be. She'd chosen him as vicar for a start – and on the recommendation of the bishop, who he suspected was her cousin.

'I'm sure all will work out exceedingly well,' he said before taking his leave. He smiled impishly. 'Once the populace have got over the shock.'

That evening he was still smiling when he thought of what her ladyship had contrived. She was a clever woman but also liked having her own way.

Before tucking into the steak and kidney pudding his house-keeper had left him, he stood looking out at the dark shape of the church sipping a glass of dark red wine. Talking about the new doctor and her ladyship's shenanigans with the hospital committee had amused him. Her mentioning that the new doctor had once been engaged to a man missing in action, a man whose identifiable remains had never been found had taken him back to a task he'd been asked to do. Soldier turned clergyman he was considered ideal for the mission, one that still filled him with remorse. He'd carried out what was required of him, praying over the bodies of six unidentified men to be reinterred. Except one of those men had carried an item of identity. He'd told no one and in his own way had honoured him as a fallen warrior should be honoured, his name engraved on a war memorial and hopefully remembered.

Grimes came along to see Araminta later.

As always, he gave her a stiff bow of his white-haired head before stating what was on his mind. 'Your ladyship, I have served this family with pride for many years but of late am finding it much harder to carry out my duties. The hours are getting too much for me. My legs—'

Araminta felt a flood of guilt wash over her. Her hand flew to her mouth. 'Oh, Mr Grimes! I'm so sorry. Is there anything I can do?'

He shuffled his feet and cleared his throat. 'Well, yes. That's what I want to talk to you about. I wonder whether it might be possible to have an assistant valet who could deal with Captain Devlin during the middle hours of the day. Not every day, but just enough to take the strain off me.'

He looked at her apologetically, his eyes a washed-out blue beneath his silvery hair. 'I'm terribly sorry, your ladyship.'

'Oh, Mr Grimes. It's me that should be sorry. You have been a good and faithful servant but really, I didn't notice that your hair was getting whiter.' She didn't add that his spine had curved into what was termed a 'dowager's hump'. Time had slipped by and although she'd noticed streaks of grey in her own ashen locks, she'd not really noticed the changes in Grimes.

'I apologise for the great burden I placed on you regarding the care of my son. I will indeed seek a solution to the situation.' She shook her head sorrowfully. 'Looking after him is not an easy task, but believe me, Mr Grimes, I am eternally grateful.'

There were no guests for dinner that evening and as Devlin had decided not to dine as he'd originally proposed she gave orders to have a tray brought up to her room.

Beforehand, in the privacy of her bathroom, she lay soaking with the steam rising around her. Her face was wet, though not just because of the steam. Tears fell from her eyes. In her mind, she cursed those responsible for the Great War. For many, it was over. Some were dead and at peace. Some had pushed those cruel years behind them and embraced the reality of whatever their life had become.

Devlin was different. Not only had the war left him blinded, but he relived the horrors of what he'd encountered every night. By day, he was blind to the world, but at night, he was eyes wide open at the battlefront, explosion and death all around. He would never regain his sight. She could just about accept that, but would he ever be able to put the horrors of those years behind him? Miracles seemed in short supply of late, she thought, before reminding herself that Doctor Frances Brakespeare was on her way. Once more she reread the letter she'd received from old friend Deborah Goldman.

'*Although not formally adopted, Frances is, to all intents and purposes, Izzy's daughter, the salve that had soothed Izzy's heart and the anger she felt for her father, which at times threatened to choke her.*'

Old memories flashed through Araminta's mind. Such times they'd had back in the days when women had first sought the vote. None of them had been spring chickens but that had been all to the good. The leaders of the movement had needed maturity plus independent means. So many women had been disowned by their parents – including Izzy, though the reason for her being disowned was more complicated.

'*I do hope you can help with this. Izzy would be extremely grateful and we did make her a promise.*'

7

The invitation to face the committee for the position at Orchard Cottage Hospital, Norton Dene came swiftly. The summons again related the stipend as three hundred and fifty guineas a year plus panel and private patients' fees, not exactly a fortune but a sum that would give her a similar level of independence to the one Izzy had advocated.

The signatory, who appeared to be a man named Mr Oliver James Nielsen, had also commented that accommodation would be provided.

'I envisage that your interview will give you the chance to better familiarise yourself with our town.'

On the way to Norton Dene, she passed rolling fields and went into a pub, where to her great joy found that she could buy a ploughman's lunch; Cheddar cheese, pickles, butter and crusty bread washed down with half a sweet cider. She asked the landlord serving behind the bar what she might expect of this town she was going to, Norton Dene.

'What's a young lady like you expecting?' he said to her.

She shrugged. 'I'm thinking it's all cows and sheep. And lots of fresh air.'

He looked at her in the way reserved for those who are not local and didn't know what they were talking about. 'It's a place of coal mines and limestone quarries. The coal mines are at the tail end of the Welsh coal seams and no more than three feet high. Men crawl with pickaxes to get it out. Then there's the limestone. That's quarried from around Bristol and all the way to the Mendip Hills and up into Gloucestershire and across the Severn into Monmouthshire. Both dangerous places to work in.'

Eating the wedge of cheese and hunk of freshly baked bread helped weigh down the apprehension that gyrated in her stomach. She was leaving the familiar behind and heading into unknown territory. Izzy had been her rock, the strong woman who had guided her every step of her life.

'She was a bit domineering,' Abigail, another of Izzy's friends had said to her.

'But all for your own good,' Deborah had countered and patted her hand reassuringly.

'Well it won't be anywhere near as exciting as London,' Abigail had countered.

'She doesn't want excitement,' Deborah had hissed. 'She wants stability and a chance to pursue her profession to the best of her ability.'

On leaving the pub she checked her luggage, the tea chests tied onto the back of the car and a small suitcase and her medicine bag bundled onto the back seat. She had considered leaving the bulk of it with Deborah just in case she didn't get the job. As it was the letter from the committee informed her that accommodation had been arranged. It hadn't stipulated whether it was just for the one night or more. *Never mind*, she thought. *I'll play it by ear.*

Her fingers lingered over the box into which she'd thrown the contents of Izzy's desk. The journal lay on top of the mountain of paperwork, books and brown paper folders. In time she might get round to reading it, perhaps when relaxing of an evening and smiling at silly little notes about her birthdays, her first day at school and going on holiday to some out-of-the-way cottage where woodland walks were overly abundant.

Two or three turns of the starting handle and the little car engine burbled into life and very soon she'd left fields and hedgerows behind and encountered terraces of miners' cottages, which in turn were replaced by the heart of the town where ranks of shops encircled a triangular green.

At the centre of the green a stone war memorial glared sepulchre white, newly erected if its unstained whiteness was anything to go by.

Frances averted her gaze from what was one of many war memorials throughout the country. Those who had served in or near those bloody fields only wanted to forget the carnage and she was certainly one of them. Instead she focused her attention on the butcher's shop which rubbed shoulders with a greengrocer's, which was next door to a baker's and there, tucked behind a red pillar box and a telephone box was a post office.

There was little traffic, few vehicles at all in fact. Compared to London, the town centre was a desert. No trams, no taxis, no bustling vans and lorries, horse-drawn carts, brewery drays or buses, though just as she thought that a woman on a bicycle dismounted in front of where she'd parked and gave her a curious glance before making for the post office. She was one of only three vehicles parked in the high street, two of which were delivery vans – one for the butcher; one for the baker. There were no cars except for her own.

A woman alighting from the bus chanced to glance in her direction before exchanging a look of curiosity with the cyclist.

Frances smiled at them. They didn't smile back but maintained shy almost wary looks.

It discomfited her to be of interest to complete strangers, but she told herself to accept what she was, a stranger in a small town. Nobody assessed who you were back in London. Nobody much cared.

A young woman pushing a pram chose that moment to walk past, her closeness and the gurgling baby startling her and stirring emotions she'd long thought buried.

If Ralph had survived, that could have been me, she thought with a pang of bitter regret. A mother with a child. Just an ordinary housewife out shopping, talking to other mothers, putting a meal on the table, keeping house for a husband whose job it was to bring in an income. Not that Izzy would have approved, of course. Izzy was all for women being independent of men even if it meant having children and bringing them up alone.

Frances could see her now and still hear her voice. 'I didn't do so bad with you did I? Managed without a man didn't I?'

Setting her jaw in a grim line and banishing the memories, she turned her attention back to the address for Orchard Cottage Hospital. It wouldn't hurt to check she was travelling in the right direction.

Winding down her car window, she poked her head out. 'Excuse me.'

The young woman pushing the pram gripped the handle more tightly and looked uncertain as to whether she should stop at all.

'The Orchard Cottage Hospital,' Frances asked. 'Am I going in the right direction?'

'Yes.' A finger pointed in the direction she should take. 'Keep going down the high street, then left at the end into Quarry Lane and straight down to the end.'

'Thank you.'

Ahead of her, ominous grey clouds hovered menacingly above the tower of the Anglican church, a Victorian pile surrounded by yew trees crowding against the churchyard wall.

The cloud followed her progress, hovering over the plainer, no-nonsense roof of the congregational chapel, which appeared to be constructed of rusting green tin.

The hospital name, Orchard Cottage Hospital, seemed at odds with Quarry Lane. She'd imagined it being surrounded by apple orchards, as its name suggested, and after all, this was a part of the country well known for its cider production. And fields. Grazing cattle and sheep or acres of golden corn. She'd even imagined milkmaids with rosy cheeks and dressed in muslin, milk pails dangling at each end of a yoke across their shoulders.

She laughed out loud at such a far-fetched vision.

To either side were terraces of red-brick houses, which were then superseded by older cottages with squat windows and low front doors.

Her laughter died and apprehension took over as the hospital came into view. So did the orchards surrounding it, nodules on boughs promising to come into bud and become pale pink apple blossom nodding over grey stone walls.

She passed through a pair of open gates where gold lettering on a dark green sign proclaimed that this was indeed the place she was looking for. Orchard Cottage Hospital. Beneath it was a dedication to a Lady Catherine Orchard, circa 1845. There went the fancy that it had been named after its surroundings. Apt then that her ladyship and the trees had worked in tandem to make it sound as pleasant as it looked.

The first cottage hospitals had been humble buildings converted from a cottage from which their name derived. Orchard Cottage Hospital was too large ever to have been the humble abode in which 'cottagers', labourers of the land, had lived. Large bay windows jutted out from the main building on either side of a set of double doors. A series of ordinary casements trailed in diminishing sizes to the outer corners of the building.

Clay rosemary tiles glowed like burnt embers on the large, hipped roof. Dormer windows jutted through the most expansive part of the roof and a mass of budding climbing plants shivered against cream-painted walls. She imagined them in flower when the summer came. The vision almost took her breath away – until the sky opened and raindrops the size of halfpennies rattled into the ground and onto the roof of the car. Engine turned off and her jacket straightened, Frances exclaimed, 'Well here goes,' swallowed her nervousness and got out of the car to face both the building and her future.

Put your shoulders back and hold your head high.

Izzy was still with her, directing how she should present herself.

First impressions count.

Of course they did.

She'd barely pushed the car door open and got out when what sounded like a clap of thunder in the distance stayed her progress. She turned her attention further down Quarry Lane. The frowning storm clouds were still there but had been added to. A dull dark grey cloud hung beneath them, tumbling and swirling up from the ground. A siren wailed, piercing her ears and setting her teeth on edge.

Stretching her neck, she turned her head this way and that seeking the source of the sound. Her action was interrupted by a welter of shouts and running feet. She turned to see a woman wearing the round white cap of a matron, ribbon tightly tied beneath her chin, come flying down the steps leading to the hospital entrance shouting at the top of her voice.

'Someone try to get hold of Doctor Walker. And someone rouse Mr MacDonald.'

The nurse running behind her shouted back that she'd sent the boy to go.

As she hit the last step, the woman she judged to be either a matron or senior sister spotted Frances sitting inside the car and stopped.

'Is that your car?' Her voice was like stone disturbed by raging water. Her manner was that of someone used to being obeyed.

'Yes. Has there been an accident? Can I be of any help?'

'Yes. You can and there has. Three long screeches of that infernal siren mean three men have been injured. You're requisitioned or at least your car is.'

Without another word or a by your leave, the front seat was levered forward, giving just enough space for the woman's short legs to clamber in and her big backside to plonk into the back seat. She shouted at the nurse to join her. 'Come along, Nurse Daniels. Don't dawdle.'

Nurse Daniels smiled apologetically at Frances before joining the senior nurse in the rear seat. 'This is very kind of you.'

'Not at all.'

'Can I have your name,' Frances asked as she scrambled back out of the car, the starting handle gripped ready for turning.

'Sister Edith Harrison. And this is Nurse Daniels. Now no more polite exchanges if you please. This is an emergency. Straight ahead. I'll direct you.' Her speedy diatribe paused as though a thought had suddenly occurred to her. 'You can drive, I suppose.'

'That's how I got here. I drove. I am properly qualified. I learned to drive ambulances during the war.'

Making her way to the front of the car, Frances slid the starting handle into the hole at the bottom of her little car's radiator and gave it a good yank. At the same time she murmured a prayer that the engine would start first time. As if sensing this was serious, the engine chortled into life. Her prayers were answered.

Foot heavy on the throttle, the little car set off at a fair lick down Quarry Lane, bouncing over its rutted surface. Early blossom and the remains of last year's fallen leaves blew in waves from the trees and raindrops sounded like buttons being thrown in handfuls over the windscreen.

Frances felt a rush of nervous excitement. Her first day and here she was racing towards the scene of an accident.

'Perhaps you could tell me where we're going.'

'To the quarry.'

'Have you any idea what's happened?'

'Not till I get there.'

'Good Lord. Let's hope we can help.'

'Can't you get this car to go any faster?'

Frances bristled. 'The old girl is doing her best.'

'Well, let's just hope we can cope.'

'When will the doctor arrive – I heard you call for him to be summoned by a boy.'

'*The* boy. Mr Elliot is our groundsman and odd job man. He's not a boy. He's over sixty-five.'

'Let's hope he finds the doctor. Do you know where he is?'

'Doctor Walker is...' The pause was telling. 'He's doing something else. He's semi-retired and his replacement hasn't arrived yet. Very tardy of the new doctor but so very typical of the young nowadays!'

Frances bristled but kept her voice even and not without a hint of triumph when she declared, 'Your new doctor is here. I'm driving this car.'

It made her smile to see her passengers exchanging surprised looks reflected via her rear-view mirror. It was followed by silence though she noticed a slightly more worried look on the face of Nurse Daniels. Perhaps she wasn't used to travelling in a car. She asked her if that was the case.

'No. No,' she exclaimed. 'I'm just hoping nobody that I know is hurt.' Not wishing to appear insensitive she swiftly corrected herself. 'I hope nobody at all is hurt.'

A shower of dust and gravel flew skywards as the little car bounced through the quarry gates before coming to a halt.

Without a moment's hesitation, Sister Harrison clambered out from one side of the car and the nurse from the other.

Stout shoes on the end of Sister Harrison's plump legs ran over the uneven ground, skirting or jumping over the puddles.

Frances grabbed her medicine bag from the back seat and ran fast enough to catch up with Nurse Daniels regardless of the Cuban heels on her snakeskin shoes.

Men appeared like wraiths from the swirling cloud of dust, features indistinguishable until they were close, when they blinked against the dirt in their eyes and swiped rags over their sweat-streaked faces.

One man stood like a colossus above the rest, his arm raised like the arm of a windmill waving them over.

'Sister Harrison!'

Without regard for the dirty water splashing up her legs, Frances followed Sister Harrison and Nurse Daniels to where he beckoned.

The eyes of the big man swept over Frances from top to toe. His look made her feel guilty that she was wearing an outfit bought in London.

'We need nurses and suchlike useful women here not no Lady Bountiful.'

'Lucky I'm here then,' she replied in a sharper tone than his. 'I'm Doctor Brakespeare and I'm taking over from Doctor Walker. Now, if you'll get out of my way, I can do my job.'

He looked embarrassed but quickly accepted that although she might look a refined city woman she could hold her own with the likes of him. *Met his kind in the East End*, she thought. *Tough men who could rule the roost if you let them.*

Three men lay amongst the dust, rocks and debris, their mates doing their best to clean their wounds and get them on their feet.

'Let me through, please.'

They looked askance but did not protest when she pushed them out of the way and examined the one man who they did not attempt to help to his feet.

Two of the casualties had sustained injuries from flying rocks and only needed patching up. The third seemed to be in a far worse state.

To their credit, Sister Harrison and Nurse Daniels took charge of the two men.

Frances chose the third and worst injured though every so often was aware of Nurse Daniels looking over, her face far paler than when she'd been in the back of the car. She knows him. That was her instant impression that this man was a relative.

The face of the unconscious man was grey with dust. His eyes were closed and a patch of blood was spreading over his flat and muscular stomach. There was also a slight bulging rather than a swelling, which worried her. She'd seen intestines spilling from a deep wound back in France and bulges caused by explosions scattering foreign objects and lodging them in wounds. A quick glance round at the scattered rubble, bits of metal and other detritus confirmed her worst fears. Her mind raced over everything she'd ever learned about such a gaping wound. Using both hands she pressed guts that threatened to erupt back into place.

The foreman's shadow fell over both her and the injured man. Behind him others had gathered looking concerned and shaking their heads.

Suddenly a voice barked through the veil of dust, subdued now thanks to the falling rain.

'Come on, you men. You don't get paid for standing around.'

With the arrival of a man who was obviously senior to anyone, the labourers standing by drifted off, some muttering, some throwing hostile looks in the new arrival's direction.

The man wore a good tweed suit and a brown trilby on a head of sandy-coloured hair. His eyes were a sapphire blue totally lacking in warmth, but oddly entranced as they alighted on the handsome young woman with dark blonde hair and lithe figure.

'And who are you, my pretty? And what are you doing here?'

His eyes stayed fixed on Frances and ignored the foreman as he named the three injured men and the extent of their injuries.

'Mr Grainger. It's Ned Skittings. He's hurt bad.'

Frances guessed he was possibly the son in Grainger and Son as depicted on the sign at the quarry gate.

She heard a sharp intake of breath from Nurse Daniels.

'Pull yourself together, Nurse Daniels. The doctor is dealing with Ned.'

So she was right. Ned Skittings was a relative.

Her hands were full and her priority was the injured man so the fact that he was eyeing her with outright lust angered her.

Grainger's lecherous look turned to one of surprise, raised eyebrows, eyes wide open. He glanced from Sister Harrison to Frances.

'You're a doctor?'

'I am. Perhaps you could tell me what happened here. This man is very badly injured. Do you have some kind of compensation scheme for your workers?'

Ignoring the question he diverted his focus to the quarry foreman.

'So what happened, Frank?'

The foreman seemed reluctant to answer, rubbing at his cheek, brow wrinkling as he tried to remember the details.

His slow response didn't go down well with Grainger.

'Well, come on, man. Somebody made a mistake. Who was it? Speak up.'

'I couldn't rightly say, Mr Grainger. I weren't yur. I was back over by the crusher.'

As she listened Frances pressed a large piece of lint onto the wound.

Nurse Daniels joined her. 'Ned's my brother-in-law. Will he be all right?'

'I think so but he needs to get to a hospital.'

Hovering close enough to hear, Grainger looked troubled.

He jerked his head at the other two men who were being helped to their feet.

'How about them two? How are they?'

Sister Harrison confirmed their injuries were not serious.

Frances had done what she could with what she had at her disposal. Hospital was the only option – a hospital with comparable facilities to London. It had to be the infirmary in Bristol.

The worried-looking foreman dared to make comment. 'Will Ned pull through, only I've got to make out a report, you see…'

'I think I too should write out a report. Once you've made enquiries can you tell me exactly what happened?'

The foreman nodded. 'I will in time. I'm only surmising for now that a row was marked out and the button pushed, but one of the detonators didn't do its job. Ned here went back with the other two to check and got too close. Gave it a prod with a wooden pole as we always do and it went off all by itself.'

'You don't know that for sure.' Grainger threw the foreman a look of dark condemnation for daring to open his mouth. Worried for his job, the foreman clammed up and stared at the ground.

The other men having been taken care of, Nurse Daniels knelt beside Frances and bent over her brother-in-law's face, her own face creased with worry.

'Ned. Ned. Can you hear me?'

The poor girl had acted professionally up until now. Frances surmised that she needed to do something to help keep her mind off things.

'Nurse Daniels. Press this lint down onto the wound whilst I apply the sticking plaster. We must keep it clean. We must keep it protected.'

Nurse Daniels bent a bit lower. 'You'll be all right, Ned. This lady's a doctor.'

She exchanged a relieved smile with Frances who knew from her training that a doctor appearing positive helped the patient do the same and this nurse understood that.

Frances noted the debris scattered over the uneven ground, the stones, the dirt, the bits of metal blown to smithereens along with the precious limestone which was as important to road building as it was to steel production.

She studied the corrupted landscape, where pools of rainwater had gathered in mud-filled gullies. All kinds of debris had been disturbed by the explosion – twigs, rope, metal, barbed wire, gravel. Any of these could have become imbedded in his stomach and it worried her.

Sister Harrison joined them but only after throwing a scowl at Mr Grainger who was still hovering too close as far as Frances was concerned.

'He needs sewing up,' Sister Harrison said sniffily.

'He needs more than that. I think an X-ray is in order. I need to know what is in there and have it taken out before he's sewn up.'

'X-rays? Good grief we haven't got an X-ray machine here, Doctor. You'll have to go to the infirmary for that.'

'I do realise that. It's about an hour to the Royal Infirmary. We need to get him there. We need an ambulance. Does the hospital have one?'

'Only on a part-time basis. Mr MacDonald's gone to a funeral in Coalpit Heath today. I can send a message but fear he won't be back until after tea.'

'He's taken an ambulance to a funeral?' Frances couldn't believe what she was hearing.

'The hearse doubles up as an ambulance. This is a small town and a cottage hospital,' Sister Harrison said, making it sound to Frances that she was just an outsider who couldn't possibly understand how things were.

Go back to London. That was the message she heard in that gravelly voice.

Ambulances were readily available in London. When it came to the provision of services the facilities were to hand whereas here...

She reminded herself that this was a small Somerset town, which suggested to her that everything would be on a make do and mend basis. It all seemed very primitive compared to what she was used to. But she mustn't appear superior. Not if she was going to stay here. She would not condemn out of hand and scurry back to London or another city hospital. If she did decide to stay she had to rise to the challenge and gain the respect of the locals. If the dual use of the funeral hearse was anything to go by improvisation was the key. She stored the information for future reference.

'The situation's too serious to wait around. I'll take him to hospital myself.' She turned to the foreman. 'I need two men to carry him to my car.'

The foreman looked at Grainger for permission to continue. Grainger met his gaze before locking eyes with her.

'Are you going to drive him there?' he asked.

'I am.'

'I can come with you if you like.'

'No thank you.' Her response was terse. She had no intention whatsoever of being alone in the company of Mr Grainger.

He offered the use of his car. 'It's bigger than this orange box on wheels,' he said dismissively.

'No thank you. I can manage.'

She found herself wanting to stand up for the little car she'd named Matron Molly, a derogatory term but her term. Her name for her car. Having her called an orange box left her seething.

The foreman stated that it was impossible to fit Ned in as the front passenger seat was in the way.

'Take it out,' Frances ordered.

The foreman raised his eyebrows. 'Are you sure?'

'If it means the man lives or dies, then yes, I'm sure. Can you keep the seat somewhere until I get back?'

The foreman promised to keep it safe for her.

The injured man was carefully manoeuvred into the front of the car so that his head and torso ended up on the back seat and his legs and feet were resting where the front seat used to be. Several blankets had been found to form a level surface between the back and front of the car. Another blanket was used to wrap around the man's guts. The bandages alone wouldn't be enough to stem the blood. The blankets too might not be enough, but never mind thought, Frances. It will scrub off. You were taught that a long while ago.

It was true. Her mind went back to the field hospital and a

mature nurse reassuring a queasy young VAD that nothing was too difficult to overcome.

The moment the patient was installed in the car, Mr Grainger nudged aside the two men who had placed him. 'I'm ready and willing to accompany you to the hospital.'

I bet you are, thought Frances. Luckily she had an answer ready and waiting.

'My car's a bit on the small side. There's only room for me. The less weight, the faster I can travel.'

Shrugging nonchalantly, he shoved off, hands in pockets to be replaced by Nurse Lucy Daniels. Her frightened gaze turned to Frances. 'Will he be all right?'

Frances patted her arm. She'd warmed to the young nurse and if everyone at the hospital was anything like her she would be content.

'I'll do my best to ensure that he recovers. The surgeons at the hospital will do what needs to be done once they know what they're dealing with. The X-ray will tell them. Can you let your sister know?'

Lucy nodded, and although she held her jaw firmly, worry lines furrowed her forehead.

The foreman turned the starting handle whilst Frances got behind the wheel.

'Wait,' she called out suddenly. 'Nurse Daniels.'

Nurse Daniels came to the car window.

'I believe accommodation is available to me overnight, but it's going to be late by the time I get back.'

'Yes. The vicarage coach house is for you. I helped clean it up. I'll tell the vicar that you'll be arriving late.'

'Thank you, Nurse Daniels.'

'Lucy. Call me Lucy.' She leaned in closer and added, 'Though not when Sister Harrison is around. She's a stickler for protocol.'

'Lucy. Nice to meet you.'

Driving off through the rain, Frances thought of her first few hours in Norton Dene. So far she could see there would be pluses and minuses in her new position. The ultimate outcome could be her staying or finding life so dull she would have to move on. On the other hand it might open doors she as yet had never discovered. Only time would tell.

8

Thunder rolled, lightning flashed and the rain slanted down like stair rods, splashing on the road and up in front of the headlights.

The windscreen wipers fought the deluge of windblown twigs and leaves and once open country was left behind the roads glistened with reflections from streetlights.

Guessing a main road would get her to the hospital proved right and her lips moved in silent prayer as she pulled up before the entrance.

Despite the foul weather someone heard her shout for assistance. Only one person came out at first but was swiftly joined by others once the alarm was raised.

A young doctor and a nurse checked her patient's pulse and breathing whilst she quickly explained what had happened. Everyone was getting soaked to the skin.

'He needs an X-ray.'

'I'll be the judge of that,' said a young doctor.

Sensitive fingers pulled back the ad hoc dressing and probed the injury. The doctor looked impressed.

'Are you a nurse?'

'I'm a doctor.'

He reacted immediately. 'Get a stretcher out here.'

A stretcher was fetched and gently – very, very gently – the injured man was extricated from the car.

'Straight to X-ray,' shouted the young doctor. 'There's something in there.' He nodded a curt thanks.

'I wrongly presumed.'

'You're not the first and you won't be the last.'

Frances quickly gave a nurse the few details she knew, which had been hastily scribbled down on a piece of notepaper by the foreman. They dashed off to their duties, leaving her there in the pouring rain, soaked through with a car that was missing a front seat.

Back she drove through the pouring rain, aching for a hot drink and a good night's sleep.

The city fell behind her and the dark road wound ahead.

'A bed,' she murmured, 'my kingdom for a bed.'

She didn't have a kingdom, but somehow a corrupted line from *King Richard III* suited the occasion.

According to Lucy Daniels, accommodation had been made ready for her in the vicarage coach house. Once back in Norton Dene it made sense that her next task was to find the vicarage.

Although the light was growing dim, Frances found the imposing edifice of the vicarage next door to the church she'd spotted earlier. Gothic perfection betrayed that its true origin was in the early nineteenth century and although on first sight it gave more than a passing nod to the Elizabethan age, it was too crisply upright to be that old.

Four very tall decorative chimneys of twisted brick sat atop four consecutive gables. Its size almost rivalled the cottage hospital, its style sprawling, as favoured by both the wealthy and the

Church. Bay windows graced the ground floor and deep eaves frowned above dark-red brickwork.

Just as she came to a halt in the gravelled drive, a cloud of steam screamed like a boiling kettle from the radiator cap. Engrossed in her errand of mercy and fearing she would not get to the infirmary in time, she'd totally forgot to top Matron Molly up with water.

After a day like today, Frances felt the need to swear and she did.

A disturbance to the curtain in one of the windows conveyed that somebody was aware of her arrival.

The front door opened and a figure stood on the top step gazing into the night. 'Can I help?'

The voice was decidedly male and warm with welcome.

'Some water for my radiator would be appreciated. I'm Doctor Frances Brakespeare. Sorry I'm late. I had to take an injured man to the infirmary in Bristol.'

'So I hear. Lucy popped in to tell me. My dear doctor. Welcome indeed.' He bounded down the steps in long, confident strides. 'Reverend Gregory Sampson. Pleased to meet you.'

He gave her hand a firm shake before turning his attention to her car.

'Ah,' he said, frowning down at the offending steam. 'Topping up the radiator is the only thing I know about cars. Leave it with me. I'll fetch some water.'

He loped back up the steps to the front door with the same long, lazy strides as he'd come down, the hem of his black gown flicking against his ankles.

His appearance and charm almost left her speechless. His presence and easy-going manner made her feel she'd arrived in an oasis of calm after a very taxing day.

He returned with an enamel jug held with both hands.

'Careful,' she said, grasping his wrist when she saw he was about to undo the cap. 'It's still very hot. Let me get a rag.'

She fancied he'd flinched when her fingers had firmed around his wrist. Now he watched with avid interest as she used a rag kept for that very purpose to undo the cap.

'Will you pour or shall I?' she said to him, the first glimmer of amusement she'd felt all day.

He laughed. 'I don't drive so assume you know better than me.'

Once the radiator was refilled and still using the rag, Frances screwed down the radiator cap.

'Now, what about you, Doctor? You're soaked through. Shall we get you settled?'

'That would be much appreciated. I was told earlier the vicarage coach house had been prepared for my arrival.'

'It has indeed.' He pointed along a narrow path at the side of the vicarage and the spot where it disappeared into the trees. 'Wait a moment and I'll get a flashlight. Can I help you with your luggage?'

'The small suitcase should be enough for tonight.'

She hoped the rest of the luggage didn't look too much as though she was hoping the position was hers and she'd had no intention of leaving the next day.

She climbed three steps to the front door and stood in the hallway whilst he fetched a torch.

The hallway of the vicarage was wide and glowed amber from an overhead light. Once he'd returned, it struck Frances that the Reverend Gregory Sampson was too young and good-looking to be a vicar. He had an outdoors freshness about him, golden streaks in his hair and laughing eyes.

Tucking the suitcase beneath his arm, he escorted her down the steps and waved the flashlight at the path they needed to take.

'I will be your light the darkness. In the literal sense.'

He also seemed to have a permanent smile on his face. Seduced by his looks alone, she decided she might be persuaded to go to church more often. But that wouldn't happen. She'd fallen out with God a long time ago when she'd learned that Ralph was never coming back.

9

The Reverend Gregory Sampson took big strides to where a small square window beckoned in the darkness. The flashlight danced the narrow path with pools of light. The arched double doors of the coach house were still hanging firmly onto their cast iron hinges. It suggested to Frances that a coach and horses might dash out at any moment.

'I lit a candle. That's why you can see a faint light in the window. I thought you might appreciate its glow on such a filthy night.'

'It looks very welcoming,' she replied, aching to get into the warmth, to kick off her shoes and sink her head into a pillow.

There was a smaller door set in the side wall of the building which he pushed open with his knee and without using a key. 'This used to be where the horses lived, adjacent to the coach itself next door. The coachman lived in the two rooms upstairs with wife and children. At least four of them, I think. It's not like that now, of course. Everything's been modernised.'

The flickering beam picked up dark crannies and lumpy furniture, both of which belonged to another age. The feeble candle flame flickered in the sudden draught from the door opening then settled once it was closed.

'The range is lit and there's a plate of bread, cheese, apples and apple chutney on the table. Apple tart too. We grow a lot of apples round here.'

His chuckle was infectious and Frances couldn't help but smile.

The torch beam flashed over several muslin-covered plates next to a brass oil lamp crowned with an etched glass bowl.

'It's a bit late and Mrs Cross, my daily help and dogsbody, has gone home. She prepared this earlier, thinking afternoon tea rather than supper. No doubt you could do with something more substantial, but I dare not go into the kitchen and prepare a proper meal. It's her kingdom, you see, and her revenge would be too terrible to contemplate.'

The warmth of her countenance matched his own. 'I like bread and cheese.'

It wasn't a lie and although she'd already consumed a ploughman's lunch at the inn where she'd stopped it seemed that he and his housekeeper had gone to a lot of trouble. She had no wish to appear ungrateful.

The glow of the oil lamp came into life and warmed the bumpy white walls. 'Only oil lamps or candles, I'm afraid, though it's hoped gas and electricity will be added before very long. Cosy atmosphere, don't you think?'

'Very,' she said as she held her hands to the glowing coals of the range.

'The range will provide you with hot water and cooking facilities.'

He insisted on showing her around. A living room with an inglenook fireplace took up most of the ground floor into which were piled logs at one end and a scuttle full of coal at the other.

Beyond the living room was a kitchen where the roof was lower and a small square window overlooked the back garden.

He pointed at the iron hooks hanging from the ceiling and the iron mangers in two of the corners. 'This was where the horses lived. There was an iron partition between here and what is now the living room. The horses each had their own space.'

'Lucky horses.'

'It wasn't as warm for them. And they didn't have bread and cheese. Possibly had apples though.'

'I'm sure you're right, Vicar,' laughter tumbling over her words.

'It's feasible.'

'Of course it is. I wouldn't expect a vicar to lie. That would be very bad form.'

'Call me Gregory outside the church, Vicar or Reverend when I'm on duty. Shall I do the same for you? Frances outside the hospital and Doctor when I'm in need of your services?' He pulled out a farmhouse-style chair and invited her to sit down. Taking the one opposite. She sighed as she sank into it.

'I don't see why not,' she said in response. 'I'm Frances and if you wish to engage me then please do. Unless you already have a doctor you're very satisfied with. I've no wish to upset the locals.'

He folded his arms. She noticed they bulged against his coat sleeves and formed the opinion that this was not a man who spent all his time writing sermons.

She dragged her gaze away and resumed holding her hands out to the fire grate.

'It's easily done. But I think they'll warm to you. In fact I'm sure they will.'

'I hope so. There was no time to wander when I first arrived. My intention had been to find out where I was to stay this evening and confirm that I was here for the interview tomorrow. Things didn't turn out as smooth as I expected. In fact I've had quite a christening since I arrived. Straight to work.'

'Yes,' he said, all trace of amusement fled from his face and replaced with one of concern. 'I heard the siren. Thank goodness there were no fatalities.'

She told him a man named Ned Skittings had had to stay in the city infirmary for an X-ray.

'Ah yes. Ned. He's married to Nancy, one of the part-time nurses at the hospital. You'll be seeing her quite a bit, as you will her sister Lucy Daniels. Seeing as they only work part-time at the hospital and in need of funds, they've agreed to take it in turns to house-keep for you.' He waved a hand dismissively. 'No extra on the rent. It's all costed for.'

Mention of rent inferred that the job was hers, that she would be staying. 'I'm very grateful. It seems you've thought of everything.'

'Shall I make tea?' he asked suddenly. Without waiting for a reply, he was on his feet and hanging a kettle already filled with water on a hook above the coal fire. 'It'll be brewed in no time.'

'I could certainly do with it. I'd not thought to find myself driving to the infirmary in Bristol. But it had to be done. I suspected some foreign object in his stomach. Only an X-ray will confirm that.'

He made comment about the wonders of modern medicine and how far humanity had come since the days of bloodletting and medicinal leeches.

'Ned's a strong lad. His strength will see him through,' he added.

Frances pushed the empty plate away and pulled the freshly brewed tea towards her. 'The biggest fear is infection. But, as you say, he is a strong young man. All should be well. And he's married to a nurse?'

'He is. Nancy.'

'That should help.'

'And they have a daughter. A baby. Not only do the sisters share their work at the hospital and here between them, but they also share caring for the baby. Along with Mrs Skittings, that is.' A broad smile almost cut his face in half. 'She's quite a character. But there, this town is full of characters.'

'I hope that in time I get to know them all – if I'm to stay that is.'

Gregory, reached across as though about to pat her hand and voice some reassurance. On realising that his timing might not be appropriate, he withdrew but still offered her the reassurance. 'Believe me. You're staying.' He sounded very adamant and went on to say, 'Whatever the committee might think it's her ladyship who'll have the last word. It's the family money that set up the hospital in the first place and she won't let them forget that. It's her baby. Her fiefdom.'

He cocked his head sidewise, his expression ripe with curiosity. 'You know, Frances, I can't help thinking I've seen you somewhere before. Don't know where though.' He was very still as he tried to remember then gave up and became as animated as he'd been before. 'Never mind. My memory's not what it was. Shall we talk about something else? How about I describe the people of Norton Dene – beginning with some members of the hospital committee?'

'Please do,' she replied feeling unusually curious about these people she had never met.

'Well. For a start...'

He went on to describe the bank manager who spent more time playing golf than in his bank, the postmistress who was a natural-born nosy parker, Ned Skittings' mother who brewed up herbal remedies, the Brigadier Grainger, who still maintained that the only gentlemanly war was one fought on horseback.

'Plus Sister Harrison, of course, who I used to think was a frustrated spinster but can't help thinking that there's another side to her.'

'That's preposterous,' Frances exclaimed, instantly thinking of Izzy and her friends. 'I met her at the quarry. She seemed very efficient, and anyway she might not like men.'

Something akin to mischievousness narrowed his eyes. 'I've seen the way she looks at Simon Grainger. The woman is hungry – and not for bread and cheese,' he added with a wicked smile.

Frances tutted.

'More tea?'

Whilst filling her cup he went on to tell her a little about Lady Compton-Dixon.

'A mighty force in this town, as you might expect from a titled lady who marched with the Pankhursts.'

'I had heard of her.' Of course she had. Izzy, Deborah and Abigail had been disciples.

'Her ladyship is quite formidable.'

The legs of the vicar's chair scraped over the uneven flagstones. 'It's late. I must be going.' He offered his hand for the second time that evening. 'I'm pleased to meet you.'

'Will Matron Molly be in your way? My car,' she said in response to his puzzlement. She told him why she was called that. 'A dragon of a matron. Cantankerous.'

He laughed. 'Of course not.'

Once the Reverend Gregory Sampson had wished her goodnight, Frances made herself a second cup of tea with hot water poured from the kettle which the vicar had left on the hob.

Holding a lighted candle in front of her, she made her way up the narrow staircase to the bedrooms where the coachman and his family had once slept beneath the eaves. The larger bedroom at the back of the house had been made up with clean white linen that smelled of lavender. Setting the candle down on a bamboo side table, she took the opportunity to test the softness of the top pillow. In doing so, she came across a whole bunch of lavender secreted between the top and bottom pillow and knew it was freshly picked from the garden and placed there for her benefit. There was a widely held belief that its scent ensured a good night's sleep. She hoped it was true.

On pushing open one half of the casement window, a flood of fresh night air filled the room. From here, Frances looked out onto the back garden, and even though it was dark – far darker than in the city – she took stock of her surroundings. To one side was some kind of building, its roof caved in and open to the sky. A dense and silent shape rose from the opening and glided into the night. An owl. Its presence was like a welcome to her new home. Norton Dene was a market town, but the countryside was close by and despite the mines and quarries, there were still fields, woodlands and patches of greenery dispersed between buildings.

It was too dark to clearly see what was on the other side, but she thought she heard animals in a field – goats or sheep perhaps?

Before getting into bed, she undid the buckles of her suitcase and opened the lid, sighing as she did so. Lying on top of everything was the sepia photograph of Ralph in a silver frame. Her heart seemed to stop beating at the sight of him and for an instant she thought she could smell the fine wool of his uniform, the masculine scent of his body and the eau de cologne he patted his cheeks with after shaving. She also heard his voice.

'We'll get married once I've got my feet under the table.'

'I don't want to wait. I want us to get married now.'

He'd laughed at her enthusiasm but insisted they should wait until he'd moved up the ranks. 'Wouldn't you prefer to be married to a major rather than a lowly captain?'

She'd replied that marrying him didn't depend on his rank in the army. In fact, she couldn't care less whether he was a common private or a civilian plain mister. Titles didn't matter. All that mattered was him and tying the knot so they could sleep in the same bed until death did them part. Death had had its own plans and had taken him before they'd had chance to be married.

The flickering candle flame made the silver frame shimmer and bequeathed movement to the handsome man in the photograph. Seeing how the light flickered over his features made Frances want it to continue with the illusion that he was moving, that those lips she'd once kissed might smile or whisper an endearment that would sweeten her sleep much more than the lavender. She lay down on her side, head propped on her hand looking at him until her eyes closed, her hand collapsed and, still fully clothed, she fell asleep.

* * *

By morning, the candle was no more than a stub in its pewter holder. Frances made a promise to herself not to let it happen again in case it toppled and set light to the hem of the curtains.

Not a good start, she thought.

Neither was the sight of her face in the single mirror hanging above the wooden mantlepiece and it failed to be improved by a second look, this time into the washstand mirror.

As for her clothes... She sighed in exasperation. They were crumpled and in need of a good pressing that no amount of smoothing out with her hands would achieve.

Before sorting out a change of clothes, she fetched rainwater from a butt outside the back door, sloshed some into a white enamel bowl and washed her face.

She'd been frugal choosing what she would wear. All her clothes had been purchased from the best shops in London and she'd avoided choosing anything looking as if it had just come out of the box. A navy-blue bolero jacket worn over a white shirt and matched with a checked skirt that skimmed her shins seemed the right choice. The outfit was a great favourite and bought some years ago and worn on many occasions. It wasn't cut in the very latest fashion but it had served her well when she'd wanted to be taken seriously. And she very much wanted to be taken seriously.

10

The entrance hall of the Orchard Cottage Hospital was cool and smelt of cleanliness and beeswax.

Wooden flooring complemented eau-de-Nil walls, a subtle shade of green that in a certain light looked almost white. There was a cosiness absent in a city infirmary and it was certainly nothing like she'd been used to back in the grim days of war in all that was left of a shelled building.

Daylight from outside fell onto the varnished parquet floor. The chair she'd been offered was upholstered in a flowery moquette in a gilded frame. It was also quite old and it crossed her mind that it might have been donated from a great house, perhaps sometime in the last century.

Frances braced her shoulders and told herself it wouldn't be the end of the world if she didn't get the position. But it would be. Everything depended on her becoming the resident doctor at Orchard Cottage Hospital.

The sound of footsteps preceded the arrival of Nurse Lucy Daniels. A look of welcome brightened her eyes and lips.

'Good morning, Doctor Brakespeare. It's good to see you again.'

'You, too.'

'Thank you. How is your sister? It must have been quite a shock when she found out her husband was injured.'

'It was. She's grateful you took him to the infirmary.'

'It was important that I did.'

'I know. But thank you again. They're almost ready in there,' she said, jerking her head to the double doors beyond her shoulder. 'Sorry for the wait.'

'That's not a problem.'

'There is an armchair,' she said. 'If you'd like to sit down.'

'I'll stand, thank you.'

Lucy hurried off noiselessly, leaving Frances less apprehensive than she had been.

However, the two nurses were not who she needed to convince that she was the right person for the job. Stiffening her shoulders, Frances prepared herself for all that was likely to be thrown at her and hoped it would not be too strenuous.

Time did not hurry itself. Keeping busy helped avoid feeling impatient or apprehensive. To pass the time she looked around her though there wasn't that much to see. One painting above the unlit fireplace of a woman wearing a low-necked crinoline dress, her eyes as grey as November. She wore a string of pearls around her neck and matching pear-shaped pearls hung from her ears. This, she surmised, was the lady who had established the cottage hospital. Quite high up on the wall in front of her, she spotted a wooden plaque. War memorials like this were quite common, but on closer inspection it turned out not to be so. The name Lady Margaret Sarah Dixon was picked out in gold lettering. Beneath that was a commemoration.

This hospital was conceived and paid for by Lady Margaret Sarah Dixon for the benefit of those of this parish who are in work but on low wages and to enable the medical profession hereabouts to treat those in need of both their expertise and charity and refer them to these facilities when needed.

In the year of our Lord, 1856.

It was hard to drag her eyes away from that notice, thinking of what this place must have been like back when it had first been established. Smaller perhaps. She'd heard that at their beginning most cottage hospitals had boasted only six to ten beds. Both the building and the surrounding populace had grown since then.

Nurse Lucy Daniels returned with the news that the committee was now ready for her.

'This way please.'

Nurse Daniels led her along a corridor that ran straight then headed off to the left and it seemed they ended up at the far end of the building. A pair of double doors opened onto a grand room with oak-panelled walls and green velvet curtains, a stark contrast with the paleness of the walls in the reception and along the more public corridors. Her feet sank into the thick pile of a Turkish rug.

Several people were seated around a highly polished mahogany table, their heads bent, eyes contemplating a small assemblance of papers in front of them.

Men predominated, with the exception of Sister Harrison, who kept her eyes averted except to nod curtly in her direction before pretending to look down at her hands when in fact she was furtively glancing at Simon Grainger.

The men mumbled muted good mornings though didn't sound that enthusiastic at doing so.

Gregory was seated closest to the window, daylight turning his blond streaks to gold and that look on his face that made it seem as though he couldn't take the world seriously.

When he winked, she winked back. It didn't seem as though anyone noticed and she didn't care if they did.

The man sitting at the head of the table had a hooked nose and white feathering on head and upper lip, which to her immediately suggested a bird of prey – an American bald eagle perhaps, which wasn't bald but white haired.

'Good morning, Doctor. I am Brigadier Stewart Algernon Grainger.'

'Good morning. I am Doctor Frances Brakespeare.'

'Quite,' he said in what sounded like an offhanded manner. 'I'll introduce everyone first before we pursue the formalities.'

His voice sounded that of a man used to giving orders, booming like a cannon.

His magnificent head of hair was immobile as he nodded at the man who sported red circles around his eyes – a sure sign that he rode a motorcycle and that his goggles were too tight. 'This is Doctor Walker, our present doctor.'

Doctor Walker grunted a wordless greeting but continued to scribble notes on the papers in front of him.

'Sister Harrison, senior nurse.'

'We've already met.'

'Indeed,' returned Sister Harrison with a curt nod, her expression nondescript and somewhat disinterested.

The brigadier inclined his awesome white head to each of the others in turn.

'The Reverend Sampson, who I believe you have also met.'

Frances turned her head and gave the vicar a smile. 'Indeed. He's been very kind.'

'It's my job to dispense the milk of human kindness,' said the vicar, perpetual amusement dancing in his eyes.

The brigadier moved on. 'Mr John Stone, our local chemist. Mr Colin Cheshire, manager of the Norton Dene coal mines at Catbrook. Mr Simon Grainger, my son who manages the quarry.'

Simon Grainger was far more subdued than when she saw him the day before. A different man when his father was present.

In turn each man acknowledged her with a curt nod whereas the Reverend Gregory Sampson eyed her openly and with a slight smile on his face. When it seemed his smile threatened to widen, he placed a hand over his lips, his fingers extending onto his cheek.

He made her want to giggle.

The brigadier waved a hand at the only chair on her side of the table and invited her to sit down. The chair was unupholstered and gave the impression of being a poor relative of the one offered her earlier out in the hall.

'Thank you.'

Brigadier Grainger seemed about to address her but suddenly changed his mind. Shaggy eyebrows sagged over piercing eyes as he jerked his chin at the offending goggles the doctor had been remiss enough to leave lying on the table. One look from the brigadier and no words needed, they were immediately removed and placed on the floor, accompanied by a soft apology.

Satisfied his order had been obeyed, the brigadier sat straight in his chair, his chest puffed out like a fat pigeon. His eyes flickering like a butterfly unsure where to land, Brigadier Grainger glanced at her then away before making another effort to clear his throat of the prickly words he couldn't quite manage.

Frances held her breath as she prepared herself for whatever came next.

'Doctor Brakespeare, I have only just returned home and do not consider I have had enough time to peruse your application as closely as I would like. As a matter of course, I would normally put this meeting back...'

'Are you going to tell me that dragging me here was a mistake?'

There was a shared intake of breath of those in the room that she'd dared to be so challenging.

He spluttered words never quite formed a sentence.

Anger gave her courage, enough to challenge any man here if she had to.

'Well? Why drag me here if you've no wish to employ me?'

The gentle but firm voice of the vicar cut through the huffing and puffing of attendees who seemed incapable of making a decision without the brigadier.

'Because you're extremely well qualified, Doctor Brakespeare. Quite outstanding in fact.'

The brigadier continued to cough and splutter until coughing into a large white handkerchief emblazoned with an initial on one corner.

She fixed him with narrow-eyed intensity.

'The problem with your throat is likely linked to the dusty air in the quarry. You should get it looked at. Do you bring up much phlegm?'

The brigadier's eyes almost popped out of his head. She fancied that if she'd been in the military she'd have been court-martialled for insubordination.

Glances were exchanged around the table.

'Nonsense,' exclaimed Doctor Walker. 'A cigarette of a morning will clear it up in no time. Best still a cigar,' he added on seeing the end of a King Edward poking out of the ashtray.

Frances shot back. 'Tobacco of any kind will irritate it...'

'Pah!' exclaimed the doctor.

The brigadier regained his composure thanks to Sister Harrison giving him a glass of water.

As the brigadier began perusing the papers in front of him, Frances found herself facing the magnificence of his mane of white hair and for a moment it felt as though she was falling into it, allying it with the disappointment to come. And there would be disappointment. She was sure of it.

'I assumed by your name that you were male.'

'Frances. Spelt with an "e".'

He grimaced. 'I am aware of that now. However, under the circumstances and taking everything into account—'

'Don't bother. I'll come back in a hundred years. You might have modernised by then and accepted that women can be doctors.'

She was just about to storm out before they could order her to go when the door to the meeting room burst open and a woman entered with all the grandeur and hauteur of a fully rigged galleon about to scatter all opponents in her path.

Frances was tall, but this woman was taller and dressed from head to foot in a grey peplumed jacket and skirt of the softest and most expensive wool. Although the outfit and enormous hat were far from the latest fashion, it couldn't help but impress.

Frances detected a slightly hooked nose and a double chin half hidden by a black net veil that fell to just beneath her nostrils. In one hand, she carried a black beaded reticule, in the other a parasol with an ebony handle.

The head, the hat and the veil turned like a ship's prow to glance off each participant as her imperial gaze swept the room.

'I trust you have considered my advice and that no decisions have been made without me.' No apology was forthcoming.

Murmurs of compliance drifted around the room.

A respectful greeting ran from one committee member to another, Frances noticing that they seemed to crumple into their seats like crabs wanting to hide beneath stones. Chairs were pushed back. The men rose to their feet and nodded their heads in acquiescence to someone they obviously considered their superior.

Sister Harrison sprang from her chair and pulled one out for the new arrival at the head of the table. 'Good afternoon, your ladyship. Would you like to sit down?'

Without a word of appreciation, the formidable woman sat down.

An awkward silence followed. Even the brigadier seemed diminished by this new presence.

It was, thought Frances, as though Queen Victoria had arrived to take charge. Or, at the very least, Queen Mary, the wife of King George the Fifth who had come to the throne in 1910, four years before the Great War had begun. Both strong-minded women.

Assuming seniority, the brigadier dared address her. 'Your ladyship. I trust you are aware that this is about—'

'Of course I am aware what this is all about,' she snapped. 'Proceed.'

The brigadier offered his argument about not having had time to give more thought to Frances's application. With military efficiency and an air of finality, he shifted papers, shuffling them like a pack of cards until picking the papers up and reappraising the wording.

Frances recognised the letter she'd sent, applying for the position. He read it avidly, seeming to test his ground and his excuses before looking at her.

'I'm afraid there has been a mistake, Miss—'

'Doctor!' The sharpness of her interruption seemed to take him by surprise. 'I'm a qualified doctor. It took me a long time to study to become one, so whatever your views might be on a woman becoming a physician, I would appreciate you addressing me by my professional title.'

The brigadier's jaw tightened. It was obvious to Frances that he was not used to being challenged – especially not for a second time.

'Now look here, young lady—'

'Doctor.' His patronising made Frances bristle.

'Doctor Brakespeare. Doctor. I'm afraid there was some confusion. Your name being Frances, I – and I think all of us – assumed you were male.'

'It's a different spelling.'

'A misunderstanding.' He shook his head as though the very idea of a woman being addressed as such was totally ridiculous. 'It is my opinion and I think my colleagues all concur, that we should hold the matter in abeyance. What do you think, Doctor Walker? DOCTOR WALKER!'

Doctor Walker had looked to be dozing. At being addressed twice, the second time more loudly than the first, he was suddenly spurred into life.

'Regarding us replacing you with a female doctor,' said the brigadier pointedly and only slightly less loud than before.

Doctor Walker shook himself into life, his podgy hands resting on his stomach. 'I've come across female doctors before; mostly attached to midwifery units. Beyond that... well. It must be borne in mind that the hospital caters to a wide variety of cases. Sickness and on occasion terrible injury at the quarry or the coalface. Look at the incident yesterday...'

'I did,' Frances snapped. 'Sister Harrison was with me when I treated those who'd been hurt. I also took one of them to the infirmary in Bristol for an X-ray.'

Someone asked what was meant by X-ray.

Frances outlined it in language laymen would understand.

The brigadier didn't exactly wither beneath her stern gaze, but with some pride waxed lyrical on the latest medical marvel of the twentieth century. 'I came across it on the Western Front,' he expounded with an air of a man who knows and has seen more than most. 'The medical profession set great store by it to show them the extent of internal injuries – bone breakages and what have you. I am not completely ignorant of such progress and understand its usefulness to the medical profession. However, we are only a cottage hospital. I think I can assure you that we will not be getting one here,' said the brigadier with a smug chuckle.

'That is not necessarily so.'

Gregory Sampson tugged at his dog collar as though up until now it had constricted him speaking out.

Doctor Walker seemed oblivious to the concentrated frown on her ladyship's brow. 'This is a cottage hospital and that is what it will stay.'

The vicar waded in. 'It wouldn't be the first time. It used to be much smaller than it is now. Six beds according to the records. And one nurse. We now have thirty-six beds, two of them in isolation.'

The brigadier looked at him as though he'd like to see him roasted on a spit.

Her ladyship, who had said nothing until now chose her moment. She lifted the black veil from her face, patting it in place around her hat. A pearl-ended hatpin stabbed into the stiff heaped net providing further security that it would not come loose.

Frances was surprised to see that her face was amazingly line-free and her eyes clear and intelligent. She was instantly reminded of Izzy. They were both of a generation that had dared use their intelligence to benefit women everywhere.

'You each have a copy of the original classified item we placed. Read it again gentlemen.'

Each of those present brought out the item from their papers and except for the vicar sheepishly bowed their heads to read it.

'May I also refer you to our original outline on which the classified advertisement was based.'

Again papers were shuffled and read.

The brigadier made the mistake of attempting to pre-empt her reading it by telling her what it said.

'I can read. I don't need you to read it for me.' Her sharp retort stopped him short.

After taking a pair of spectacles from her reticule and perching them on her nose, her ladyship read it quickly.

'There,' she said, slamming the paper back onto the table with an air of finality. 'It doesn't specifically state that we will only take on a male doctor.'

Doctor Walker dared to jump in. 'Correct, but what it does say...'

Emboldened by the doctor's interruption, the brigadier finished the sentence for him. 'It says that preference will be given to someone who served in France. I'm sorry,' he said, apology and triumph etched on his face and blooming in his eyes. 'I'm sorry, Doctor Brakespeare, but—'

'I did serve in France.' She felt immense pleasure seeing their faces drop. 'So that's one impediment out of the way. Is there anything else that might prevent me from carrying out the duties of the position?'

For a moment, rears fidgeted in chairs and uncertainty brought nervous tics to some faces and lolling tongues capering along dry lips.

'Are there any other objections?' asked the vicar, who looked to be enjoying baiting the men too full of their own self-importance.

'Well...' The brigadier wasn't finished yet. He was used to having the final say and he was going to have it now. 'I fully accept that you are a woman, but that in itself raises another problem. If you should decide to marry your tenure with Orchard Cottage Hospital could be very short indeed.'

'And we wouldn't want that,' added his son Simon Grainger, the quarry manager and a man she'd taken an instant dislike to. Her blood boiling, Frances pushed the chair away from her as she got to her feet. 'My fiancé, the love of my life, was killed not long before the end of hostilities. My hopes of marriage dashed, I am married to my profession and always will be. Now, if you'll excuse me, I'll leave you to discuss the implications of taking me on and await your decision elsewhere.'

A pin could have dropped in the room behind her and although her cheeks were aflame and tears of anger stung her eyes, Frances couldn't help feeling triumphant. With grim determination, she marched out with her head held high, unsure of what might happen next but suddenly determined that she would win them all over, that as a woman she would take this job no matter what. She left the door open behind her, a small act of defiance towards those who had belittled her. Whatever would be would be.

In the hope of finding peace, she headed for the church. Fronds of honeysuckle piled like an old-fashioned hat on the lych-gate tickled her face as she passed beneath it. The flagstones beneath her feet were green with moss and small wildflowers pushed their happy faces through the cracks.

Out of reverence, or perhaps because she needed to be alone, she slowly and carefully closed the gate behind her before walking on. The path wound through battalions of tombstones, some newly erected and some coated in lichen, the names carved centuries ago blurred by time and weather.

The heads of bright red poppies and ears of seed-bearing grass nodded their welcome. Poppies. Back in France, in that last August before she'd left for home, they had burst into bloom once the land was no longer being torn and battered.

Bees and butterflies parted at her passing. The grass became shorter in a place of grander mausoleums seeming to proclaim that those who had been important in life were just as such in death.

Walking around helped clear her head and bring her to a decision. A short while ago she had determined the position was hers. Now her pride kicked in and although she knew it to be contrary she considered refusing them.

Her contrariness remained with her as she headed back out of the lychgate and headed for the high street and the triangular-shaped green at its heart.

Face still flushed, Frances circumnavigated the white kerbs enclosing the green before stepping onto the grass and heading for the war memorial standing at its heart. Its glaring whiteness and cold stone seemed to send the high street and the present day into a mist, a sad mist, a mist reminiscent of the yellow-tinged fog that had swirled over the battlefield in the aftermath of a barrage.

Memories took shape in that mist until she could shake them away and bring herself back to the here and now.

The names engraved in its shining edifice were picked out in gold. The heading noted that these were the names of those known only to God, the ones whose last resting place was unknown.

Standing there, the old pain squeezed the breath from her chest and the blood from her veins. Her eyes ran down the list of names, knowing none of them – or so she thought.

The very last name, one that looked as though it had been engraved as an afterthought, leaped out at her.

Captain Ralph Porter

The stone memorial was stiff, cold, and so was she.

A dizzying array of questions whirled in her brain. Ralph had been born and brought up in Suffolk. So what was his name doing here?

All thoughts of leaving Norton Dene vanished. She couldn't leave until she knew why his name was there. But most of all it seemed like a sign from him that this was the place for her because he was here too – if only in name.

11

Two o'clock in the morning according to the chimes of the clock in St Michael's church tower clock and sleep still evaded Frances.

Why was Ralph name on the war memorial? Why, why, why? She knew that even if the committee couldn't agree on her staying, she couldn't leave.

The candle had burned low but gave enough light to see her way back down the twisted staircase. Before touching a taper to the embers of the range, she removed the etched glass globe of the oil lamp, turned up the wick and a more substantial light fell over the table.

Sliding her fingers into the interior side pocket of her old medicine bag, she found the pen, ink, notepad and envelopes she'd placed there.

Her mind was in turmoil and the first person she felt a great urge to write to was Deborah Goldsmith, her closest link to the past.

Dear Deborah,
   Finding myself unable to sleep, I am writing this in the early

hours of the morning. I won't go into the first dramatic event that met me on arrival in Norton Dene, but I must report the second, for it is this discovery that prevents me from sleeping.

Ralph's name appears on the war memorial of those who never returned and I don't understand why, thus, even if the committee decide not to take me, on I must stay until I discover the reason for it being here. Perhaps it is fate that has lent a hand. Or perhaps something much more mundane and explainable. Either way, seeing his name made it seem as though he was close by, so even if I never find out the reason, the very fact that it appears is a kind of omen, telling me this might turn out to be the place where I belong.

In a flourishing hand, she signed off and waited for the dawn.

* * *

Not a bite of breakfast passed her lips, though she did manage to drink half a cup of tea. After replenishing the fire bed of the range with a shovelful of coal she sat staring as the coals began to glow red, waiting as though the tongues of red, yellow and bluish green flames might give her some idea of what the day would bring. Meeting the hospital committee had been very important, though not as much as discovering Ralph's name on the cenotaph. Who could she ask about it and what could she ask? Did you know him? Have you any idea why his name is there? Anyway, there just might be a local man with the same name though somehow she didn't think so.

A shower of hot cinders leapt crackling from the fire and necessitated her brushing them up and throwing them back into the grate.

The tea she'd made had gone cold when the knock came at the door.

Swallowing her nerves, Frances swung the door back, took a deep breath and readied herself for whatever decision had been made. If the committee had been swayed she would unpack the rest of her belongings from the car and make her home in the coach house. If not she would find lodgings. Going back to London now she'd found Ralph's name on the war memorial was no longer an option.

'Good morning, Doctor.'

The voice was chirpy and the face fresh as a peach. She recognised Nurse Lucy Daniels, her presence both a surprise and a relief. It didn't seem likely that she'd brought the committee's decision to her doorstep. She had a little more time yet. Anticipation turned to a puzzlement that showed on her face.

'I didn't quite finish the dusting and besides I wanted to know how you were settling in.'

'That's very kind of you. But I might not need to settle in. The committee might decide they don't want me.'

Lucy Daniels burst out laughing. 'Not if Lady Araminta's got anything to do with it. It's her hospital. She makes the decisions. The rest of them don't count.'

'I admire your confidence.'

Lucy's dark eyes danced with merriment. 'It's not confidence. I've lived here all my life. I know who runs things and it isn't the likes of them on the committee.'

It felt to Frances as though a ray of sunshine had come through the door and made her dare to hope. Her attitude had changed since yesterday. She needed to stay. The name on the cenotaph intrigued her and besides her ladyship seemed to be out of the same mould as Miss Izzy.

'I haven't made much of a mess so far. Are you sure you don't have something better to do?'

'I'm instructed to help you settle in,' she said brightly. 'I might as well make a start.'

'That's very kind of you.'

'Dust, dirt and spiders run for cover when they hear that me and my sister Nancy are on the case,' Lucy chortled.

Frances couldn't help but join her. Lucy was one of Mother Nature's natural tonics, indomitable and put on earth to brighten a grey day and lift a grey spirit.

Frances stood to one side as Lucy swept in with an energy about her that was both admirable and amusing.

'It's so wonderful to have you here,' declared Lucy, setting down a woven shopping basket and slipping off her coat. She placed both in one of the copious armchairs. 'Don't get me wrong, I've nothing against Doctor Walker, but having you here... well...' She heaved a happy sigh, her face glowing. 'You're what this town needs. A lady doctor.'

'I'm glad you think so. Though I'm hardly a lady. Not titled anyway.'

Lucy eyed her approvingly. 'You look like a lady. It shows in your clothes. Everyone who's seen you says so.'

Frances made no comment. Being from London, her arrival was bound to have led to local gossip.

Lucy tied the strings of her apron and knotted a kerchief around her bouncy auburn curls so that they were pulled away from her heart-shaped face. 'Nancy and I split duty at the hospital and here between us. She's married to Ned and we've also got Polly to look after. She's Nancy's baby.' Her exuberance turned to concern. 'She's gone on the bus to Bristol to see him.' She shook her head. 'It should not have happened. Something went very wrong but nobody's saying anything. Nobody wants to lose their job.'

Frances frowned. 'You think it wasn't an accident?'

'It was, but somebody did something stupid to cause it.'

'That's very bad.' Frances didn't like what Lucy was implying if it was based on hearsay rather than fact, but then she could hardly tell her so. Lucy was the local. She, Frances, was the outsider.

Lucy plucked a feather duster from her basket and put it to work. It slowed when she asked Frances if Ned would be coming home any time soon.

'He will be all right, won't he?'

Frances made the effort to sound and look reassuring. 'The X-ray will reveal whatever it is that went inside and the surgeon will take it out. Your brother-in-law will be home to convalesce in the cottage hospital as soon as that's done.'

'Thanks to you,' said Lucy, gratitude shining in her eyes. 'I really meant what I said about being glad you're here. Me and Nancy.'

'Thank you. Your opinion means a lot to me.'

Lucy's face shone like the sun. 'Ahhh. That's lovely. Really lovely.'

'I meant it.'

'Yes. Right,' she said rather breathlessly, then with an air of resolution said, 'Oh well. Must get on.'

Lucy's renewed energy behind the feather duster sent spiders scurrying and buzzing bluebottles bolting for an open window or door.

At the sudden sound of a motor car pulling up outside, her head bobbed to one side and her moony brown eyes fixed on the scene through the window which was just beyond Frances's shoulder. 'That's her ladyship's car that's just pulled up. I'll leave you to it and go and mop the kitchen floor.'

Like a rabbit off to hide in its burrow, Lucy and her feather duster disappeared into the kitchen, the iron catch on the pine-planked kitchen door rattling as it firmly closed behind her.

Feeling apprehensive but forbearing, Frances opened the front door. Fresh air sucked the heat from the room. It was tinged with the cloying smell of gardenia worn by her visitor whose height and breadth filled the doorway. The grey outfit from yesterday had been replaced by one of sage green, although a black veil still half covered her face.

'Doctor.' An imperious voice delivered from a great height.

Frances looked up at her hoping she couldn't hear the thudding race of her heart. 'Your ladyship. I take it you come bearing news.'

'Yes, but I am not partial to imparting news on the doorstep. May I come in.'

The small living room seemed even smaller once she was in it.

'Now,' she said, taking off her gloves with the flourish of a knight about to throw a challenge in the opponent's face. 'Everything is decided. As of now you are resident physician at the Orchard Cottage Hospital. You start as of now.'

Frances reined in a look of surprise. 'As a doctor?' A silly question, she thought, but such was her relief.

'Of course as a doctor! Just because you're living in a coach house doesn't mean to say you're to be a coachman!' The imperious voice was matched by an imperious look.

'Well, that's a relief.'

'The hospital does not have a surgery and I have suggested to the committee that you implement one forthwith.' She looked around the living room at the furniture, the fireplace, the oil lamp dominating the centre of the dining table. 'Is this all there is? Rooms, I mean.'

'Plus a kitchen and a lean-to scullery out the back. Are you suggesting I see patients here?'

'Difficult, I know but you'll have to manage as best you can until a proper surgery is set up at the hospital. It's about time it was.'

'I can't wait to get started.'

'Can you manage in the interim with what you have here?'

Frances nodded emphatically. 'I dare say I can.' Her visitor sauntered around the room, her eyes travelling over the old but sturdy furniture, the vase of flowers on the table, the medical journals she'd left lying on the dining table.

'I would suggest that private patients and those who pay into the insurance panel are seen here in the front room. Those unable to pay – and believe me there will be several of those – can be received in the scullery at the back. Bear in mind, Doctor Brakespeare, that your private patients of greater social standing will require you to carry out house visits. You drive a car so that shouldn't be a problem. Those who pay into panel arrangements or as income dictates will present themselves at the back door. Whether you visit them at home is up to you. Though, I would warn you that some live in circumstances that are far from congenial hence my advising you to have them visit at the rear. Both parties will feel more comfortable that way.'

Assuming her ladyship had never visited a poor man's hovel in her life, Frances felt the need to point out that she had and thus make it clear that she had every intention of treating all patients with the same level of care and consideration.

'I used to visit such places in London. Believe me, I've seen bugs and cockroaches walking the walls and smelt the stench of the outside privies.'

'So have I.'

'I didn't know that.' Frances was genuinely surprised.

'Well you do now. Never judge a book by its cover, Doctor. My experience with the poor is far ranging. I have had some experience of such places and people when I sat on the board of governors of workhouses and such like.'

In a flurry of words Lady Araminta headed for the kitchen door which she flung open as though thinking to find sin being committed behind it.

Frances expected to see Lucy on the other side still holding her feather duster, but there was no sign of her.

'Would you like some tea?' Frances asked as her ladyship proceeded through the kitchen and out into the lean-to scullery where she undid the top half of the back door, the bottom half remaining closed. Her head bobbed through it before being withdrawn.

'Yes. I think as a temporary measure this structure should be perfectly satisfactory.'

'Tea?' Frances asked again. At the same time wondering where Lucy was hiding.

A gloved hand waved casually. 'Good grief, no. It's too late for that. If I don't call in again or see you in the high street, I'll see you in church.'

'I'm not a regular church goer.'

Her ladyship raised her eyebrows but made no comment and Frances gave no reason though there was indeed one very good one. Abandoning faith and not attending church was her way of showing God that she hadn't forgiven him for Ralph's death.

'Lady Araminta, can I ask you something?'

'As long as it's not too personal, you can ask me anything you like.'

She swept back into the living room, sliding her hands back into her kid gloves.

'I noticed the war memorial – very similar to the cenotaph in Whitehall, unless I'm very much mistaken.'

'You are not mistaken. I insisted we replicate the much larger structure here in Norton Dene. I even got that man Lutyens to adjust the measurements for a smaller version of the original to suit.'

Ah. So her ladyship had been involved in its construction.

'I noticed the list of names of those whose last resting place is unknown. Known only to God, as such inscriptions are fond of saying.'

'Get to the point, my dear. I have a busy day ahead,' she stated in a matter-of-fact manner.

'One particular name sprang out at me.'

'Indeed.'

Her ladyship concentrated on doing up the tiny buttons that would fasten her gloves.

'Captain Ralph Porter.'

Her ladyship frowned. 'I don't recognise the name.'

'He wasn't a local man. Not the Captain Ralph Porter I knew,' Frances said wistfully.

The already arched eyebrows rose some more. 'I must admit I do not think him a local man.'

'He wasn't. He was from Suffolk. We were engaged to be married. He never came back, but...' She frowned and a bitter taste flooded her mouth before she could swallow and put what she was feeling into words. 'It was quite a shock seeing his name listed there.'

Her ladyship tossed her head. 'At least it's there. That was the whole point, you see, to list those men from the town who never came back and whose last resting place was unknown. It was, and is, a focal point for their families to grieve.'

'Very commendable, but I still don't understand why his name is there seeing as he wasn't a local man.'

Her ladyship stood in front of the door, waiting for Frances to open it. 'I'll make enquiries for you and see if there's been some mistake. In the meantime, might I suggest that you do not look a gift horse in the mouth. You have a job to do and the sooner you get on with it the better. Welcome to Norton Dene and the Orchard Cottage Hospital, Doctor. Let us look forward to a long and lasting commitment. Good day to you.'

Once the front door had creaked shut, Lucy appeared from the kitchen, an impish look on her face. 'You ready for that cup of tea, Doctor?'

Frances adopted a stern and unsmiling pose, then burst out laughing.

The kettle was already boiling on the blacked hob at the side of the range.

'Where were you hiding?'

Lucy grinned. 'Under the table. She used to be our Sunday school teacher. Fire and brimstone with every word and a smack of the ruler if you didn't pay attention.'

'I can well believe it.'

Frances sighed with satisfaction as she took the cup of tea from the very likeable Lucy Daniels.

'I think I'll take her ladyship's advice and start right away. I want to see everything!'

'I'll come with you if you like.'

No little girl receiving the present of a doll's house could ever feel as excited as Frances was feeling now.

'I can think of nobody better to show me around. Let's finish this tea and get going.'

12

Frances drove the car to the hospital with Lucy Daniels sitting beside her keenly observing the passing scenery. Nancy, Lucy's sister and a nurse was on duty this afternoon so Lucy had a little spare time. In answer to the questions Frances asked her Lucy told Frances of her family history and the fact that there were Daniels buried in the churchyard going back to the fifteen hundreds.

Armed with notebook and her favourite tortoiseshell fountain pen and followed by Lucy, Frances strode purposefully into the hospital smiling like a Cheshire cat.

'My own hospital,' she whispered to Lucy. 'In a manner of speaking.'

Lucy added that she was looking forward to it and that she would do everything she could to fit in with whatever Frances wanted.

'I know you will.'

A weak and watery sun was penetrating the many windows of the reception area. A sign on the wall above a brass bell invited it to be rung to gain the attention of a member of staff.

'No receptionist.'

'Doctor Walker said it was a waste of money to have someone sat there just to say hello to anyone who came in through the door.'

'Didn't he consider using a receptionist to also keep patient records?'

Lucy shook her head. 'I don't know and anyway us nurses are not told much unless it's bedpans and bandages. That's us.'

The comment made Frances laugh. From the very first she had warmed to this young nurse who although accepting of her status wasn't afraid to speak her mind.

'I'd like a quick tour around first before anything else.'

'Pleased to oblige,' she responded and looking very pleased to do so.

They entered a ward where patients' eyes followed the pair of them around the ward.

'Are you a new nurse?' some asked.

'No. This is Doctor Brakespeare. The new doctor,' Lucy responded before Frances had time to do so herself. There was pride in her voice which Frances greatly appreciated.

She shook hands with some of the patients.

'I've never 'ad a lady doctor before,' exclaimed one old man.

'Then ain't you the lucky one,' remarked another. 'And at your time of life.'

Chuckles pervaded the pristine cleanliness of the wards and went some way to improving the spirits of those who were sick.

Nurse Nancy Skittings, Lucy's sister, came over to shake her hand.

'Well we were thinking we'd get someone better looking than Doctor Walker. We just didn't think it would be a woman.'

Dimples appeared at the sides of her mouth when she smiled.

'Well I'm certainly that, and this lady doctor would like to meet everyone here. I know I can't gather everyone all at once and in the meantime your sister is doing a very good job of showing me round.'

'Where would you like to see next, Doctor?' said Lucy, her face fired with enthusiasm.

Frances thought about it. The wards were important. The staff were important. But so too were the medicines she was required to prescribe.

A voice suddenly rang out stopping them in their tracks at the far end of the ward.

'What's all this noise about might I ask?'

Sister Harrison came stomping into the ward, her heavy work shoes making as much din as a set of iron horseshoes.

The stern look dropped from her face when she saw Frances.

'Ah. Doctor Brakespeare. I wasn't expecting you.'

It was quite satisfying telling her that she and Lady Compton-Dixon had agreed that she should start straight away. At mention of her ladyship's name her expression changed.

'Of course.' She glanced almost contemptuously at Lucy Daniels before saying, 'What would you like to see?'

'Everything. Nurse Daniels has already showed me the wards. Now I would like to inspect the dispensary.'

It was difficult to read the look on the senior sister's face except to think that it was guarded in some way.

'This way, please. Carry on with what you were doing, Nurse Skittings.' She then turned to Lucy. 'I can take over here, Nurse Daniels. You can go.'

'I'd like Lucy to stay.'

A barely perceptible wince appeared then disappeared on Sister Harrison's face.

'As you wish. Come this way.'

The dispensary was situated off the main reception where Frances was already thinking a receptionist would deal with visitors, suppliers and keep patient records – unless there was already an efficient routine in situ though she doubted it.

Glass doors lined the whole of the longest wall inside of which were shelves of glass and ceramic jars, the latter with blue lettering on a cream background. There were also more modern cartons and all manner of pill boxes of differing sizes.

Frances tried one of the cupboards but found it locked. She tried several others but they were locked too.

Before asking the obvious, that is the whereabouts of the keys, she spotted a notice on the opposite wall above a desk.

ACCESS TO SOME CUPBOARDS AND THIS DESK IS RESTRICTED.
PLEASE ASK SISTER HARRISON FOR THE KEYS.

'Where are the keys?'

Sister Harrison was a picture of indignation. 'They're my personal responsibility. I keep them under lock and key as I've always done.'

'The way things have always been done isn't necessarily the way I want to do things.'

She could have added a new broom sweeps clean but didn't think it would go down well. Ultimately, she wanted to fit into her new vocation and getting Sister Harrison's back up would not be a clever way to start.

'So show me where you keep the keys to the medicine cabinets.'

'I keep the keys in here.'

Frances watched in amazement as Sister Harrison took a small key from her pocket and slotted it into the desk drawer.

'You keep the keys in the desk.'

'Yes. For safety's sake.'

'Does anyone have a duplicate key to open the drawer?'

'No. It's a security precaution. We wouldn't want items from the dispensary to go missing.'

'Neither would we want patients to die for lack of medicine.'

Her lips set firm Sister Harrison's expression remained devoid of response.

The small key protruded from the top drawer of the desk, a shining interceptor against the grim dark wood. Sister Harrison gave a great huff of indignation that she also wore on her face as Frances turned it and pulled the drawer open.

A bunch of keys lay on top of a paperback book – likely one of those from the Boots library by the look of it. Frances glimpsed the title, *Love in the Moonlight*. Sister Harrison's reading matter was none of her business but had come as something of a surprise.

After grabbing the keys, Frances slammed the drawer shut and turned to Sister Harrison, dangling the keys in front of her face. 'Is this the only set of keys?'

'There were two.'

'So where is the other set?'

'Doctor Walker had them.'

'I see. Then we need to get them back from him.'

'We can't.' Sister Harrison's manner was taut and dismissive. 'He can't remember where he put them.'

Frances sighed. Not having access to the one set of keys they had was bad enough. Her predecessor having lost a set was irksome, though not as much as Sister Harrison's attitude. 'Is there a locksmith in the town who can make us copies?'

'I dare say Mr Lewis at the hardware shop could do so.'

'Good. We need it done quickly. Please deal with it.'

Sister Harrison was not an ugly woman but petulance made her look as though she might bite given half a chance. 'If you wish, Doctor.'

Frances had no wish to make an enemy but suspected that the

hand of friendship wouldn't be readily accepted. The woman was a good nurse – at least she'd seemed so at the quarry accident. In time a more amenable side might surface but time was exactly what it would take – though goodness knows how long.

'Right,' said Frances. 'If you could give me the rest of the guided tour, Sister, and we can discuss what else needs to be done.'

Frances fully accepted that change was never welcome by those who'd followed the same routine over a period of time. Harmony was never achieved by feeding animosity.

Each of the wards was neatly kept, the linen sheets pristine white and folded-over coverlets of the same light green as the walls. There were six beds on the women's ward, six on the men's, plus a three-bed facility for expectant mothers. There was also another small ward, with only one bed tucked into a corner, plus a few chairs and other items stored for future use.

Frances ran her eyes over the facility. 'Is this ward never used?'

'It only has one bed. We use it purely for isolation.'

'Including the storage of chairs?'

Her inference fell on deaf ears or a disinclination to make comment. Plans were forming thick and fast in Frances' head as to the way forward. There were so many things she'd like to instigate. What were the chances, she wondered, of setting up a hospital clinic where expectant mothers could be monitored on a regular basis? And what about a clinic for the men suffering from the effects of the dust from the mines and quarries? And how about extending home visits and even visits to schools, administering doses of cod liver oil, weighing and measuring the heights of children, checking their hair for nits and the advent of ringworm? There was so much she wanted to do.

By the time she'd inspected the sluice, the laundry cupboards and the small cloakroom where the nurses hung up their cloaks, she knew very well that her enthusiasm for improvement was not shared by Sister Harrison but consoled herself that it was something to be worked on.

The warmth of her office just off reception was a welcome break after being in the company of Sister Harrison, whose world seemed coldly preordained. Yet the woman read romance novels! The fact still surprised her.

* * *

It was three days later when Ned Skittings was discharged from the infirmary in Bristol and brought to the cottage hospital to convalesce. Mr MacDonald brought him in the hearse, where a stretcher had been fixed in the back for live bodies as opposed to dead ones.

Nancy had come on duty by then and almost fell over him before Mr MacDonald pushed her to one side, demanding that him and his assistant be given room to do their job.

'You can fawn over him once he's in a bed,' Mr MacDonald laughed. 'But not too enthusiastically. Intimacies must wait until you get him home – otherwise you'll have Sister Bedpan and Bloomers after you! Or the doctor.'

On seeing Frances, he muttered an apology and touched his forelock.

Nancy hovering by her husband's head, Frances perused paperwork passed to her by Mr MacDonald's assistant and followed on.

Sister Harrison stood by the door, hands clasped in front of her ample hips and a broody mouth pouting over the white bow stiffly prominent beneath her chin.

Frances asked Ned how he was.

Although still suffering, somewhat Ned's face brightened as his wife clutched at his hand. 'A lot better now I'm here with my Nancy.'

'That's good. Sister Harrison. If you could just pull the screens around the bed.'

With cold reluctance, Sister Harrison did as ordered though it was obvious she thought it a lesser person's job.

To help make amends, Frances took her to one side and whispered, 'Let them savour this sweet moment. We all need romance in our lives, don't you think so, Sister?'

She couldn't be sure whether Sister Harrison read the message in her eyes, that somewhere she had an inclination for romance herself.

Frances waited outside the drawn curtains, studying the notes sent by the hospital.

Sister Harrison went to each of the other beds in the men's wards checking thermometers, pulses and pillows even though they'd been checked by Lucy Daniels just before lunch.

After giving Ned and Nancy a little time on their own, Frances stated her intention to investigate the wound and after counting to five drew back the curtain.

Nancy's face was flushed and Ned's smile was wide enough to almost crack his face in half.

Giving no sign that she'd noticed their flushed faces, Frances instructed Nancy to pull back the bedclothes so she could inspect the stitches inserted by the surgeon at the infirmary.

First Frances examined his chest with her stethoscope. 'You've a strong heart, Mr Skittings.'

She saw a look pass between the young couple that she believed referred to something other than the passage of blood. This young married couple were still in love. She envied them and determined to do all she could to get Ned back up on his feet.

'I'd like the wound bathed with Dakin's fluid every four hours. I trust we have some in the dispensary?'

Nancy looked unsure. 'I don't think we do, Doctor. In fact, I don't think I've ever heard of it.'

Frances took the stethoscope from her ears and fastened it more securely around her neck. 'You may not have. We used it on the battlefield to keep infection at bay. I don't say it's likely that the wound will be enflamed, but better safe than sorry. Please take a set of keys from the drawer and look for some.'

Nancy said that she would check.

A good nurse, Frances thought. Caring and methodical about both nursing and her husband.

In her imagination, she saw herself as Nancy and Ned as Ralph, two people who would forever be in love.

Thinking of Ralph brought the name on the cenotaph to mind and made her puzzled all over again. But it's only his name, she said to herself. He's not there. He never was. He never will be.

It had been four weeks since she'd arrived in the middle of an accident at the quarry and although she still missed Izzy and everyone else back in London, she was so busy that the present and her ideas for improving the hospital dominated her waking hours – and sometimes also her sleep.

The following morning she received two letters with London postmarks. One of them was from Deborah saying she needed a short holiday and could she come down and stay in June?

Frances smiled and thought how wonderful that would be. Yes, of course she must come to stay.

The other letter was from the same firm of solicitors who had given her notice to leave the house she'd lived in all her life.

Dear Doctor Brakespeare,

It has come to the attention of the Brakespeare family that you have a car in your possession purchased by the late Miss

Isabelle Frances Brakespeare. The family would like this to be
returned to them forthwith.

Frances had come home to the coach house, tired but happy.
Now she was fuming. The little car, Matron Molly, had moved with
her down here to Norton Dene. Silly as it might seem but Frances
couldn't help bestowing the temperamental Austin with human
traits hence giving her a human name. She would not give her up.

Tomorrow she would write two letters, one to Deborah asking
her to name a date for her visit and one for the solicitors
explaining that Matron Molly was a present from Izzy to her, her
adopted daughter. She would not give in.

13

MAY DAY

The expanse of green in the centre of the town was big enough to have its war memorial at one end and a maypole at the other. The May Day festivities had been formally opened by Lady Araminta Compton-Dixon, who had happily accepted an ice cream cone once her duty was over.

It came as no massive surprise that her son had not accompanied her. He was rarely seen, except in the back seat of the limousine, from where he saw none of the town, none of the townspeople, but looked sightlessly ahead. They said he was taking the air, a small break from being holed up in his rooms at Orchard Manor.

The miners' band from Catbrook colliery was belting out the 'Trumpet Voluntary' and a few other familiar tunes that people either sang to, danced to, or both.

The bank manager, Oliver Nielsen, was strutting around like a turkey cock, clipboard in hand, keen to handle the admin side rather than run a coconut shy or a tip-the-man-into-the-barrel sideshow.

A carpet of children dressed in their Sunday best scampered

between the hoopla stall, the hook-a-duck stall and their very favourite place where gobstoppers, strings of gleaming liquorice and other goodies were displayed. For the first hour, everything was free, thanks to the generosity of her ladyship.

Miss Flower and Miss Parson, teachers at the Lady Orchard Junior and Infant School, were shepherding their charges into position around the maypole. After all had visited the toilet and had a ribbon in hand, they readied themselves until the Morrismen shook their bells and batted their sticks and everyone began to dance.

There would not have been room for all the attractions if the road around the perimeter hadn't been closed. Space had been made for a series of six swing boats at one end, plus a carousel and a smaller roundabout adorned with pink pigs and yellow giraffes for the small fry.

Nancy had opted to take the early shift at the hospital so she could keep Ned company, leaving Lucy free to go to the fair with Polly strapped into the pushchair sucking a strip of liquorice.

Normally Mrs Skittings, Ned's mother, would have been caring for the little girl, but she had taken up her annual place beneath a bower of fresh willow branches woven into an arch. Above where she sat looking splendid in an extravagant costume of purple, orange and green, a pair of old brass curtain rings hanging from her ears, a sign read, *Gypsy Lily. Fortune Teller.*

Like everyone else, her efforts were to raise cash for the Orchard Cottage Hospital and other local charities, including school trips and equipment.

With a few of her old friends behind her, one snuggling a six-month baby to her breast, the other looking as though she was going to drop her expected offspring at any moment, Lucy leaned into the opening and asked Ma Skittings if she was going to read her palm.

Ned's mother eyed her spuriously. 'Only if yur going to cross me palm with silver.'

'What about your crystal ball? Can you see my future in there?'

The ball was a genuine crystal, shiny, clear and looking as if it had been polished that morning.

Ma Skittings waved a dismissive hand. 'Go on with you.' As soon as the words were out of her mouth, her manner altered. 'Someone of importance wants to 'ave a word with you.'

'What...? Is it someone tall, dark and handsome?'

Ma Skittings grinned and in doing so showed the gaps in her teeth. 'You could say that.'

Lucy turned round and saw her friends were putting distance between her and them. The reason was approaching in a dark green dress with beaded embroidery around the neckline, sleeves and hip-hanging waist.

'Nurse Daniels. I'd like a word with you. Let us repair to the tea tent. We'll share a pot of tea and some fruitcake.' Lady Araminta smiled down at the sticky-faced Polly. 'Perhaps we can get a biscuit for Nancy's little girl.'

Caught off balance, Lucy stuttered a reply and pushing the pram in front of her followed the tall striding figure as the crowd parted to let them through.

Hats were raised, acknowledgements exchanged and people folded away to make a path. Her ladyship thanked them accordingly.

There was enough time before reaching the tea tent for questions to be asked about how Ned was doing and how Nancy was managing without him at home.

Lucy said that they were managing as well as could be expected and luckily they did have Ned's mother to fall back on. 'She's very good to them.'

'But you have the child today and for obvious reasons.' Her

ladyship directed an amused look in the direction of the fortune teller's tent of woodland greenery.

'Mrs Skittings does like to do her bit. Her family's lived in Norton Dene for hundreds of years.'

'So have mine,' said her ladyship. 'It could very well be that her ancestors and mine were on more than passing acquaintance.'

Lucy agreed, though had no idea whether it was an accurate statement. The thought of her ladyship and Ma Skittings being related way back was enough to make her choke on her cake.

Lady Araminta took a mouthful from the piece of cake on her plate. 'Jolly nice fruitcake, don't you think?'

'Yes.'

Regardless of the small talk, Lucy was certain that something else was going on here.

'I want to know what you think about Doctor Brakespeare. And please be honest. Do you like her?'

Lucy was surprised. After all, she was only a nurse and didn't think her opinion held much weight.

'Honestly?'

'Of course honestly. I want to know what you think of her. Your opinion matters.'

Lucy washed down a mouthful of fruitcake with tea.

There was no point in beating about the bush so she got straight to the point.

'She's a new broom.'

Eyebrows were raised. 'And you think she'll sweep clean?'

'Yes. I do. Not that I didn't respect Doctor Walker but...' She paused, unsure whether her ladyship might think her disloyal. She decided to put what she was thinking into words. 'I'm not being disloyal, but I have to say that the hospital needs fresh blood – if you don't mind me saying so.'

'So you don't agree with Sister Harrison that things should stay as they are?'

So. That was it. During the new doctor's inspection at the hospital, Sister Harrison had looked as though she'd been about to explode, but it seemed she'd not voiced her feelings to the new doctor but had gone straight to her ladyship.

Frances Brakespeare had aroused a sleeping viper.

Lucy had never made a speech in her life, but she felt like making one now. First she took a deep breath.

'Nothing was going to be the same following the Great War, not for life in general or for men and women. Everything is changing, and to my mind for the better. Some people can't bear the thought of things changing, but nothing stays the same and if the new doctor makes changes that improve things, then all the better. I'll adapt and so will everyone else.'

She stopped then, aware that her ladyship looked not just impressed but amazed.

A slight smile twitched at Lady Araminta's lips and then slowly and quite softly, she clapped her hands. 'Nurse Daniels, I couldn't have put it better myself.'

'So I'm not in trouble.'

'Good grief, no. Why should you be?'

Lucy looked beyond her ladyship's shoulder to where Sister Harrison was standing like a statue. Behind her, dancers whirled around the maypole, the white streamers shorter now as the end of the dance approach. Simon Grainger approached her, said something that made her look at him and change her icy glare into something more amenable. A smile followed before she took his arm and they walked off away from the green, past the bank and into the shadows.

For his part, Simon Grainger looked very pleased with himself. If Sister Harrison thought she was Simon Grainger's only paramour, she was very much mistaken. He was like the dancers around the maypole, twirling around from one lady friend to another.

The eyes of both women, the titled lady and the nurse followed the pair before they disappeared. Neither made comment, at least not about Sister Harrison and Simon Grainger though it surprised Lucy that Sister Harrison could be so gullible, so infatuated with a man who wasn't worth bothering with.

Lady Araminta was speaking again and interrupted her thoughts.

'I very much appreciate your honesty.'

Lucy plastered a smile back on her face. 'I had to be.'

'I hear you're a good nurse. Now, after us having this little chat, I think you're also a very good person. Good morning, Nurse Daniels.' She bent down and smoothed Polly's hair back from her face. 'Enjoy the rest of your day and do give your sister my best wishes for her husband's recovery.'

* * *

Once in the shadows, Simon placed a warm hand on Sister Harrison's back and guided her to where he'd parked the cumbersome car that belonged to his father.

Even before he had closed the front passenger door, she went on and on about how the new doctor was changing things and that nothing good would come of it.

'I won't have it. Simon. You must do something about it. Tell the committee that it will not be good for patients and that change is not always for the better.'

Simon had been in the mood for something other than her string of demands that he influence the committee to stop the new doctor in her tracks.

'Edith. My darling.' He attempted to kiss her mouth shut, but she was in no mood for compromise. No mood for anything else either.

She hit his hand away. 'Don't bother trying to sweet-talk me. I'm not in the mood.'

'So I notice,' he said, folding his arms, looking glum and thinking of more amenable arms and a woman not obsessed with the bloody Orchard Cottage Hospital.

'Are you going to do something about her?'

Glummer still, he looked out of the windscreen at the empty street. Edith's worries were nothing compared with his own. 'No. I'm not.'

Edith looked dumbfounded. 'You can't mean that.'

'I have no choice,' he said grimly. 'The accident at the quarry could have severe repercussions. I will need a doctor in my pocket who will toe the line.'

'I don't understand.'

When he sighed, the car filled with cigar-smelling breath.

'I might need you to help me persuade her to be on my side.'

Edith held her breath as she tried to work out what he was saying.

'Are you saying it wasn't an accident, Simon? That business with Ned Skittings getting injured?'

'It was but could be construed as negligence. I don't want the truth getting back to my father or – more importantly – her ladyship.'

'Oh dear,' she said, her outward expression hiding her conviction that sharing his secret had placed him in her power – or so she thought because that's what she wanted. She wanted him, she wanted him for her and her alone.

Simon was of another mind. A woman in love was easy to manipulate and he would do just that.

14

Ned had been asleep, but when Nancy, looking professional in her clean uniform, touched his shoulder, his eyes opened and a rueful smile came to his lips. 'You're a sight for sore eyes. How are you, me darling?'

'Never mind me. You're the one in hospital. How are you?'

'Missing you and our little girl. Longing to go home.'

They exchanged a sad smile and for a moment held hands, before she adopted a more professional demeanour, setting an enamel bowl and squares of lint onto the side table. Taking a deep breath she said, 'I'm to bathe your sore belly.'

Ned groaned. 'Not too heavy-handed, if you please. It's feeling a bit sore.'

She smiled reassuringly but was alarmed to see that his face was shiny with a thin sheen of sweat.

Hiding her concern, Nancy whipped aside the dressing that covered his stitches and saw the inflammation encircling the wound. Her heartbeat quickened, but she determined he wouldn't see she was worried.

'I'll get the doctor. I know she wants to keep her eye on this.'

Frances had been in her office writing plans in her notebook which she hoped one day to put into operation.

She looked up when Nancy knocked then outlined the problem with Ned.

'It's inflamed. I don't like the look of it.'

Out on the ward Frances slid silently behind the closed screens and peered at the sight that had so worried Ned's wife. It worried her too.

'Is this the first time the wound has been bathed today?'

'Yes. Sister Harrison did it yesterday.'

Bearing in mind that Ned was Nancy's husband, Frances guided her out of earshot of Ned and kept her expression neutral. 'You were right to tell me, Nurse Skittings. As you've already surmised, the wound is infected. That yellow around its edge is becoming redder. But thanks to your keen observation, it's early days although it's a shame there's no Dakin's in the dispensary. It proved very effective in the treatment of battlefield infections. We must be able to get some from somewhere.' Although Nurse Skittings appeared under control, Frances was in no doubt that her discovery of infection must have alarmed her.

'Continue with what you're doing.' She gave the young nurse a reassuring smile. 'I need to pop out for a moment.'

Ned winced when Nancy started bathing the circular wound progressing carefully over the yellow and redness around its jagged edges.

Ned's eyes followed the movement of her hand and although he might have had an idea that something was wrong, he made conversation about family and general things.

'Is Polly all right?' he asked.

'She's in safe hands. Your mother's looking after her.'

Ned smiled. 'Nothing bad can come to anyone when my mother's out and about.'

'That's true. And she's been thinking of you.'

Ma Skittings had asked that very morning whether there was any sign of infection in her son.

'I wouldn't be surprised after something nasty got blasted into his body.'

It turned out that his mother's words had been prophetic. She'd asked what they were giving him – inside or out. Nancy had mentioned aspirin for the pain and bathing the wound with carbolic and hot water.

Ma Skittings had drawn in her chin and looked totally astounded. 'Aspirin and carbolic?'

Ma Skittings had deferred to her own medicine cabinet. 'Yur,' she'd said in her strong Somerset burr. 'Take this. Smear it on. You've used it before.'

In the absence of both the doctor and Sister Harrison, Nancy fingered the small bottle in her pocket. 'Your mother's sent something that might help you get better more quickly.' She looked about her before taking the cork stopper from out of the bottle. 'Lift up your pyjama top.'

Incapacity failed to dampen expectation. His grin widened as she undid the cord of pyjama trousers and pulled them down enough to expose his belly. 'Nance. You're a wife in a million.'

Nancy arched an eyebrow and smiled as though only pleasure was on the agenda. 'You ready for this?' She already had a smudge of honey on the tip of her finger.

'You know me, Nance. I'm always ready.'

'Less of your sauce. Right. Here goes.'

'Arghhhh!' His back arched and his lips pulled back hard, exposing his teeth. 'Core blimey! That hurts.'

'I haven't finished.'

He hissed through his teeth, lips still stretched with the pain.

The hissing continued with his words. 'It better be doing some good.'

'Of course it is. Your mother swears by it.'

Nancy placed the stopper back in the bottle and slid it into the pocket beneath her apron.

'Stop complaining. You're on the mend. That's all that matters, isn't it?' She said it blithely without regard to the discoloured skin around the wound which she knew from experience could be trouble. Hopefully the honey would work or, better still, the doctor would get hold of the solution she swore by.

Ned grumbled his agreement.

Nancy patted her husband on the head like she might their daughter. 'That's a good boy. Let's get you comfortable, shall we?'

She felt his eyes following her as she folded down the bedsheets, tucking the loose ends firmly beneath the mattress. Unlike a lot of others of their age group, they'd wanted to get married. It hadn't been a case of her expecting. They'd been childhood sweethearts and at times they still acted as though they were still fourteen and not twenty-four.

He caught her wrist suddenly. 'Nance. Will the doctor be all right about you plastering me with me mother's stuff?'

She set about busily plumping up his pillows. 'Of course. So long as we don't tell her.'

Still not meeting his eyes, she pushed him back into the pillows.

'Nance! It won't get you into trouble, will it? You won't get the sack or whatever?' He looked worried. Her income was going to be very important to them in the weeks ahead.

Her hands rested to either side of his head on the newly plumped-up pillow. 'What the doctor don't know, she won't grieve about.' She kissed him on the forehead. 'Now get some rest and stop worrying. Everything will be all right.'

All she hoped was that Sister Harrison wouldn't find out. If she did, there could be trouble.

'Now rest. You need to get better. I've got other patients beside you.'

Other patients would have to wait. Nancy's footsteps diverted into the empty staffroom, where she grabbed the tea towel and held it to her tear-stained face. The tears had been held at bay whilst still in Ned's company. Now they flooded out.

The red skin encircling Ned's operation scar was worrying. The doctors at the infirmary had wanted him to stay there after surgery, but he'd opted to go back to the cottage hospital where he would be closer to his family.

His temperature was up too.

She took several deep breaths. Crying like this was unprofessional, but Ned was her husband. A lot depended on him getting better.

Nancy sobbed a little bit more before drying her tears when the door suddenly sprang open and there was Doctor Brakespeare.

'Nurse Skittings.' She didn't ask something stupid like what was wrong, but without hesitation took the sobbing young woman into her arms. 'I know it's hard, Nancy, but Ned will get better.' She held back a moment and looked at her. 'Sorry. You don't mind me calling you Nancy, do you? It seems only fit seeing as I call your sister Lucy.'

Nancy smiled through her tears and shook her head. 'No. It's nice and friendly.'

'And you can call me Frances, though only in private. And not when Sister Harrison is around.'

Nancy blew her nose and almost laughed. 'I wouldn't dare when she's around. She scares me.'

Frances joined her in a moment of subdued laughter. 'She scares me too!'

15

Visiting the chemist in the high street had not yielded the solution she needed, but the dispensary at the infirmary in Bristol had come up trumps. The pharmacist at the end of the phone had asked her to hold whilst he checked what he might have. Waiting seemed interminable and the longer it went on the more she prepared herself for him to come back and tell her that he couldn't help.

To her boundless joy, he'd told her that he had quite a large stock.

'We treated a great many injured servicemen both during and after the war, so many in fact that some had to be laid out on the grass bank next door. Not all of it was used. How much would you like?'

His words were music to her ears and she told him so. In response, he sounded bashfully pleased. She told him how many and he told her that he would send it by train the very next day.

'Can you get it collected from Norton Dene station?' he asked.

'Yes. Even if I must collect it myself.' Seeing Nancy crying and exchanging first names had changed something between them. They'd become friends and she wanted to help.

A sudden banging invaded her thoughts.

Another series of knocks was conjoined with the rattling of the scullery's glass roof at the rear of the coach house.

The cold flagstones were a treat to her aching feet as she dashed through the kitchen and into the scullery. The top half of the door was wide open and there stood Mrs Skittings in a shabby dress and sackcloth apron. The trilby hat she wore was set at a jaunty angle, the brim baggy and battered.

'Evening to you, Doctor. Hope I ain't disturbing your dinner, but I wanted a word.'

Frances shook the surprise from her head. 'Of course. Do come in.'

She reached for the bolt to slide it back to let her in.

'No need,' said Mrs Skittings. 'Top half is all we needs.'

'Oh dear. I didn't realise I'd left it open,' remarked Frances.

'Oh you didn't, Doctor. It's never locked. I pushed it open. Knew it would give easily.'

'It doesn't lock?'

'Not very securely. Still, don't matter much. We all leaves our doors open 'round here.'

'Ah,' said Frances. The sudden thought that she might have been murdered in her bed came to mind but was discarded when she remembered where she was. This wasn't Whitechapel or some other equally down at heel part of London. It was the small country town of Norton Dene. Nothing like that could happen here. 'So what can I do for you?'

Mrs Skittings leaned forward to whisper into her ear, though there were no neighbours around to hear anything. 'I went in to visit my Ned before coming yur and noticed he's got a bit of redness on his belly and Nancy said you were 'aving trouble getting 'old of something to sort it out. I took the liberty of giving me own salve to Nancy.' A flash of sheepish embarrassment crossed her face but didn't last. 'Hope you don't mind. Only we was all worried. Nancy will do anything for my Ned.'

The moment the words were out, Frances guessed that Nurse Nancy Skittings had already applied whatever it was to her husband's wound. Should she be angry that they hadn't asked her? She decided not.

'You're his mother and I can't blame you for trying. I only wish I'd...' She stopped herself from continuing that if she'd found what she'd been looking for in the first place there would have been no need for 'quack' medicine. 'Never mind.' She shook her head.

Mrs Skittings carried on. 'I 'ope you don't take offence. Far be it from me to interfere in the job of a proper doctor, but I've brought some more so you can see it ain't going to do 'im no harm. He's my boy, I'll move 'eaven and earth for 'im, that I would.'

Most doctors' first inclination would be to tell Mrs Skittings that her home-made medicine was of no use whatsoever, but Frances stopped herself. She was a new force in this town and loath to upset anyone.

She nodded approvingly. 'You're a very observant woman, Mrs Skittings. I do know of something that would help but it isn't in the dispensary. It's being sent for collection at the railway station tomorrow.'

Mrs Skittings' tired old face brightened. 'I'll collect it for you if you like, seeing as you're such a busy woman, Doctor.'

'That's very kind of you but no need for you to walk when I can drive there.'

'Oh I won't be doing that. I've got a bicycle.'

The thought of the very wide Mrs Skittings riding a bicycle brought a smile to her face. 'I'm not yet sure what train it will be arriving on.'

The corners of Ma Skittings face turned downward.

She thinks I'm fobbing her off, thought Frances and immediately attempted to make amends.

'I'll let you know which train. How can I let you know?'

She wasn't so cross as to ask whether she had a phone. Of course she didn't.

The corners of her mouth turned upwards. 'Run up the flag on the roof. That's 'ow it used to be done.'

'Seriously? I didn't know.'

A mischievous look came to the nut-brown face. 'No. Phone Mr MacDonald the undertaker. He's only along the road. In the meantime, I better give you a sample of my salve… healing honey – that's what I calls it.'

With something akin to a fanfare, she brought out a small glass bottle from inside the copious hessian apron. The glass was deep blue in colour and marked 'Poison'.

Mrs Skittings saw the look of alarm on her face, laughed and then explained. 'The bottle's been washed out. See?' She took out the stopper, turned the bottle upside down and emptied a dot of its contents onto her finger.

Frances held her breath when she licked it, then sucked until her finger was clean.

'Honey,' said Mrs Skittings, once her finger was out of her mouth, her grin wide and toothless. 'Just honey. I keeps bees, you see. Them bees make sweet things and magic things. That's what this honey is – not the sweet one you spreads on yer toast or puts in yer porridge, but the one that works magic. Take it.'

Still a little wary of the bottle's original use Frances took it gingerly. 'Thank you.'

'Now I'd better be off. Oh, and I left something on account for whatever I might owe you in future. Them and the honey. No charge.'

Frances stared after her as she waddled off. Honey on account and whatever it was she'd left on the other side of the back door. On peering over, she saw half a sack of potatoes.

'At least I won't starve,' she murmured, shook her head and laughed.

After dragging the potatoes into the kitchen, Frances headed for the vicarage, where Gregory Sampson had offered her the use of his phone whenever she needed it. Her first task was to ring the station and find out the time of the trains from Bristol. After that, she would ring Mr MacDonald.

If there was time and he didn't mind, there was another person she badly wanted to speak to if she was to make progress and benefit the population of Norton Dene.

16

Gregory's face shone with delight on seeing her standing at his front door.

'Frances. How delightful. I've just put a pigeon pie in the oven. And I've a bottle of home-made parsnip wine.'

'I came to take you up on your kind offer for me to use the phone.'

'Oh. Yes. Of course.' He looked slightly disappointed at first but quickly recovered. 'Please come in.'

'I need to phone the train station and ask about train times for tomorrow.'

'No need,' he exclaimed. 'I have the latest timetable.'

'Then I need to phone Mr MacDonald.'

'The undertaker? Nobody's died, I hope. If so, nobody thought to tell me so I can make the necessary arrangements.'

She laughed. 'No need to involve you.' She went on to tell him about Mrs Skittings offering to fetch the package from Bristol on her bike.

'Who needs modern communications when you've got the

likes of Mrs Skittings,' Gregory laughed. 'Now about breaking bread with me – well, not just bread. Pigeon pie.'

The smell reminded her that she'd had little to eat that day and there wasn't much in the larder – except for half a sack of potatoes.

'That would be wonderful.'

After rummaging through a bureau in the front parlour which, judging by the books and papers lying around and spilling from shelves, served as a study/office, he pulled out a copy of the Great Western Railway timetable. 'Here you are.'

'That's wonderful. Thank you very much. There's someone else I need to speak to – in private.'

'Here,' he said, indicating the phone hanging from the wall in the hallway. 'I'll leave you to it whilst I lay the table.'

He smiled and for a moment she considered that he was waiting for her to tell him who she was calling. When she stood purposefully with her hand resting on the device but not taking the earpiece out from its cradle, he left her there.

She dialled her ladyship's four-digit phone number, heard it ring and then a male voice answer in a resonant manner, so loud that she was forced to hold the device half an inch from her ear.

'Doctor Brakespeare here. I would like to speak to her ladyship if possible.'

'Doctor? I'm afraid she's indisposed at present. Can you call back?'

'I'm sorry. I should have known she was having dinner.'

'Hello? Can you hear me? It's Grimes here.'

'Grimes.'

'Can you hear me?'

'Yes!' she shouted back. Either this man Grimes was deaf or distrustful of telephones in general. 'Can you tell her I called?'

'Doctor? Is that you?'

'Yes.' Her shout reverberated around the vicarage hallway, so loudly it brought Gregory out from wherever he had been. 'Can you tell Lady Araminta that I called? I need to speak to her urgently.'

Grimes repeated that she was indisposed. 'I don't think she needs a doctor. She's rarely off colour and has never been seriously ill.'

Frances rolled her eyes in exasperation. Gregory, who had discarded his dog collar in favour of an unbuttoned check shirt and sleeveless pullover, shoved his hands into his pockets, looking casual, amused and totally engaged.

'Tell her I'll be in touch.'

She replaced the earpiece in its holder. 'I think I could hear Mr Grimes well enough without him using the phone. He shouts loud enough to burst my eardrums.'

'Her butler. Been with her for years.'

Frances eyed the phone and speculated whether her saying that she was phoning from the vicarage had got through.

'He's not deaf,' said Gregory as though reading her mind. 'Just a bit suspicious of modern gadgets.'

Frances rubbed at her ear. 'My ear is aching and my head's ringing.'

Gregory laughed.

Frances threw him the sort of glance a schoolmistress might a naughty pupil.

He looked suitably contrite. 'Sorry. You're being serious.'

'It's not funny. I really need to discuss a few things with her ladyship.'

'About the hospital?'

'Yes.'

He took his hands from his trouser pockets and straightened. 'How about you lay your troubles on me? That pigeon pie is too much for one. So's the parsnip wine I've just opened. I made it myself. Two years ago. It's just about ready to be sampled.'

Defeated by her telephone encounter with Grimes, Frances allowed herself to be led into the vicarage dining room. The table was large and looked quite capable of seating twenty. This evening it was set for two.

'Were you expecting anyone else?' she asked on eyeing the settings placed at the far end. 'I'm not interrupting anything, am I?'

He patted her hand. His expression was sublime, his eyes dancing with secrets. 'Yes.'

She unclasped her hand from his. 'You don't mean that?'

'Of course I do. The moment I opened the door to you and your request to use the telephone. That's when I laid the table.'

A smile threatened, but she held it at bay. She had come to realise that Gregory's sense of humour was a big part of his character. He liked to amuse people and most certainly had a way with words.

'Grimes said that her ladyship was indisposed. I do hope she's not unwell though he did say that she was never sick.'

He held a dining chair away from the table for her to sit down. 'I saw her earlier today. She was quite well.'

He poured wine into her glass and did the same to his.

She couldn't see his expression, but he had fallen to a sudden and unexplained silence.

As he ladled a portion of pigeon pie onto her plate, she asked, 'Does she live at Orchard Manor alone?'

It could have been her imagination, but for the slightest slip of time his hand paused over her plate.

'No.'

That one small word spoke volumes.

Once both their plates were full, he sat back down at the head of the table and next to her.

'Tell me more,' she said as she tucked into the melting pastry and pigeon pie. Wild mushrooms, small new potatoes and dark curly greens accompanied what was a very fine repast.

She saw the hesitation on his face, the slight slowing of his cutlery.

He looked at her with knife and fork in hand. 'Devlin lives with her.'

'Devlin? Her son?'

Never since meeting him had Frances seen the vicar's expression veer away from good humour. Rarely had she seen him without a smile on his lips and laughter in his eyes. This time it wasn't humour she saw there but sadness.

'Captain Devlin Compton-Dixon. Late of the King's Regiment of Rifles. He was injured in France.'

Frances's heart leapt in her chest. Her first thought was that he might have known Ralph. But it wasn't possible. He'd been in a different regiment. Still, there was always the chance.

'Where did he serve?'

'Here, there and everywhere. He was brave, perhaps headstrong. He loved being a soldier. I don't think he ever thought he'd end up a casualty. But he did. Badly so.'

'I'm sorry.'

She waited for his eyes to meet hers, but he seemed suddenly indifferent to where he was and who he was with. A memory from the past sent a shiver down her back. It was behaviour she'd come across before. Which could mean only one thing.

'You were there too. Am I right?'

He seemed to think about it before answering. Laying down his cutlery, he looked into her eyes.

'I should have remembered that it takes one to know one.'

When their eyes met and held, it was as though the present had vanished and they were back there experiencing not just the horrors but the passion for life, to see this through, to gain a lasting peace – and more. Much more.

Frances felt her face burning, for she knew without doubt the reason why. From the very start, she'd thought Gregory a beacon of light in a world that a few years ago had been very dark indeed. Dare she say it – or even think it – but in some ways he reminded her of Ralph, though better able to laugh at the world and all those in it. On top of that, he made people feel very at ease with both him and the Church.

Her wine glass was empty, though she couldn't be quite sure when she'd gulped the first measure back. Gregory poured more of the spicy, sweet brew into her glass. Half of it vanished down her throat.

'Do you want to talk about it?' he asked.

'About what?'

'Anything.'

Should she tell him about Ralph? She was about to, but a sudden reluctance stopped her. Instead she transferred her concentration to the lengthy list of items she wished implemented at the cottage hospital.

'I've listed areas at the hospital in dire need of improvement.'

'You wish to make changes?'

'I do.'

'If that's the case, then an EGM seems in order. An extraordinary general meeting where you can put forward your ideas.'

She sighed heavily.

Gregory immediately understood why and voiced what was in her mind. 'Some members of the committee are not open to change.'

'Sister Harrison for one. She holds the keys to the dispensary door and the medicine cabinets – or did – until I snatched them off her.'

'Oh dear. She won't like that. Old iron drawers is an unchanging force in a changing world – or was – until you came along.'

Frances curbed her smile and adopted a more serious expression.

'I've other plans. I think the hospital should be busier than it is, but then it can only offer the most basic medical care. I want it to do more for the community. Modernising won't happen overnight, but given time, introducing modern methods and ways of thinking will bring benefits to the townspeople. Or so I hope. Do I sound too pompous? I do hope not.'

'Not at all. But this is a small, sleepy town. It certainly isn't London, or Bristol for that matter. You coming here is by way of a stark awakening that the twentieth century is here and things are moving on apace.'

She fixed him with her slate grey eyes, concern flickering along with fringes of dark lashes. 'But they will come round. Won't they?'

'In time. Do you want me to set up this meeting? This EGM?'

She smiled. 'I'll still mention it to her ladyship. The final decision will no doubt rest with her, but your support would be much appreciated, so if you would be so kind.'

'I'm required to set an example of being kind. It goes with my calling.'

* * *

Using his trusty flashlight to see their way, he escorted her back along the path that led to the coach house. Halfway there it began to rain, a light slow drizzle that could well increase by morning.

Frances couldn't help smiling and then laughing lightly before saying, 'For a moment back there, I completely forgot that you're a vicar.'

He adopted a thoughtful silence before saying, 'I'm a man first and foremost, just like many others. Being a vicar is just my job. Just as you're firstly a woman and your calling is as a doctor.'

He sheltered with her at the front door beneath the porch roof where climbing roses and honeysuckle fought for space.

She fumbled for the four-inch-long iron key before realising she hadn't locked the door. 'Fancy forgetting to lock the door. Perhaps I'm becoming a true local,' she laughed.

'I hope you will.' His glance was swift but intense enough to almost make her blush.

With the confidence of someone familiar with the route, Gregory followed the beam from the flashlight over the flagstone floor to the oil lamp and lit it. A small glow came into being that seemed particularly puny once the flashlight was turned out.

'There you are. You need to get your wet things off.'

'My shoes first.'

She sat down and slid her right foot out of her shoe without unlacing it, then used that one to prise the left one off the other without bending down.

She fancied his eyes were on her and when she met his gaze found she was right. His look was intense and what he said next was even more so. It dug into her and brought buried emotions to the surface.

'Is that him, the one who lives in the sadness in your eyes?'

He jerked his chin at the silver-framed photograph which she'd left sitting on the table.

Was her sorrow that easily read in a room where the only light came from candles and – at present – the round bowl of an oil lamp?

'You're very observant.'

'It's part of my job.'

She could see from his expression that he knew he'd opened a raw, unhealed wound.

'Forgive me for being so personal. Would you like me to leave?'

'No need.' She gulped. The wound had been opened and this was a vicar asking her, a man who was used to listening to secrets and deeply buried hurt.

'There are some glasses in that cupboard and a bottle of brandy. If you could do the honours.'

He found the bottle and glasses, poured into each and passed her one.

She took a hefty gulp before the words came.

'We were engaged. I was going to give up nursing so we could marry. The battle of Cambrai intervened not that long before the war ended. I was numb. I threw myself into the filthiest jobs that an auxiliary of the Voluntary Aid Detachment could do, but dealing with gangrene and resultant amputations threw me in a different direction.' Her eyes lit up with evangelical strength and met his. 'Did you know that limbs were amputated as a precaution against a man losing their life? There was horse manure and filth everywhere. Infection was ravenous. It seemed acceptable – or did... but the filth – flicking at flies, trying to keep wounds clean...'

They fell into a shared silence before she spoke again, her words hanging like snowflakes in the air, cold but soft.

'His name was Captain Ralph Porter. Losing him changed my life. I resolved to marry a profession rather than a man.' She shook her head disconsolately. 'Nobody could replace Ralph, so I enrolled to become a doctor. My guardian had encouraged me to become one for a very long time. I was adopted you see. Taken from a workhouse.' She swallowed. 'She's gone now. I believe she was acquainted with her ladyship. At least I think so. Both were suffragettes, leaders of younger women in the fight for equality.'

Gregory eyed her silently before saying, 'I'm sorry for your loss.'

'Thank you.'

She drank the last of the brandy and declined a refill when the bottle was hovering over her glass.

Regardless of her refusal he poured himself one and held the amber fluid over the top of the oil lamp to warm it.

'I admire them, those women who wanted things to improve. There is still a lot to do. You at least got to be a doctor. I admire you for that.'

'I was top of my class but was downgraded purely because I was a woman.'

'That must have been very hard to accept.'

Her expression turned sour. 'It was.' When she lifted her head, he saw that her eyes were shining. 'But I secured a good post at St Aldelm's. But it didn't work out. I was too outspoken.'

'Outspoken is just another way of saying that you were honest. And now you're here and I'm glad you're here. If there's anything I can do for you, please don't hesitate to ask.'

Frances's thoughts clicked into place like a set of dominoes. In her mind she had ticked off the items on the list she had written in pen. Lady Compton-Dixon first regarding the introduction of new methods and facilities at the hospital. Having the vicar's support was an added extra. There was also the letter from the solicitors regarding her car. The very thought of returning the present Izzy had given her was monstrous – but it was personal and at present she was disinclined to share.

The last item, however, was something Gregory might be able to help her with. All the same she felt nervous at the possible answer.

'There is something. I was looking at the list of names on the war memorial.' She frowned. Thinking of what she'd seen pained her but voicing it might help her understand even if she he didn't know why it was there.

Faltering over her words, she expressed her surprise on seeing Ralph's name listed on the war memorial.

'He's not from here.' She shook her head. 'He was one of those missing, resting place unknown, but he wasn't from here and that is what I cannot understand.'

His expression was subdued, even reflective when he said, 'Leave it with me. I'll see what I can do.'

* * *

Closing the door of the vicarage against the night, the Reverend Gregory Sampson caught sight of his reflection in the mirror on the hallway coat stand and swore.

'How can you face yourself?'

Shaking raindrops from his hair, he stowed the flashlight on the bottom shelf of the hall stand, took off his coat and hung it up. He needed a stiff drink, and parsnip wine wouldn't be good enough. From a tantalus of three-cut glass decanters, he poured himself a large brandy.

Forgiving sins was one of his jobs as a vicar but could that possibly include self-forgiveness? Why had he done what he'd done? It had been no onerous task to add one more name to those listed on the war memorial. It had all begun with the exhumation of bodies for a top secret mission meant to heal national pride.

Once the brandy balloon was empty, he made his way into his study where church records and accounts were kept. The captain and his name should have died with him on the battlefield and he would have remained yet another man whose remains should have been known only to God except finding that locket with her picture inside had altered everything. He couldn't help himself engraving his name on the war memorial, the silver locket in his pocket enclosing that beautiful face that he so clearly remembered from the field hospital. The fates had decreed that it should be Norton Dene.

The six men they'd exhumed had carried nothing that might identify them. Or so they'd thought. It transpired that one of them had carried a silver locket between battledress and mouldering flesh. Gregory had been alone when he'd found it, had opened it up and cast his gaze on a woman he'd thought an angel when he'd first seen her in the flesh back in the war. And now... the fates had indeed been working overtime. She'd turned up here. He'd been slow recognising her, thinking he could have run across her anywhere and besides photographs could be very deceiving. As time went on he slowly accepted that it was her, the young woman who showed such kindness to those for whom life was over. And then when she had mentioned Cambrai...

A battle, a kind young woman and a silver locket. They were all connected with that terrible task he'd been ordered to perform. On a whim, he'd kept that locket with their names etched on the back. *Frances Brakespeare and Ralph Porter. With love.*

The photograph in the locket had been taken some time ago, but the years had been kind. Doctor Frances Brakespeare was still a beautiful woman.

He'd remembered her but she wouldn't have remembered him – not even his voice when he'd made comment about her compassion for a dying boy in a field hospital, though she didn't recognise him.

Given time, he would break the oath he had taken never to divulge the sanctity of what he and a team of others had done. He knew he couldn't avoid it. He wanted everything to be out in the open with this woman, one he knew he was swiftly falling in love with.

* * *

Although it was late Frances found the energy to write a letter to Deborah informing her that the Porters' solicitors had been in touch demanding the return of the car.

Dear Deborah,

Izzy gave me that car when I passed my finals. She stipulated it was a present. How dare the family demand it back! I will do all in my power to retain my car and it is with this in mind that I ask if you can think of anything I can use as proof that it was a present. They are saying there is no paperwork. If there is none perhaps you might consider putting your hand to a statement saying that she discussed the matter with you. If there is no other evidence to confirm my ownership then I fear there is nothing else for me to do – except perhaps to drive away into the sunset, to somewhere nobody can find me. That would, perhaps be too drastic.

I'm making inroads here. I'm making The Orchard Cottage Hospital my own.

17

GRAINGERS' QUARRY

First there was the noise of rattles and whistles followed by the shout, 'Fire in the hole!' The shouted warning was nothing compared to the explosion of sound that followed. Shattered stone flew over twenty feet up into the air, particles of stone rolled and dust billowed in giant clouds before finally cascading to earth.

Though the walls of the office trembled, making it seem as they too might crumble to dust, Simon Grainger rubbed his hands together gleefully. Prior to the explosion, he had taken great delight in hearing the new drills made in Cambourne, Cornwall by Messrs Holman Brothers, digging into limestone. It was possible to assess with each hour that passed how deep they had gone. Twenty, thirty, forty feet. The deeper the drill bit into the deposits of stone laid millions of years ago, the more money was made. Each foot represented greater tonnage and thus greater profit and Simon Grainger assessed just how much money the total represented.

Windows closed firmly against the dust meant the office was stuffy with stale air and male sweat. It was also the busiest it was all week. Not only were invoices being sent out for loads already supplied, but today was Friday. The wages were being counted out by his jack-of-all-trades clerk, James Forester, and placed into small brown envelopes, along with a slip declaring the amount to be paid. The wage packets were then placed in a row in a tin box, ready for allocation, and a signature in the wages record book.

Everything had gone as smoothly in that department as it had with the blasting, although James was hesitant with the last amount of money to be paid to one man on the list.

'Mr Grainger. Excuse me if I sound a trifle obtuse, but Ned Skittings' wages are a little over the weekly average he receives – even with overtime.'

'Don't you worry about it, Jim.'

James swallowed the riposte he wished to make, that he preferred to be called James. There was no point. Simon Grainger already knew that. Calling him Jim against his wishes made Simon feel superior. As for James Forester it was a case of put up with it or get another job.

Feeling well satisfied that yet another load was on the ground and that he'd reaffirmed his superiority over his clerk, Simon lit up a cigar, one he'd taken from the balsa wood casket his father kept on the study desk at Newton Friars – a house built in the early Victorian age in the gothic style, an imposing design but less than tasteful.

He blew a cloud of smoke into the air and smiled with pleasure as he watched it twirl and twist upwards.

'Just pay what's listed, Jim. I have my reasons.'

'Of course, sir. So this is a bonus – to make up for the accident?'

Simon bit down on the end of the cigar and glowered at his clerk. 'Call it what you like, it's what I want to do. That all right with you, Jim? Don't have to ask your permission, do I?'

'No, sir.' Wincing and clenching his jaw James bent his head back to the job in hand.

'That's my man.'

Simon's tone was condescending. He liked making lesser mortals – that is poorer and in less comfortable circumstances – look small. Especially when at one time James had held a higher station in life than being a menial clerk in a filthy and dangerous limestone quarry.

James Forester was a well-educated man who'd once taught piano at a ladies' college – until he'd run off with the head girl. The college had fired him, the girl's father had disowned her when she'd refused to give him up and although he had been middle-aged and she'd been little more than a girl, they were still together and had produced six children. However, explaining away his background and continually coping with assumptions that his wife must be his daughter, jobs where the two of them could live in peace and quiet without fingers being pointed had proved difficult to come by.

Simon Grainger had recognised this and taken full advantage.

'You owe me,' he'd said to James with great relish on several occasions. 'I took you on when nobody else would. And don't you forget it.'

Having had no alternative but to accept his lot or inflict poverty on his family, James had accepted. He knew very well that charity had nothing to do with Simon giving him the job. He might have thought so at first, but it became patently obvious that his boss was a bully.

'Excuse me, Mr Grainger. But seeing as Mr Skittings is in hospital, can we expect his wife to collect Ned's wages or shall I get one of the men who lives that way to deliver them?'

Already feeling as though the world was his oyster, Simon blew another cloud of smoke from pursed lips that sat in a self-satisfied expression.

Everything comes to those who wait, he thought to himself. *Like the cigars.*

Taking the advice of the new female doctor, his father had sought advice for his chest problems from a private doctor in Harley Street. The doctor had advised him that smoking was good for the lungs, that it lined them and made them stronger. For some reason known only to himself, his father had ignored this advice. Instead of smoking like a chimney as he always had, he'd chosen to abide by the advice of Doctor Brakespeare. A woman doctor! What was the old fool thinking? Was it possible that he was still susceptible to a pretty face, a pair of neat ankles and grey eyes that made his knees buckle? Simon chuckled to himself. Silly old fool. His father had certainly changed his tune from when the lady doctor had turned up for her interview.

Simon hadn't berated his father for suddenly becoming aware of his own mortality. The old man was getting on. He wasn't going to last forever, so it didn't matter to him which doctor was right. Either way, he was the beneficiary of whatever ensued. To start off with he'd inherited the box of Havana cigars, said to be the same brand smoked by King Edward. It was just a matter of time before he ended up with everything else.

James asking what he should do with the money due to Ned Skittings and whether his wife was coming to collect made him smile. Ned was in hospital and when she wasn't on duty at the hospital, Nancy was alone with her baby. A vision of her pretty face and curvaceous figure came to mind. Before she'd become a mother she'd been too skinny for his tastes. But now!

'Give it to me. I'll save her the journey. I'm driving that way. Got a little business to do. I'll drop it off.'

'She does have a bicycle.'

Simon's clenched fist thudded so hard on the desk it sent the inkpot jumping in its stand, the pen sprinkling blue spots over the blotting paper.

'Are you deaf as well as stupid? Come on. Give it here.'

Head bowed and cheeks aflame, James Forester handed him the wage packet.

Only after Simon Grainger had left the office did he show any sign that he understood what his boss had in mind and thoroughly disapproved. He feared for Nancy Skittings alone in her house with her baby. The boss wouldn't dare do anything if Ned wasn't in hospital, but he'd try his luck now and face the consequences that might or might not come. The fact was Simon Grainger considered that he was entitled to anything he desired – and that included women.

18

Nancy Skittings had taken the opportunity to pull in the zinc bath from the back wall and place it in front of the range. Kettles and saucepans full of water bubbled and steamed on the side hobs. There was also a large bucket hanging from a hook over the fire bed.

Polly was sleeping, so it was the ideal time for her to take a bath, to relax after a long day which had begun early this morning at the hospital.

Her little girl had been suffering teething troubles of late and the usual solution hadn't been working. Along came mother-in-law with something she swore would work.

Having a modern approach to medicine, Nancy had asked her about the ingredients.

'Rose hips and tincture of mushroom.'

'Are you sure?'

'Well, if you don't want my 'elp...' Ma Skittings had said in a thoroughly affronted manner.

Tired and unwilling to upset her mother-in-law, Nancy had allowed her to rub the little girl's sore gums with the pinkish elixir.

Training as a nurse had made Nancy a little distrustful of medicine that didn't come in a bottle from the chemist, but Polly hadn't slept for nights, and neither had she.

The warm water was glorious and the steam rising from the surface smelt of Lifebuoy soap. For a moment, she closed her eyes and wished it was Ned rubbing her over with the flannel. It came as something of a disappointment to open her eyes and see the familiar rose-scattered curtains, the scrubbed wooden floorboards, the bread board, butter and cheese dish sitting on the pine kitchen table.

When the water had cooled and was no longer so soothing, she got out. Once she had donned her upper clothes and armed with a large enamel jug, she tipped the tepid water from the zinc bath onto the garden where Ned had planted a row of runner beans, carrots and cabbages.

'Now don't forget to keep them watered.'

She smiled at the vision of him lying in bed, more concerned about his vegetables than himself.

Once the bath was hanging back on its nail, she went into the house to finish brushing her hair. Next, she checked on Polly and found her sleeping soundly. It was the first time she'd seen her sleeping so deeply for days and made Nancy wonder about the gum rub Ma Skittings had used but Nancy was assured everything her mother-in-law made was from natural ingredients. Of course it was. Ma would never chance doing anything to harm her only grandchild.

Feeling reassured, she closed the doors and went back downstairs to get fully dressed. Her stockings and garters were the only things left to put on, but they were being awkward. Just when she was about to give up on an elastic garter that decided to snap, the front door, which was rarely locked, burst open. A figure almost as wide as it was high filled the gap between the dim interior and the daylight outside.

The figure swept off his hat and she recognised Simon Grainger, the man Ned worked for.

'Mrs Skittings. Nancy. You don't mind if I call you Nancy, do you?'

Taken by surprise, she gave a little gasp and let go her skirt, which had been above the stocking top of one leg. 'Mr Grainger! What are you doing here?'

Fondling his hat with both hands, his smile spread like treacle across his wide face. His eyes gleamed and stayed fixed to where he'd espied the flash of stocking top.

'I've got something for you,' he said, his wet tongue flicking at the corners of his mouth. 'Something I think you'll be very glad of.'

'Oh. Will I?'

He kept smiling, his smouldering gaze sometimes seeking her eyes, sometimes falling back to where he'd glimpsed naked flesh when she'd been dealing with a garter.

She'd been a nurse long enough to have experienced men's lust and was immediately on alert. Even when they were ill, some men simply couldn't help themselves. But Simon Grainger was not sick. He was fit and healthy and she recognised the threat.

He brought a small brown envelope from his pocket, which she immediately recognised as a wage packet, identical to the one Ned brought home every week.

'Ned's wages.'

'Thank you for bringing them. You shouldn't have troubled yourself. I could have come in and collected them.'

He looked somewhat contemptuously around the simple terraced cottage where she and Ned had lived since they were married. 'I thought I'd save you the trouble.'

She feared stepping forward to take it, preferring to wait until he placed it on the table.

Disappointment flickered on his face but was batted away as anyone else might a fly. The smile of overwhelming confidence and belief in himself returned.

'I've put in a bit extra. Thought you might need it, what with Ned still being in hospital.'

'That will come in very handy. Thank you.'

He looked around again before his gaze came back to her.

'Any idea yet of when poor old Ned will be coming home?'

Her response was swift and sharp. 'Shortly. It could even be within the hour.'

The truth was that Doctor Brakespeare hadn't yet given a definite date, but she wasn't going to tell him that.

'You must be missing your man. Every woman wants a man about the house – to chop wood, dig the garden. Warm her bed.'

Her face warmed. She couldn't find the right words because she feared where this was going. He was waiting for her to express more than gratefulness. That's the kind of man he was.

He twirled the envelope in his hand like a playing card – and to some extent it was.

'Ned's always been a good worker. That's why I'm going to make him an offer he can't refuse – an upgrade. I'm going to make him foreman at one of our other quarries. Monkswell over in Monmouthshire. There's a cottage to go with it.'

This was something she hadn't expected and it took her back to hear that Ned was being rewarded for working hard.

'I'm not sure we'd be happy to move.'

'It's your man's job.'

'Even so, we have family here. I'm not sure I want to live among strangers.'

'Strangers have a habit of becoming friends in the fullness of time.'

Her eyes narrowed as she thought through what this might really be about. Why now? Why when Ned was laid up in bed recovering from a blast that had gone wrong? Ned suspected what the problem had been but was keeping it to himself until he was absolutely sure.

Her attention went back to Simon Grainger. Was it her imagination or had he taken two or three steps closer to her?

Nervous of his intentions, she took a few steps back until her fists closed over a kitchen shelf behind her. Her back arched as she realised she could go no further.

Simon's wet tongue licked along his lips, hovering at the corners of his mouth as his eyes roved over her.

'I love nurses. It's not just the look of the uniform. It's the swishing of the skirt, the apron pinned over a caring breast. And the stockings. Black stockings and a prim and efficient way of handling people.' He chuckled. 'Wouldn't mind you giving me a bed bath any time – or anything else, for that matter. What about you? Fancy that, do you?'

'No. I do not!'

Behind her, she felt for anything she could use as a weapon. Simon had a reputation with women – not a good one.

'Here's some money.'

In the blink of an eye, he pushed Ned's wage packet down the front of her blouse.

'I believe in paying for what's worth having.'

Used to handling people in and out of bed, supporting them when they were relearning how to walk, Nancy was stronger than most women. Clenching her fists, she beat at the wide expanse of his barrel chest.

'It's Ned's money! He earned it.'

Simon laughed. 'There's more where that came from. Play your cards right and you could earn more than your husband.'

She turned her head to avoid the wet leering lips that sought hers. 'No!'

Whilst his fingers grappled for her breast, she kept pummelling his chest and kicking his shins. He towered above her, but she would keep fighting. She'd leave her mark on him and not tell Ned until he was out of hospital.

In the meantime, she needed a miracle. If only Polly would cry. Perhaps then his conscience might be moved, although she doubted he had a conscience.

Her skirt lifted. She felt the scratching of blunt fingers forcing their way up her leg. Cold air came too, still at first, but then blew a bit more forcefully, as though the edge of a gale had entered the front door which had remained open.

Engrossed in shoving one hand up her leg and the other into her blouse, Simon betrayed no sign that he'd noticed any change – until there was steam rising from one of the hob kettles and scalding water pouring over his head.

'Aaghhh...?'

His white shirt was soaked through, as was his jacket. As his neck and face turned scarlet, he whirled round and came face to face with Ned's mother, Ma Skittings.

'You stupid old cow!'

Ma Skittings seemed to grow in stature as she faced him head on, her expression dark with loathing.

There was an unhealthy clang of metal against bone as she swung the iron kettle against the side of Simon Grainger's head.

'Get out of this 'ouse,' she shouted, 'or I swear I'll pour more boiling water over a far worse place than yur head!'

Nancy joined her, a rolling pin held high above her head.

'My mother-in-law says nothing that she doesn't mean. I suggest you get out. Now!'

Red eyed and scalded, Simon Grainger clutched at his soaking wet and very hot shirt. He turned on Ma Skittings with hatred and disbelief in his bloodshot eyes. 'You old hag! I'll get you for this. You just see if I don't.'

He turned on Nancy, seemed about to say something in a similar tone to that handed to her mother-in-law, but then thought better of it when the black hob kettle connected with the other side of his head, that side which had escaped the first onslaught.

At the same time as taking steps to the door he half turned, glaring at Ma Skittings with a mixture of disbelief and fury.

'I only came here to deliver Ned's wages. And to say that he's been paid a bit extra.'

Ma Skittings cocked her head. 'Have you now. And why might that be? Blood money, is it? A bit extra to keep his mouth shut.'

'And he's offered Ned promotion to a quarry called Monkswell which is on the other side of the Severn,' Nancy added.

Ma Skittings moved steadily towards him swinging the empty kettle above her head, grievous intent etched on her face.

'Oh, want to get rid of 'im, do you. Well, we're family, Mr Grainger, and families stick together. So whatever your reason for paying extra money and offering my boy the earth, you'd better think again. Or own up to the true reason you're being so bloody generous. You ain't known for it. Neither you nor yer old man!'

Eyes out on stalks and jaw stiff with rage, Simon stormed out, leaving the door hanging open, a chill blast blowing in his wake.

Ma Skittings eyed her daughter-in-law. 'You all right, Nance?'

Scrabbling to fit buttons into buttonholes, Nancy nodded. 'Yes.'

The fierce expression on Ma Skittings face changed to one of concern. 'Now don't you go telling Ned will you.'

'No.'

Nancy's voice was smaller than usual. She tidied her hair back from her eyes and rubbed a hand across her eyes.

Swaying from one plump foot to another Ma Skittings went to the water pump in the backyard to refill the kettle with water straight from the pump.

Feeling greatly relieved, Nancy cupped her hot face with her cool hands. Simon Grainger's attack had come as no great surprise. He had always looked at the female staff at the cottage hospital as though he owned them. Sometimes he'd followed them out into the sluice room where they washed bedpans and other medical instruments. Up until now, nothing had happened, mainly because Sister Harrison had followed like a mother hen, looking out for her chicks, though she'd always blamed them for his behaviour – as if they'd had any choice.

Ma Skittings came back in, her bowed legs giving her the exaggerated gait of a drunken sailor, her sack apron heavy around her belly. She placed the refilled kettle on the range without looking round at Nancy.

'Now that is a man with secrets that will never be shared. He's dangerous, spiteful and never forgets a slight.'

There was controlled worry in her tone.

Nancy sighed. 'I'm just so thankful you came in when you did. He's a big man.'

A pair of watery grey eyes met hers. 'In more ways than one. His type bide their time and they're nasty.' On seeing her daughter-in-law's alarmed expression, she offered the only reassurance that she could. 'You've nothing to fear. Ned will be out from the hospital soon, so he'll behave himself when he's around.'

Nancy fingered the wage packet thoughtfully. 'Why extra money? Why this promise of a better job with a cottage and everything? Do you think it might have had something to do with the accident? He seemed a bit nervous about it.'

'We'll have to wait and see.'

Ma Skittings did not disclose that she had a friend on the inside at the quarry. She'd had the good fortune to assist at his wife's confinement. Miriam Forester had given birth before but this last one had been more difficult. She should really have been in hospital but had pleaded with Ma Skittings to step in and do what she could. Ma Skittings had done. The child had died but she had saved the mother and for that both Miriam and James Forester were extremely grateful. James Forester had told her that Simon Grainger had stopped paying the health insurance that had been part of his employment agreement, hence seeking out her help.

'Little 'un all right, is she?' Ma asked her daughter-in-law, purposefully changing the subject.

'Sound asleep.'

'Just rub her gums when needed. I told you it would work.'

19

Simon Grainger swept through Newton Friars, the Victorian pile that was the family home without acknowledging Smith, the valet, a servant shared between him and his father, or Molly Tucker the parlourmaid. If they'd noticed that he was dishevelled and soaked through, Simon's manner was a clear enough signal that this was not the right time to make comment.

Molly did relent and call after him that his mother was entertaining guests and wouldn't see him until dinner time.

He didn't bother to reply. All he wanted to do was get out of the ruined clothes and swill his face with cold water.

Once he'd poured enough from the blue enamel jug into a matching bowl on the washstand, he stood staring out of the window plotting the downfall of Ned's mother. Throughout his charmed life, nobody had dared abuse or injure his person and that included his father. He'd never raised a hand to him, and when he'd been sent away to boarding school, strict instructions had been given that no master or prefect should harm him.

One master had dared point out to the brigadier that the British army weren't averse to corporal punishment. Plus he'd also repeated the old Victorian saying, spare the rod and spoil the child. The brigadier had opted to spoil his son whilst his mother was an aloof figure who took immense pride in holding soirées and planning closer ties with the rich and titled of the country. The only person she didn't seem to impress was Lady Compton-Dixon, something she badly wanted to do. In her opinion they were both the upper class of people, the elite personages in the town. They should be closer, meet for tea more often. That was what his mother suggested. Her ladyship did not seem to agree.

As for a wife. A few had been trotted out to him, but once he'd shown his true colours – that he was far from being a gentleman and apt to grab bits of their bodies when they least expected it – he had remained a bachelor preferring to pick his women wherever and when he wanted them.

'And I'll bring my children up the same way,' he'd repeated laughingly to his friends in London when he fancied a flutter at the casino or the loose creamy limbs of a willing woman.

The dinner gong sounded from downstairs at roughly the same time as he had made himself look presentable, though his face was still a deep shade of rose.

* * *

His father sat at the head of the table his eyes half hidden by his bushy white eyebrows.

'Good evening, Father.'

'Good evening, Simon. A good blast today?'

'Very. Good evening, Mother.'

His mother turned her head, thus allowing her to kiss him on her chilly cheek.

Doctor Walker and his wife had been invited by his father, much, no doubt, to his mother's indignation. They were lesser people, but what could one expect in such a small country town? One had to make do.

She sat stiffly, cutting her food into tiny bites, quaffing her wine in small deliberate sips as though it might sting her tongue if she took bigger ones.

Doctor Walker was bleating on about the medical profession going to the dogs.

Simon decided to add his own view on the matter. 'It comes to something when we are forced to engage a woman doctor.'

Doctor Walker nodded as he dabbed a linen napkin at each corner of his mouth. 'Not that I have anything against women doctors, especially in obstetrics, but I do not foresee them ever making inroads into orthopaedics for instance. It takes strength to saw through a bone even when the patient is anaesthetised.'

Simon noticed that his mother baulked at the doctor's comments, showing her disapproval by pushing what was left of her lamb chop to one side of her plate.

As the brigadier launched into his chest problems, Simon's eyes met those of his mother in mutual understanding. Both would be somewhat relieved – and better off – once the old man was dead.

'I made the decision to quit smoking of my own accord. Good health is very important to me.' He laughed. 'Anyway, my son thought it an opportune moment to take over my horde of top-quality cigars. And he's welcome to them,' he added, beaming at Simon, who made the effort to look extremely privileged.

'Very generous of you, Father.'

'Not at all, my dear boy.'

Simon comforted himself with inner thoughts that his father was attempting to face his own mortality and in that respect was clutching at straws.

A dessert of rice pudding was ladled into shallow dishes and a bowl of plum jam passed around.

Simon reached for another glass of claret to make the conversation more interesting. If he drank enough, he might blot it out altogether.

Before his brain was lulled into self-imposed isolation, he caught a scrap of conversation that made him prick up his ears.

Doctor Walker was waxing lyrical whilst knocking back his third glass of sherry.

'Even in this century the old "gamps" are still peddling their dubious medicines. Take Mrs Skittings for example. I've nothing against her attending women lying in at home when giving birth and unable to afford a professional nurse or doctor, but I'm dubious as to the ingredients of her so-called medicines. What does she know of medicine? Nothing.'

'Herbs and snake oil,' remarked the brigadier, his bushy eyebrows so highly arched that his eyes were totally exposed.

Doctor Walker reached for another sherry. Once he'd wetted his lips, he set forth to explain, his manner imperial and certainly pompous. 'I was reading an article from America regarding a medicine called Paregoric, presently peddled by so-called herbalists. At least, I think it was called some such name. Anyway—' he took another sip of sherry '—it was instructed that a spot of this Paregoric was dotted onto a finger and rubbed onto the gums of a baby suffering discomfort from teething. The baby stopped crying almost immediately and following many sleepless nights fell into a peaceful repose.'

'Very useful,' stated the brigadier.

Simon grasped that there was more to this story. 'I sense there's more, Doctor.'

The doctor blinked, sucked in his lips and setting his head to one side spoke of something that Simon latched onto immediately.

'It got banned. Apparently some babies went to sleep, never to wake up again.'

'Terrible,' said Mrs Walker in support of her husband. 'What was in it, my love?'

Doctor Walker sighed heavily at the same time as imbibing yet another sherry. Too quickly, it seemed. A fleck of the dark red liquid dotted his shirt.

'It contained opium. All supplies were immediately withdrawn.'

Mrs Walker tutted, then reached above her ample bosom and belly for a second portion of rice pudding and plum jam.

Simon sat numbly, his eyes glittering as a plan took root in his mind. However, he wanted to be sure he was on firm ground.

'And you think Mrs Skittings is out of the same mould?'

Doctor Walker nodded. 'More or less. She peddles potions she makes herself. Has done for years.'

'How very interesting,' said Simon as he let the information sink in. 'As you say, she's not trained in medicine. She's just a woman who makes potions – like gypsies at fairgrounds or...'

'Witches.'

It wasn't often his mother said anything much at dinner, certainly not in the presence of lesser souls like Doctor Walker and his wife. All eyes turned to her.

A cruel smile curled Simon's lips. 'Mother. Surely our Mrs Skittings isn't a witch. Goodness gracious, you'll be suggesting next that she should be burned at the stake!'

His mother averted her eyes whilst delicately dipping her dessert spoon into the small portion of rice pudding set in front of her.

'She would have been in times gone by. Norton Dene might seem a quiet place nowadays but in times gone by...?'

A silence opened like a deep well waiting to be filled, everyone entertaining their own thoughts and visions. Eventually, it was broken by the sound of the brigadier clearing his throat.

He turned to the doctor's wife. 'How are the roses this year, Mrs Walker? Good enough to take a prize at the horticultural show?'

Simon wasn't interested in hearing Mrs Walker trilling coquettishly about her roses and the chances of beating those grown in the sumptuous gardens of Lady Compton-Dixon.

Once their guests, had left his mother apprehended him at the bottom of the stairs in the hallway, where she touched his reddened skin with her cool fingers.

'What have you been doing, my darling boy?'

He winced and took a step back. 'I got too close to the blast at the quarry.'

His mother narrowed her eyes until they were pinpricks of grey steel. Her thin lips formed a hard, straight line. She always looked at him like that when she didn't believe him.

Unwilling to be drawn, he remarked, 'Just an accident.'

The incisive disbelief in her look made him nervous. His mother noticed. She knew him well.

Her eyes glittered. 'I do hope so. If someone had done it deliberately, I would take instant and deliberate revenge.'

She said nothing more but turned on her heels and was gone, leaving him feeling she knew the truth and had given him carte blanche to do something about it.

* * *

Later whilst blowing cigar smoke out of his bedroom window, Simon considered his mother's suggestion that Mrs Skittings was a witch. His skin still tingled from what she'd done. His pride smarted even more. If that old bat hadn't come along, he would have had his wicked way with Ned's wife. He would have paid her to keep her mouth shut, of course. Wasn't he already paying Ned off by way of his wage packet for an accident that should never have happened, that he was ultimately responsible for?

But there it was. Everything had a price and even if Ned found out about his visit to Nancy, he could always attempt to grace his hand with promotion and money. More money. Everyone had a price.

20

It was with a surge of great relief that Frances had watched Ma Skittings wobble up to the front of the hospital on her bicycle.

'I've got it,' she'd called out, waving one hand – which had sent the bicycle wobbling even more.

That was yesterday and already the application of Dakin's solution to Ned's wound was reaping results.

Last night, Frances had slept well. Today, she threw open her bedroom window and welcomed the cool air along with the smell of flowers from the garden.

In the hour or two before she went to the hospital, was the allotted time when she was available for any patients who called. Her eyes strayed to the front window, through which she could see the narrow path winding down between masses of cornflowers, roses and lupins, all the flowers one expected to see in a cottage garden.

Frances occupied herself by checking through her medicine cabinet – which was in fact a carved cupboard, part of a Welsh dresser and set at the same level as the shelves displaying willow patterned crockery.

Looking around the room, she suddenly realised that something important was missing. The photograph she had up until now taken everywhere with her, including bringing it down to breakfast first thing on a morning, was nowhere to be seen. For the first time ever, she'd left it upstairs.

What were you thinking of? she said to herself as she dashed up the narrow winding staircase.

The photograph was in its usual place on the bedside table, alongside a small vase of flowers picked from the front garden.

'Things are not going too badly,' she said to an image caught by time in the silver frame. She listed several things she intended altering – improving. She might have gone on further, but a clattering of crockery and the smell of hot coals on the range drifted from downstairs and she remembered that Lucy Daniels had a key.

The kettle was puffing clouds of steam up into the chimney and a fresh loaf of bread together with curls of butter and a jar of honey with a paper cover tied with string sat on the table. Cup, saucer, milk jug and a bowl of sugar cubes completed the setting and something was bubbling in a saucepan set on a hob at the side of the range.

'Lucy. I'm not sure that I've got room for breakfast...'

The figure she'd thought was Lucy turned round and she saw it was Nancy.

'Oh. Nancy. I was expecting Lucy.' She shook her head. 'Silly me. It's not her day. It's your day today. Isn't it?'

Nancy's curls bounced when she nodded, though a pensive look persisted. 'Yes. I mean it should have been Lucy, but not today.'

Although she tried to brighten, there was a veiled expression on her face.

'I've made porridge. And there's honey. Will that be all right?'

Frances couldn't help thinking of the honey Mrs Skittings had given her. The jar marked poison had put her off, but she'd dared taste it and hadn't dropped dead.

Nancy dribbled a yellow blob of honey off a small wooden device onto the creamy porridge.

'Thank you, Nancy. Now sit down and pour yourself a cup of tea.'

At first, it looked as though she was about to decline the invitation. Another urging from Frances and she deigned to sit down and pour herself a cup of tea, which she gripped with both hands. It wasn't difficult to guess that something was wrong.

'Are you going to tell me about it?'

Eyes downcast and the fingers of her right hand fiddling with a lock of hair, it didn't seem as though Nancy was going to divulge whatever was troubling her.

Even when she raised her head and held Frances's enquiring look, her expression failed to brighten.

'Sister Harrison told me that in future the hospital could make do with just Lucy. They didn't need to employ a married nurse – even part-time.'

Frances let her spoon wallow in the dish of porridge. 'On whose authority?'

Nancy shrugged. 'I presume the committee.'

Shocked at the revelation, Frances sat back in her chair. There was a pretty good chance of the porridge going cold and the rest of the food untouched.

'She said that Ned should accept Simon Grainger's offer and move over to the quarry they own in the Forest of Dean. I told her we didn't want to go. Our families are here. My mother would be devastated.'

Frances felt herself turning cold. Something was going on here that she couldn't quite understand. 'And what did Sister Harrison say to that?'

Nancy's dark lashes fluttered. 'That we shouldn't look a gift horse in the mouth. That we'd never get a better offer – not the likes of us...'

Frances frowned. 'What did she mean by that, I wonder.'

It wasn't really a question for Nancy, more a wondering quite what was going on.

'I'm willing to let Ned go home tomorrow. Another week or so and he'll be fit for work. Do you have enough money to cope for a week or two?'

It seemed for a moment as though Nancy's whole body shuddered.

'Nancy? Is something wrong? Has something else happened?'

Although Nancy shook her head emphatically, Frances sensed when a woman was holding on to a secret too fearful to declare. She'd seen women responding like this before.

'I'd like to know why Sister Harrison has taken upon herself to do this. I have not been told and, as far as I am aware, neither had Lady Compton-Dixon or she would have told me.'

Or would she? The question came unbidden into her mind. After all, she was an outsider.

Usually wide-eyed, Nancy's expression was more guarded than usual. There was anger in her face and she seemed to be holding on to whatever was troubling her with grim determination.

'Believe me, Nancy, I'm going to make enquiries about this. I've been quite happy having you and your sister working part-time at the hospital. Part-time here too.' She smiled. 'How would I cope without your mother-in-law's honey?'

She gave a little laugh, which brought a corresponding one, though Nancy's sounded more forced.

'I expect you're glad to know that Ned is about to come home. Have you everything prepared for that?'

A wan smile, but there was happiness there, plus what looked like relief. 'I can't wait.'

Frances's mind went back to what was previously said. 'And you won't have any money worries?'

Nancy shook her head. 'No. We'll be all right.'

'I take it his employers will be supporting him as promised?'

If Nancy's taut expression was anything to go by, it seemed she'd struck a raw nerve.

'Has Simon Grainger gone back on his promise?'

Nancy shook her head. 'No. He's been very generous.'

Frances eyed her speculatively and was reminded of a volcano about to erupt. Just a few words would perhaps open the floodgates.

'Nancy. We're friends, remember? I promise that whatever's troubling you won't go any further.'

Nancy looked as though she'd been woken from a deep sleep – or was coming to a decision.

'Simon Grainger came round with the wages yesterday.'

Frances paused and guessed that something bad had happened.

'Were you alone?'

Nancy nodded. 'Yes, except for Polly, but she was asleep. The poor little mite's got teething problems.'

Again, Frances took a considered pause before asking, 'Did he make himself disagreeable?'

Nancy looked stronger when she took a deep breath and told Frances the first portion of what had happened.

'He thought that handing over my Ned's wages had to be paid for by me being nice to him. Nice! The man makes me sick.'

'What happened next?' asked Frances, keeping her voice even although she felt sick with anger.

Suddenly the face of Nancy Skittings shone with happiness.

Not just any ordinary happiness but a triumphant happiness that brought her to the brink of boundless joy.

'Ned's mother arrived. I didn't see her come in, but never have I ever been so pleased to see her. She's a funny old thing with funny ways, but she always does what's right. She's always been one for sticking up for them that can't stick up for themselves.'

'The underdog.'

'That's it.'

'So she gave him a piece of her mind,' said Frances saying the first thing that came into her head.

Nancy burst out laughing, then covered her mouth with one hand as if she'd overstepped the mark or was being rude. She shook her head and her eyes glowed like jewels.

'She emptied the kettle over him.'

'Hot water?'

'You bet it was. My, but did he holler.'

'Oh dear. I wish I'd been there.' A mischievous impishness curved her lips and glittered in her eyes.

She knew she sounded as exuberantly girlish as Nancy had until a thought came to her.

'Will Ned lose his job?'

Nancy looked thoughtful. 'I don't think so. I had a letter this morning still offering Ned the job at the other quarry.'

'Will Ned take it?'

Nancy shook her head. 'No. If he goes, I won't. This is my home. I don't want to live anywhere else. I want Polly to grow up here, just as me and Ned did.'

Having finished her breakfast, Frances began picking up the dishes for taking to the sink in the kitchen.

'Doctor, it's me that should be doing that.'

'I'm not helpless. I'll give you a hand.'

The kettle had retained some hot water which they used to

wash up. As Nancy washed and Frances dried, she asked the capable nurse about her mother-in-law and the honey which had done a good enough job until the Dakin's solution had arrived.

'Some say she's a witch,' Nancy said laughingly.

Frances laughed too. 'What other potions does she make?'

Nancy nodded her head from side to side. 'This and that. Things for coughs. Sore feet. Liquorice mixture for that bunged-up feeling. If you know what I mean.'

'I believe I do.'

'She gave me something to rub on Polly's gums for her teething. Poor little mite hadn't slept well these past two nights and neither had I. Her teething mixture worked a treat.'

'What's in it?'

The blunt question took Nancy unawares. She had to think.

'Herbs. It's always herbs. And a few old-fashioned medicines.'

'Like what?'

'Things from her cupboard shelf. Some of them were handed down by her mother, even her grandmother. The women in her family have always been healers.'

It was not the first time Frances had heard of such women. For the most part, they were harmless and gave people solace as well as medicines.

'I have to say that her honey and willow salve worked well enough on Ned's infection.'

'Yes, and her tincture for Polly's teething has worked. I know you don't agree with such things, Doctor...'

Frances stopped her right there. 'That's not entirely true. I do not condemn them out of hand. In fact, I'd like a few samples of her medicines. They wouldn't have lasted over the centuries if they didn't have some value. Do you think she'd mind?'

Nancy looked surprised at Frances's interest. 'I'll ask her.'

Nancy went in one direction, looking determined to keep the old coach house spick and span despite everything.

Frances went into the living room, where she sat at the pretty little bureau that Gregory had brought over from the vicarage.

He'd said to her, 'It's a bit too feminine for me and there's not enough room for storing my lengthy sermons.'

She'd pointed out to him that on the few visits she'd made to church she'd heard his sermons and their length was quite reasonable.

His face had dropped. 'In that case, I'm a failure. It's a well-known fact that a church sermon should be capable of sending the severest insomniac into a long and peaceful sleep.'

They'd both laughed and even now, just sitting at it, thinking of his chirpy response made her smile.

Her thoughts wandered to Nancy's run-in with Simon Grainger. Why was he so keen to get Ned to transfer to another quarry far away from family and friends? It didn't seem that either Ned or Nancy favoured the move, even though it would bring a bigger wage. Being new to the town she was still getting used to people and practices and knew nothing at all about quarrying.

Simon's behaviour had angered her. Women came across this kind of thing all the time – men trying to take advantage of women. In this instance it seemed an act of stupidity. On the one hand, he was trying to persuade the little family to accept his offer, then he'd done this. What a contemptible fellow he was!

The smell of garden flowers wafted into the living room along with damp earth. Nancy popped her head around the door.

'Mrs Lynch is at the back door.'

'Mrs Lynch?'

'Your first patient of the day. She's not likely to pay much, mind,' she whispered. 'Well. Not likely to pay anything if she can avoid it.'

'Right,' said Frances. 'Regardless of the ability to pay, in future, I want all patients to come to the front door. I heartily dislike this two-tier system.'

'You're very generous, Doctor. Shall I fetch her in?'

'You may.'

As she waited, she looked around the small but cosy living room and thought of her predecessor. Not for Doctor Walker the close confines of the coach house. Burlington House where he'd seen patients was a late-Georgian pile that dominated a road lined with sycamores behind the high street. Classically styled windows looked out from each of its three floors.

Nancy returned quickly. 'She begs your pardon, but she accidentally trod in horse manure on the way here, so thinks it best you see her out back – and in private.'

'She's got seven children, so I expect you can guess what she's come here for,' whispered Nancy.

Frances picked up a notepad and pen. 'I'll need to make some notes. Can you type?'

'A little, though that could be a problem. We don't have a typewriter.'

'Another thing to add to my list,' said Frances with a sigh.

'I do write well.'

'Good.' Frances handed her the writing implements. 'I'll examine her. You take notes.'

Mrs Lynch had the typical look of a woman who'd had too many children. Her hair was lank, her face grey and skin stretched tightly over prominent cheekbones.

'I've got a bit of belly trouble, Doctor,' she said, bending forward as though imparting a great secret. 'If you could give me a strong laxative, sure it would set me up fine and get rid of this belly ache once and fer all.'

The pen that had only so far scribbled the patient's name paused. Nancy exchanged a certain look with Frances.

Frances concentrated on the job in hand. 'Is that so, Mrs Lynch? I believe Nancy knows your address, but can you please confirm your age?'

'Thirty-seven.'

'And how many children do you have?'

'Seven. And that's plenty enough.'

'Quite a handful, I should think.'

'That it is, Doctor,' she said, bobbing her head to one side as though she was a spritely seventeen-year-old, not a woman of thirty-seven who'd had too many children. 'I told my old man it was more than enough, but you know what men are like...'

'Different to women.'

Mrs Lynch laughed. 'Well ain't that true!'

Her laughter tinkled like the sound of fragile bells, delicate and pretty.

Years ago, she'd probably been a beauty, as blonde and vivacious as a girl could be.

Frances noted the streaks of grey in her dark blonde hair and the fine wrinkles around her sharp blue eyes, which must have sparkled when she was younger. Now they were dull, as tired as her skin and edged with the same yellow as the stains on what remained of her teeth.

Frances had seen it all before in the East End of London. The worn-out women who'd given birth at the lying-in hospital with the hollow look of resigned hopelessness in their eyes. The true miracle was that once the newborn had entered the world; their faces had lit up with unconditional love. She'd felt for those women most of all, for their fertility, for their weariness and for the sex their husbands considered their due rights without a thought for the consequences.

'This belly ache just won't go away. I can't go, you see,' she whispered with controlled embarrassment. 'I need something stronger than senna pods, to be sure I do.'

Mrs Lynch was playing a game she'd heard before, not exactly telling the absolute truth, but giving the facts so Frances could conclude what was only hinted at. The woman was after heavy laxatives that she would take in quantity in order to bring on a miscarriage.

'A belly ache, you say. Now what kind of belly ache would that be, Mrs Lynch,' she asked lightly as though she had no idea what was ailing her.

'Well,' said Mrs Lynch, blushing profusely as she tilted her head in the opposite direction to before, carefully avoiding the doctor's gaze. Finally when her gaze wandered off some way to the left, she came as close as she dared to what was troubling her. 'It's an ache that wasn't there last month but is there now and I can't seem to get rid of it!'

'You mean you need a strong laxative, Mrs Lynch. Strong enough to be rid of a heavy problem?'

Mrs Lynch blushed like a virgin. 'It's very embarrassing to talk of it, Doctor. It's all in the private parts, in the regions below the waist.'

Frances turned away, praying for the time when women gained a bit more control over their lives and their bodies. Marie Stopes had made a start with her clinic in Holloway, London, where she gave advice on birth control.

Poor Mrs Lynch. Seven children and another on the way. Perhaps in years to come effective birth control would be readily available. For the moment, abstinence was preached from the pulpit and contraception was a word barely breathed by the medical profession. Not that there was much on offer anyway.

Frances didn't need to open one of the glass-fronted doors of her medicine cabinet to find what Mrs Lynch was after. The tablets regularly prescribed to women with the same problem were kept in a white porcelain jar. Liberally laced with senna pod and liquorice, they were responsible for easing the lives of women worn out with childbirth and desperate enough to do anything rather than having another mouth to feed. Taken in copious quantities and washed down with strong spirits, they were about all that was on offer.

Despite the teachings of the Church, the backstreet abortionists were there if Mrs Lynch cared to look for them. Thinking of such women brought a question to mind. Ma Skittings peddled home-made medicines, but did she also carry out abortions? It wouldn't surprise Frances, but what she didn't know about she wouldn't try to find out.

Seeking such a service if there was none to be had locally meant a bus ride to the nearest big town. The outcome was not always favourable, women bleeding to death after the insertion of soapy water, a long thin knife or a knitting needle.

Frances placed the pills in a brown paper envelope and wrote the directions on the outside and, in case Mrs Lynch could not read, also gave her the instructions verbally.

'Four taken with a hot bath every night for a week should do the trick, though of course there's no guarantee,' Frances said to her.

'Oh thank you, Doctor. Everyone's saying what a grand doctor you are.'

Frances flinched. 'Are you a Catholic, Mrs Lynch?'

'I am that, Doctor.'

'In that case, all I ask is that you don't mention it during confession. Your excuse is that you have a bowel problem. Constipation. Such things are best kept private.'

The tired-looking Irish woman was over the moon. 'Doctor,

you're a saint, and that's the truth of it.' She wrapped the bag of pills in the hem of what had once been a child's dress recut for use as an apron. 'Mustn't let the old man know,' she said with a wink. 'Mustn't have him worry about something that's not likely to be – not now – not with your kind help, Doctor.'

Frances waved her towards the back door. 'You take care of yourself, Mrs Lynch. And if you need to come again, knock at the front door. I won't tolerate divisions between my patients.'

If anyone expected Frances to feel a shred of guilt at what she'd just done, then they'd be sadly mistaken. Too many babies. Too many women grown old before their time. Babies should be blessings. There should never be an instance of not wanting a child.

Her spirits rose when more patients trailed in. Having tossed the prepared vegetables into the bubbling stockpot, Nancy stepped in as receptionist, scribbled down names and addresses before asking them what their problem was.

Frances dabbed gentian violet on a six-year-old boy with warts on his hands and scabies down his back. His mother paid her with three still-warm hens' eggs.

She used the same treatment on a twelve-year-old boy who worked in one of the nearby coal mines at Catbrook Colliery. Conditions there were grim and wages low, but his widowed mother needed every penny to feed her family of five. After handing over his wages, Horace Joy was left with next to nothing and certainly not enough to buy a pair of boots. So he worked barefoot on sharp surfaces and his feet suffered for it.

Frances winced as she cleaned his wounds and applied the salve. She advised that it was not wise to work in a coal mine with bare feet and asked him if it was possible to get hold of a pair of second-hand boots.

'I would have thought there must be someone with a pair their own son might have grown out of. Perhaps you could ask around.'

The boy sniffed and shook his head. 'The gaffer gave me a pair. Belonged to 'is son they did. 'E got killed in the war.'

'I take it you grew out of them?'

'No. They were too big for me. Me mum got two bob for them down at the pawn shop.'

Although knocked sideways, she continued to apply salve to his ravaged feet. Some cuts had healed into scabs, only to be replaced by new lesions.

'Do you have soap at home, Horace?'

''Course we do,' he exclaimed, seeming somewhat slighted. 'Sunlight. Me mum uses it for everything.'

There was no need to ask what else it was used for. Everything meant just that. Laundry, washing dishes, cleaning floors... Everything.

'I would suggest that if you can't get another pair of boots that you wash your feet after coming home from work. Do you have a bowl you can wash them in?'

He thought about it. 'There's the pig trough.'

'How about the pig? Is he likely to object,' she asked with a smile.

'Nah! Killed and cooked years ago.'

'Hmm. Horace, you have a very hard job. You really need to wear boots. You could get a serious infection and end up losing your foot – and perhaps your job if you're not careful. How would your mother cope then?'

'Send the kids tip picking.'

'Tip picking? What's that?'

'Picking up bits of coal from the slag 'eaps outside the coal mine and selling it door to door.'

'To my mind, that's a poor return for a lot of effort. Take my advice and if someone gives you another pair of boots, tell your mother from me she's not to pawn them.'

'I'll tell 'er to pawn me trousers instead? Is that what you're saying?'

Getting anything for the shabby trousers he was wearing seemed unlikely. They were big and baggy, far too large for his spare frame.

'Let's hope it doesn't come to that.'

Who am I, she thought, *laying down the law like that?* If his mother had to choose between her son wearing a pair of decent boots to work and a meal on the table for the whole family, she was bound to choose the latter. *And so would I*, Frances admitted, *though it would pain me to do so.*

She waited for him to dip into his pocket for a shilling or even a few coppers, but no fee was forthcoming and she wasn't going to ask for one. It was obvious that she was never going to earn much from these people but she wanted to be there for them, to be a beacon of hope amid their poverty.

By midday, the patients had all gone and the coach house reverberated with the sound of creaking beams. Outside, a flock of sparrows, tits and wrens took it in turns to hang from the water pump to catch the drops.

Nancy came in with a cup of tea, the notebook and pen.

'I've written down all the details of your patients who came this morning. There were six altogether,' she said brightly. 'Things are looking up, don't you think?'

'Did any of them pay?'

'Yes. Mr Forester. He's the wages clerk at the quarry. He said that if his family took ill this is where they'd be coming. I kept a record of them that paid – though it's not much,' said Nancy whilst eyeing the shillings in her hand. 'Mr Forester paid half a crown.'

Frances eyed the half-crown with raised eyebrows. 'That was most generous.'

'I went round to the back path and asked the others for

payment before they reached the front gate. You can't always trust them, you know, especially that Mr Crouch. He doesn't pay for anything if he can help it. Still I got a shilling from him and a shilling each from the others. There's three shillings...' She placed them on the desk. None of it was silver but a collection of pennies, half-pennies and farthings. She looked at the eggs Mrs Lynch had left in payment. 'I'll put those in the kitchen cupboard. I've put the rabbit in the shed for now.'

Frances looked up. 'Rabbit?'

'Horace brought it. He said he was very grateful and that there are plenty more where that one came from. There's a lot of rabbits around this year. Do you want me to skin it for you?'

'If you don't mind.' Frances was not going to admit that she'd never skinned a rabbit – Izzy had had a cook to do that.

'I'm used to it. I'm off home now. I'll see you in the morning.'

'Thank you.'

After she'd gone, Frances looked around her. Every room had a low ceiling, flagstone floor and overstuffed furniture of dubious age and solid construction. It would do for now until something better was set up at the cottage hospital, which was only a case of converting two rooms next door to each other, one as a waiting room and one as her surgery. And no matter status and ability to pay, everyone who wanted to see her would wait in the new waiting room. Sickness laid low poor and rich alike. They were all in need of her care and she wouldn't hesitate to provide it.

21

It was the day for James Forester to go to the bank in person and place an order for a cash withdrawal for next week's wages.

He hadn't been feeling too well of late and the day before had asked Mr Grainger if he could go early that evening so he could call at the doctor's surgery.

'Which doctor would that be, Jim?' Simon had asked scathingly.

'The new doctor is closest.'

'The lady doctor!' Simon had thrown his head back and laughed before all merriment was replaced by a look of pure contempt. 'Fancy her, do you, Jim?'

James had blushed as Simon had intended him to. 'Certainly not! I've got this—'

'Itch for her,' said Simon without giving him time to respond. 'On the surface, she's a good-looking woman. But who knows what lies beneath, eh? Acts like a man and might be one under her skirts. Now wouldn't that be a shock once she was in the buff.'

Amused by his own crass joke, he'd chuckled so hard he'd nearly choked. James wished he would.

Simon had carried on chortling and making fun. 'Though you shouldn't have any problem with that, Jim, should you. Experience counts. You shouldn't have any trouble at all.'

James had swallowed ripostes that would have put Simon in his place. Unfortunately, he couldn't afford to do that. He badly needed this job. After all, he had his family to think of.

'So would it be all right...?'

'No. It would not.'

James had become used to Simon's bullying, so much so that guessing his request would be denied, he'd made other plans. He had to go to the bank and if he left early enough, he could call on the doctor at the coach house.

Counting on the bank clerks being more efficient than usual, he'd marched into the bank, pleased to see there was no queue and so, to his great delight the job was done in half the time it usually took.

'All well with you, Mr Forester?' asked the bespectacled cashier on the other side of the cash desk.

The cashier was young and made James feel old. Perhaps that was why he snapped back, 'Why shouldn't it be?'

The real cause was the headache he was suffering. They were becoming more and more persistent, though mostly during the working week. At the weekend, they dissipated but slowly built up on Sunday evening prior to turning in for work the next day.

The doctor had opened the door of the coach house and looked surprised to see him there. 'Oh. Do you want to see me?'

'If possible, though if surgery is over I can come back again...'

He sounded dejected but looked at her hopefully.

It seemed to work. She invited him in.

The room she showed him into was an oasis of calm after the office back at the quarry. He sat in the chair offered, the cash bag he'd taken to the bank hugged close to his chest.

'I keep getting headaches.'

'Right. If you would like to set down your things and take off your coat...'

Her hands were cool on his forehead and the sound of her voice was a healing balm to the banging going on inside his head.

At the end of the physical examination, she asked him about his job, his family, his day-to-day life.

An avalanche of details came out of him, his tone affectionate when speaking of his family, anxious and helpless when detailing his time in the offices of Grainger and Son.

'He doesn't let up. If he can put me down, he will. He even refuses to call me James, my preferred name, but insists on calling me Jim.'

Slights and name calling, laughing in his face and behind his back, making him climb up a pile of aggregate to tell someone they were wanted in the office – or fired. The brigadier's son took immense pleasure sacking people on a whim – only to re-employ them at a lesser wage.

'He plays with people. He's a bully.'

The doctor was mostly silent as she listened to the catalogue of wrongs wrought on his person.

'Take these aspirin when needed.'

He was about to say that he already had some but didn't want to offend her. If all she was going to give him was aspirin, it seemed he'd wasted his time. Not that he would say so. He wasn't a man for upsetting people.

Hands clasped on the desk in front of her, she held her head to one side and began to speak. 'I know it's only aspirin and perhaps you were looking for more. Physically there's nothing wrong with you. You've told me that your headaches are confined to weekdays – workdays. Your job is causing you anxiety. Is it possible to find employment elsewhere?'

At first, he stared at her in disbelief before shaking his head. 'No! I have a family you see and there are circumstances which...' Unwilling to divulge the scandal of his marriage and former employment from which he'd been dismissed, he got swiftly to his feet. 'I can't,' he said, continuously shaking his head, though goodness knows that would do nothing to disperse what he'd done and what he was.

'I understand, Mr Forester. Might I suggest you do nothing at weekends except to take walks in the country with your family. Fresh air and being with those you love is as good an antidote as aspirin.'

Her advice stayed with him as he'd hurried back to work and his headache had diminished. She was a doctor in a million, he thought. One in a million!

On the other side of the road to the Moon and Sixpence, an ancient pub of black and white timbers and twisted windows, he'd espied Mrs Skittings on the other side of the road.

'Mr Forester!' She waved him over.

Her florid expression leaned into his, giving the impression that she was about to impart a secret.

'Mrs Forester asked me for a pick-me-up. I've prepared her a tonic that should do the trick.'

She handed him a small bottle of brown fluid that he thought looked like vinegar, though of course it couldn't be. His wife saved money by referring to Mrs Skittings when it came to medicines. A lot of people did.

He thanked her and hurried on his way. Mr Grainger had an appointment with the director of a steelworks earlier that morning, so James could get away with being a little late.

As it worked out, he was just hanging up his overcoat when he saw the black Bentley cruise into the yard. He'd only just made it in time – or thought he had.

The moment James saw that smug smile, he knew he was in for a roasting.

Simon stopped by his desk and looked down at him. 'I stopped off at the Moon and Sixpence.'

James said nothing. He knew full well this was leading somewhere he wouldn't like.

'Saw you with Mrs Skittings. Any reason for that?'

The straightforward answer would be for James to tell him to mind his own business. But this was Simon Grainger and for the foreseeable future he was compelled to hold his tongue.

'Mrs Skittings prepared a tonic for my wife.'

Simon smirked. 'Did she now.'

A minute of thought and Simon Grainger's expression changed.

'My mother could do with something like that. Might go to her and see what she advises.'

'She's very good,' James said, feeling that this might be a better day with the boss than he'd envisaged.

'So I hear.'

Simon was thinking nothing of the sort but perceived the seeds of a plan taking root in his mind.

'Yes,' said James, hoping for improvement between them. 'A lot of people swear by her elixirs and potions.'

Elixirs and potions. Simon recalled what his mother had said about the old biddy being a witch. 'Mind if I take a look,' he asked.

James gladly took the bottle from his pocket and gave it to him.

Simon turned it over in his hand, noticing that the bottle was reused and might once have contained something far more deadly than a tonic for a run-down disposition.

'She's got a wonderful reputation with the locals,' James expounded, warming to his subject.

Simon eyed the bottle. 'Is that why everyone calls her Ma Skittings, because she looks after them like a mother does her children?'

Up until now, James had felt the sun had finally shone on him. But on seeing the narrowed eyes in the fleshy face, he shivered. 'I wouldn't know.'

Simon weighed the bottle in one hand, then the other. 'How much did you pay for it?'

James hesitated. Should he tell the truth or lie that it was double the true sum?

Telling a lie was alien to him. He decided to tell the truth.

'Threepence.'

Simon raised his eyebrows in surprise. 'Is that all?'

James, wondering what would happen next nodded. 'Yes.'

He felt a sense of relief when James handed the bottle back to him.

'On second thoughts, I don't think I'll bother. My mother wouldn't take it.'

'It is good,' James exclaimed as reassuringly as he knew how.

Simon grinned. 'My mother has expensive tastes. She's of the opinion that if a medicine costs less than ten shillings it can't be any good.'

* * *

The plan Simon had conceived grew like a poisonous weed in his mind. Every time he pulled down his shirt collar and viewed the red rawness of his skin, his thirst for revenge was bitter on his tongue. The redness was lessening, but the deed had been done. How dare the Skittings woman assault his person. He plotted her downfall, a downfall from which the old crone would never recover.

Ma Skittings was well thought of and the lower classes

certainly put great faith in her cures. But what if they discovered that some of her cures were downright dangerous? What if someone was made seriously ill or even died after taking one of her potions?

The most delicious part of this plan was that he would be able to join in the condemnation. In this regard, it was imperative that no suspicion should fall on him. Everything he had in mind had to be done secretly, though he did need assistance from someone outside the family, someone who he could fool into thinking they were doing good when in fact...

He smiled. Tonight he was meeting just such a person. Her name was Marian Murray, a maid in Lady Compton-Dixon's household. She was as besotted with him as Edith Harrison and like her believed herself in love with him and him with her. She couldn't be more wrong. The only person Simon loved was himself. Lady Compton-Dixon's second maid was young, ripe and impossibly naïve. Ideal for what he had in mind.

22

Trees in the churchyard soughed in a slight breeze that flicked Frances's skirt to one side around her legs and sent a few wisps of hair tickling her brow and cheeks.

After selecting a posy of wildflowers – yellow rattle, feathery grasses and foxgloves that had hidden for longest in the shadiest places, she made her way to the expanse of grass in the centre of town where the war memorial threw its melancholy shadow.

For a moment, Frances paused, closed her eyes and buried her face in the flowers. Perhaps when she opened them, she would not see Ralph's name there. Wishful thinking. There were supposedly many cases of wishful thinking in one's life and her most intense wish was that he'd come back from the war. But he hadn't.

Frances lay the flowers at the base of the list of names and in a strange way was glad there were no bodies buried beneath the stone construction which was not a grave but a benediction to the brave.

Her attention was suddenly distracted to where a coffin, followed by a crocodile of black-robed mourners, was making its way into the church.

Coffin delivered and the hearse no longer needed, it was on the move, slowly proceeding over the cobbled road.

'Rest in peace,' she whispered, as much for the recently deceased as for all those whose names were listed in stone.

* * *

On the following day a letter arrived, this one from Deborah.

Darling Frances,

I received your letter about the Brakespeare family's solicitors requesting return of the car. Dreadful people the lot of them. They ought to be ashamed after all that happened. But there, it cannot be altered. I've spoken to an old friend who also happens to be a solicitor. She suggests you hunting down the birthday card, the bill for the car if you have one and any piece of paper on which she may have written down her intentions, i.e. a will. A will? Just because her family snatched back the house doesn't mean to say that there isn't a will. Do a thorough search, my dear.

Sincerely yours, Deborah

Frances set the letter to one side. In time she would do as suggested but not today. Today she would carry on rearranging things at the hospital to her satisfaction. It was also the day the new surgery would be completed and she couldn't help but feel a frisson of excitement.

The only thing that did stay with her from the letter was Deborah's comment that Izzy's family were dreadful people and ought to be ashamed of themselves but then Deborah had always been very vocal.

* * *

Ned was at last coming home. Consequently, Nancy was bursting with excitement.

'I can't believe it. My Ned is coming home at last.'

'I can take you in my car if you like. I'm sure we can fit Polly in too.'

It amused Frances that a ride in a car could contribute to the excitement of the moment, but then few people ever got to ride in a motor car even one as humble as Matron Molly.

'I couldn't have him being taken home in Mr MacDonald's hearse. He deserves better.'

Nancy was the picture of a doting mother as she leaned over the child, folding the knitted blanket that covered her and smoothing it flat. Her heart-shaped face glowed with motherly pride.

Dressed in day clothes, Ned leaned on Sister Harrison, who was hovering attentively and telling him to walk slowly.

'You can't go from cart horse to racehorse overnight,' she added, not unkindly.

A porter tied the pushchair onto the car roof, whilst Frances and Nancy helped Ned into the back seat.

Sister Harrison stood looking on.

Frances tried to read her expression but gave up. Was she annoyed that she was giving the family a lift, or was it something else? She had no idea.

Ned and Nancy could not have sat any closer in the back of the car, Polly sound asleep between them.

Ned remarked that his daughter looked a bit red in the face and asked if it was normal that she slept so much.

'She's been teething. Babies and toddlers sleep a lot when they're teething.'

'Are you still rubbing her gums with the potion your mother-in-law gave you?' asked Frances.

'I've only got a bit left.'

Frances refrained from questioning anything about the tincture provided by Mrs Skittings. There being little left gave her the opportunity to hand over something she knew was safe.

'I've got something you can use.'

On arrival at their home in Waterloo Terrace, Frances fetched out a small bottle of recommended soother for babies.

'Take this.'

Ned left nursing the baby, Nancy and Frances untied the pushchair from the roof of the car. Ned carrying Polly and Nancy dragging the pushchair behind her, they said goodbye. If they didn't exactly skip up the garden path they did hold hands as best they could and gazed at each other like star-struck lovers.

Lucky them, thought Frances and wished she'd been as fortunate as those two.

* * *

The car seemed empty and quiet as Frances drove back to the hospital, where patient notes needed to be updated and a few patients had come in on the off chance.

One patient had cut her arm – quite a deep cut in need of stitches. The other had a boil that needed lancing. Neither of them were serious nor had come via their general practitioner.

The wards were oddly quiet and surprisingly empty. In one way, Frances was a little perturbed at the lack of patients. On the other hand, perhaps the health of the local population was improving and hospitalisation was not needed.

Although the dispensary wasn't very untidy, she applied her time putting things in order. She tidied away the jars of liniment, the boxes of powders, the jars of pills and the bottles of syrup. Small noises echoed in the still air. Although there were staff around she felt almost alone until somebody called, 'Doctor!'

A large frame filled the doorway from side to side and top to bottom.

Simon Grainger swept his trilby hat from his head.

'Mr Grainger. You startled me.' She wondered what he would want here at this time of night.

'I wanted a word.'

He didn't apologise for startling her.

Wiping her palms on a hand towel she'd brought in for the purpose, she adopted a professional smile. Not a welcoming one. She found it difficult to be pleasant to someone who so unnerved her. She hoped he wasn't here on a health matter. Even though all patients were equal he was one she would prefer to avoid – although she couldn't say that. Instead she adopted a blank expression and asked what she could do for him.

Without being invited, he pulled out a chair on the opposite side to her own, placed his hat on the desk and sat down.

She noticed that his hands were smooth, his nails neatly trimmed and polished. His neck, however, was still very pink from the boiling water Ma Skittings had poured over him.

'It's about Ned Skittings.'

Ah. Now we're getting somewhere. 'What about him?'

'I hear he was discharged this evening.' He sniggered. 'Back in the crumbling hovel that's loosely termed a house.'

She was about to enlighten him on the concept of patient confidentiality, but he beat her to it.

'I know you can't say too much. Him being your patient and all. But it's like this...' He leaned forward, his hat resting on one knee after he'd crossed one leg over the other and leered at her.

'Ned's a good worker but wasted doing what he's doing. I need a man like him at Monkswell – it's another of our quarries over in the Forest of Dean,' he explained. 'I can offer him a better wage and a cottage to live in free of charge. And I wouldn't insist on him starting work right away. A week of convalescing before taking charge would do him some good.'

'And you're doing all this out of the goodness of your heart?' She tried not to sound sarcastic.

Grainger chose to ignore her arched eyebrows and the scepticism in her tone of voice. 'He's been through a bad patch. The brigadier – my father – and I thought it our Christian duty to do right by him.'

'By sending him away from his family and friends.'

Grainger shook his head harshly enough to send his oiled hair slipping from over the bald patch hidden by a few stray strands. 'No, no. That isn't it at all.' He tried to sound genuine but didn't come across as such.

'Your charitable actions are your concern, Mr Grainger. What I'm wondering is why you came to me. You hardly need my permission.'

A slight fluttering of his eyelids betrayed his discomfort. 'I... We thought you might advise him – seeing as his wife is one of your nurses.'

'I see.'

Grainger sneered. 'Excuse me for saying so, Doctor, but she's not got much work to do here at present. As you may have noticed, there's not enough patients being referred to the hospital to make any difference to staffing. It's likely to change of course.' He paused to give her time to let the veiled suggestion sink in. 'I'm sure that banded together, myself, the committee and my father could persuade the local doctors to refer patients to the cottage hospital just as they did—'

'Before I came! Which gives rise to the question, Mr Grainger, as to why they were persuaded otherwise in the first place.'

A stunned expression was swiftly banished. Grainger and his father – with the connivance of the committee – were used to running things as they saw fit.

'Things could improve a great deal for the hospital. For instance, my father and I could contribute more money to its running. That way, you can have more nurses – I won't say lots more – but the financial situation would improve and facilitate doing so. All I ask is for you to persuade the family that moving to Monkswell would be good for his health.'

Frances shook her head adamantly. 'I'm sorry. I cannot intervene. It would be unprofessional.'

Grainger looked taken aback, though the confident expression swiftly returned.

'I must admit I'm rather surprised. Under the circumstances.'

Frances held firm, her tone and general demeanour leaving him in no doubt that she would not collude with his plans.

'Under the circumstances, specifically the Hippocratic Oath, I cannot disclose a man's health matters to you and neither can I interfere with a patient's decision of where he should work and live. I can only advise as a friend and then only if he asks me.'

A blank surprised expression hid what Frances countenanced as clockwork cogs and gears whirring in his mind.

'Well,' said Grainger, drawing in his chin and seeming somewhat relieved. 'Then we both now know where we stand. Thank you for your time, Doctor. I'll let you get on with your work – such as it is.'

His parting shot stung her. She knew what he was saying. You haven't got much to do at the hospital. All you can attract are the poorer segments of the town, those paying into an insurance scheme or unable to pay at all.

* * *

Evening was setting in and shadows from fluttering leaves splattered the hospital walls. In the quiet solitude of the small office, Frances thought about her reasons for leaving London, coming here and how best to make her residency a success.

Perhaps she might have headed back if she hadn't seen Ralph's name engraved on the war memorial. It intrigued her and at the same time held her here, the name alone clinging onto her heart. Sometimes at night, she swore she could hear him whispering in her ear, saying how glad he was that they were together again. In a way, she agreed. They were together in spirit if not physically.

Norton Dene had seemed inconsequential at first until she'd met the people. The town might be small but the character of the people was writ large. Their ways brought a smile to her face and a warm tingling in her heart.

As for Gregory. Now there was a surprise. A vicar who could charm the birds from the trees – he'd certainly charmed her.

Because? It was an obvious question with an obvious answer. He made her laugh.

Thinking of Lucy and Nancy, nurses and new friends, turned her mind to what to do about the lack of patients. How could she persuade people to take her seriously?

The idea of a cottage hospital was for general practitioners in the vicinity to refer those patients who needed it to the cottage hospital. Instead they were either treating them themselves or sending them to the city's infirmary. Yet the cottage hospital was much more convenient. She wondered whether people's hostility was really down to a female doctor. Perhaps she had to give them time to get used to her.

'It's not London,' she muttered to herself. Yes, she had run into male hostility there, retaliating rather than eating humble pie.

Women doctors were becoming far more numerous than they had been. Not overwhelmingly so but on the increase.

Her mind went back to Simon Grainger's visit. The meaning of his words were obvious. If she persuaded Ned to accept his offer and move away, then he would make it his business to persuade every doctor in the town to refer patients to her. Anger rose like bile in her throat as she recalled his sneering at her predicament. But why was getting Ned to move away so important? Simon Grainger was not the sort to do anything for free. There had to be a good reason for him doing so, a reason hinted at by Nancy Skittings.

She'd learned from Nancy that she and Ned were already aware of the offer, although both had expressed reluctance to leave their hometown. She suspected that within a few days Ned might mention it to her just as Simon Grainger had done. It made her feel like an umpire at a cricket match between a slick professional and an amateur who simply enjoyed the game. She dreaded it happening simply because she didn't know the full facts. She wondered who did, but the hospital was top priority and she most certainly knew to whom she could turn to for help as far as that was concerned. Too late in the evening now, but first thing tomorrow...

23

Her ladyship did not hear the telephone ringing through the downstairs hall because she was in Devlin's room holding his hand and trying to maintain a stiff upper lip. Ladies of substance did not break down or show their true feelings in front of the servants. One of her maids, Marian Murray lingered in the room, fussing around, trying as usual to ingratiate herself in the absence of Grimes.

'You can go now, Marian. I can manage quite well, thank you.'

Marian hesitated until her ladyship said it in a more commanding and crisp manner. 'Go!'

Araminta suspected the girl's fussing around to be nothing but a delay tactic, a chance to listen in, and she was having none of it.

It tore her heart two to see her beloved son staring into the distance, his body shivering slightly. Not because he was cold but because he wasn't in the room – or at least his brain wasn't. He was back there, back in that terrible maelstrom that was the Great War.

During the war, she'd been as patriotic as most people, but on his return she'd cursed those who'd encouraged millions of young men to go over the top for a lost cause. At her age, she had concluded that the concept of glory, national pride and patriotism were not worth dying for. Hadn't Nurse Edith Cavell said that shortly before the enemy shot her? Patriotism was not enough.

'Darling...'

It was all she said. At times like these, Devlin wasn't really listening and when he did speak it was to describe the scene he was reliving, in which he saw men who were no longer recognisable, blood mixed with mud and even the limbs of dead men and horses.

Grimes came to tell her that Doctor Brakespeare was on the telephone.

'Is it urgent?' she asked, though her candid look remained focused on her son.

'She didn't say.'

Relinquishing Devlin's hand she got to her feet. 'Sit with him until I get back, Grimes.'

'Yes, your ladyship.'

Araminta took a deep breath before speaking into the mouthpiece and placing the plug-shaped device for hearing flat against her ear.

'Doctor. What can I do for you?'

'I would like to call a meeting with all those concerned with the day-to-day running of the hospital. I've made a list of several items that need attention.'

'Our monthly meeting isn't due to be convened until next week, but I see no reason why it cannot be brought forward. Wednesday afternoon in the board meeting room would be best for me. I'll get Grimes to contact all those concerned.'

'Thank you. Whatever date and time you decide, I will endeavour to fit in.'

Araminta placed the listening part of the phone back in its cradle.

Seated in her favourite chintz ruffled chair, she gazed out at the night falling like an immense black curtain over the rose garden. Her thoughts were always the same and coupled with sad regrets. What if things had been different? She might have been a grandmother by now.

When Marian brought tea, she asked her to summon Grimes. Devlin should have settled down by now and was probably listening to music on the gramophone. She'd purchased a good stock of records and he could wind up the device himself. She'd even managed to get hold of the recorded books, a new phenomenon so not many yet, but they went some way to occupying her son's time.

Grimes entered the room in his usual courteous fashion, bowing his head whilst her ladyship continued to stare out into the night.

'Grimes. Summon the hospital committee to a meeting on Wednesday afternoon. Telephone or send a message. I don't care which. Just get them there.'

'At the hospital, my lady?'

'Yes. Of course at the hospital. Not here. I don't want the likes of Grainger eyeing up the silver.'

His departing bow seemed stiffer than usual. She reminded herself that he was getting old and had requested an extra pair of hands to take care of her son. Taking on extra duties since the end of the war hadn't helped. Before then, there had been twice as many staff at the house: maids, cooks, butlers, valets and footmen. It hadn't been a huge household compared to some of the great houses of titled families, but there had been many more staff than there was now. Unlike some wealthy people, she did not bemoan that people were less inclined to enter domestic service than they had been, especially women. She welcomed the fact that with increased education they could improve their lives and attain careers denied to them in the not-so-distant past.

At first the slowing down of willing servants had been a trickle. Now it was becoming a deluge. Grimes had remained, but she could see by his encroaching stiffness that his days of service were numbered.

The slight throb of an impending headache pressed on her brow when she looked at him. Her life had been one of privilege, yet her heart was not completely hardened to those who had to serve others for a living.

'Grimes, referring back to our previous conversation, I am of the opinion that you are doing too much.'

'Oh no, your ladyship!'

There was alarm on Grimes's face at the consequences of what might be on the horizon. It wasn't unknown for elderly servants to be 'let go' when age enfeebled their usefulness. Her ladyship couldn't bring herself to do anything like that, but new plans were forming, plans that might make things easier for both.

'I am of a mind that you should carry out lighter duties that require less physical effort. I have it in mind that you aid me with paperwork and related duties.'

His shocked expression dissipated to one of welcomed surprise. 'If that's your ladyship's wish.'

A sigh of relief seemed to flow through his whole body and for a moment he staggered a little, though quickly regained his balance.

'Are you all right, Grimes?'

'Sorry, my lady.'

Her ladyship's smile was sad and thin. 'My legs are not so good either. Let's face it, Grimes, we're both getting old.'

* * *

It pleased her that evening when Devlin came down to the oak-lined dining room with its deep red carpets and the sound of clocks ticking time away.

Joining her for supper depended on his mood, on the stick he used to probe his way down each carpeted stair and the unwavering attention of Grimes, who hovered within easy reach to catch him if he should fall.

Her son was cheerful this evening, a fact that raised her spirits and brought a little more colour to her face with each sip of sherry.

'So what did you listen to today?'

'Mozart. Paul Robeson. Some jazz.'

She was pleased to hear it and, having him being in a happy mood, was keen to keep the conversation going.

'Anything else?'

'*The Murder of Roger Ackroyd*. Again.'

She laughed lightly. 'I wish we could get more. It's a very new thing this telling of stories on a record. I was lucky to get that one.'

'Goodness me, don't they realise how many men came back from the war blinded? Isn't it obvious that those who were avid readers are no longer able to delve into literary worlds via a book!'

'There is Braille.'

'After a while, my fingers go numb. More records. That's what I want.'

His mother touched his hand, fearing he might totally lose his temper and spoil this precious moment. 'I'll enquire of the London publishers to see if any more are being recorded. In the meantime, either myself or Grimes are willing to read to you.'

'Grimes!' Devlin laughed. 'Poor old chap. He can manage about an hour of reading before he falls asleep.'

'He can't help it. He's getting old. And that's something else I want to talk to you about. I've spoken to him about reducing his duties. The time might now be ripe for bringing in a younger man to act as both your valet and companion. How do you feel about that?'

'As long as he's got a good reading voice,' her son grumbled. 'Not too cut glass an accent for a start. And not too mundane a tone that sends me to sleep.'

'What about the valeting side of the duties? What preferences do you have for that?'

A pair of dark eyebrows flinched above her son's sightless eyes. 'Physical assistance carried out in silence. I don't want a continuous flow of small talk whilst he administers to my more intimate requirements.'

'That doesn't sound unreasonable. A personage with an attractive voice that does not send you to sleep and the sensitivity to keep silent when dealing with your more personal needs.'

Devlin laughed. 'A Gemini. Two people wrapped in one.'

She laughed with him. The evening had gone well and her heart had lightened to have him close and acting almost like his old self.

It wasn't until later when she was braiding her hair that a vision evolved from what he'd said. Two people wrapped in one. Perhaps dividing his needs between two people was what was needed. She would sleep on it for now. Night-time was for sleeping and the morning for revisiting ideas which like seeds might germinate in a very short time.

24

Lucy hummed to herself as she slipped her cloak over her uniform, her mind fixed on having a bath the moment she got home. The wards were half full, something they hadn't been for a while, and Lucy couldn't help wondering what had changed.

There had been scepticism when Doctor Brakespeare had first arrived, but of late, only the last week or so, something had shifted. Those who'd been treated by the 'lady doctor' had spread the word. It was a slow process, but both Lucy and her sister, Nancy, were locals and had their ears to the ground. Both believed that word of mouth would win out in the end.

Lucy was looking forward to a night off and to that end Sister Harrison had summoned Nurse Bennett who lived in Radstock to cover the night shift.

Nurse Bennett only came in part-time and always said a prayer on her way in that nothing serious would happen. Her habit was to pass the night in the nurses' snug with her cup of cocoa, a pile of magazines and an unending supply of knitting.

Lucy had no option to sit and wait, ready to rush home as soon as Nurse Bennett arrived.

Unfortunately, Nurse Bennett didn't arrive but Sister Harrison did.

'Nurse Bennett has gone down with an infection. She can't make it.' Her expression turned shrew-like. Lucy sensed there was reluctance to say what she had to say next.

'I've sent a note to your sister asking her to come in and she sent a reply that she will. I would be obliged if you would wait until she gets here.'

'But... I've got a date at half past seven...'

'Then the young man concerned will have to wait until eight. You can still go to wherever you were going, but your duty is to wait until Nurse Skittings gets here.'

Sister Harrison emphasised Nancy's married name as though it were a sour taste to be spat from her mouth. She was obviously not happy that she'd had to retract on her decision and call her in.

After uttering a hasty goodnight, she took her leave before Lucy had chance to ask her if she would be so kind as to wait in her place, but it seemed Sister Edith Harrison had foreseen that possibility and made a hasty escape.

Lucy sighed. In her mind the hot bath she'd envisaged seemed to grow colder. Her aunt Rose with whom she lived had promised her that the kettles would be on the range and the zinc bath pulled in front of it. Just thinking about it had shrouded her in a warm glow. The kitchen would be the warmest place in the house and the bath towel, plus a hand towel for her hair, would be hanging on the wooden clothes horse just to the side of the range.

She sat down, folded her arms and thought about how unfair life could be – especially if Sister Harrison was involved. Why did she go out of her way to be difficult? Why indeed did she seem to dislike her and Nancy so much? Or was it just Nancy? It was hard to tell.

Time ticked by. Lucy glanced at the grim-faced clock. Tired of sitting and waiting, she bobbed back and forth between the window and the door to reception. Nancy was later than she'd expected her to be. Had something happened to hold her up?

Tonight of all nights had promised many things. Brian Faulkland had asked her out. She'd been enamoured of him for as long as she could remember. All the girls hereabouts carried a torch for his full lips, dark blond hair and velvet brown eyes. Fixed in a permanent pout, his lips were plush, pink and promised a kiss to die for.

'Hey, darling,' he'd said to her when he'd asked her out. 'Care to have some fun with me?'

Did she? Yes! Of course she did!

At long last, Nancy came bustling in, breathless with apology and her daughter Polly in the pushchair. Her cloak was whisking about her and her flowing starched headdress was a bit askew, but at least she'd arrived. The pushchair and baby were an added extra.

'What's this?' cried Lucy eyeing the baby with round-eyed dismay. 'Where's Ma got to?'

'Can't be helped,' exclaimed Nancy, tucking the blanket higher around the pink face of the sleeping child. 'Either Polly had to come or I couldn't.'

'Nancy! Edie Harrison will go mad if she sees Polly here.'

'And Sister Harrison would be mad if she heard you calling her Edie. Anyway she's gone home, hasn't she?'

'But why can't Ma have her?'

Nancy waved her hands dismissively, though it was easy to see that she was a mite distraught herself. 'Couldn't be helped. Mr Painter's passed. Ma's gone to lay him out.'

'Poor chap. Do you remember how worried he was the other day when Mr MacDonald picked him up from here to take him home?'

Lucy said that she did. The old chap wore a truss and his chest was caving in thanks to the coal dust choking his lungs.

'He warned Mr MacDonald not to take a wrong turn and him end up in the cemetery by mistake.'

Nancy grimaced. 'Looks like he had reason to be worried. And before you ask, Ned's gone for a pint with Cyril Parker. He deserves it,' she added before Lucy had chance to get annoyed.

Lucy slumped back down into the chair she'd only just vacated, dejection drawing her face. 'Brian was taking me out tonight. There's a dance at the Miners' Institute.'

Nancy looked around. 'Has Sister Harrison been in?'

'She stopped just long enough to tell me that she'd asked you to come in.'

'Ordered more like. I could hardly refuse.'

'In which case I can't see you being dismissed what with more patients being referred. It won't work.'

A worried look creased Nancy's forehead. 'Just when I need the money, what with Ned not being able to work for a while. She told me he should take the job in Monkswell that Mr Grainger keeps pressing him to take.'

Lucy expressed surprise. 'What's it got to do with her?'

They exchanged knowing looks as the same explanation came to them at one and the same time.

'He wants Ned to take it and she's helping him persuade you both.'

'Well it won't work,' Nancy said adamantly. 'Norton Dene is our home. We won't be moved.'

Lucy sighed. 'Let's see what happens. In the meantime it won't hurt for Polly to stay here with you. I've done most of the tidying round. There's little else to do.'

'Seems I'll have to chance Sister Harrison coming in.'

Nancy held her head to one side as another relevant thought

came to mind. 'Can you ask Aunt Rose if she can collect Polly and have her, at least until Ned gets back from the pub.'

'It's a thought, but you know she's not very well.'

Although they both tried to keep it away from wagging tongues, Aunt Rose wasn't exactly ill but far too fond of barley wine. Though she'd been recommended it by Doctor Walker for medicinal purposes years ago, the sisters were wise enough in medical matters to know that she drank too much of it and that Doctor Walker had made a mistake. But then he'd made a few of those as he'd got older.

They concluded it would be best if Lucy took Polly home and for Ma Skittings to pick the child up from there.

Apprehensive but glad to have some sort of plan, Lucy tied up the ribbons on her cloak. 'I'm off to my bath, my date and a bit of dancing at the Miners' Institute.' She gave her sister a kiss on the cheek and the sleeping Polly one on the forehead.

She laughed as she headed for the exit and a night of fun. 'Don't work too hard.'

'And don't do anything I wouldn't do,' Nancy shouted after her.

Rose Daniels had the traditional look of a country milkmaid or farmer's wife, her face pink and plump, and over the years, her figure had grown to the size of a Jersey cow. She assured Lucy that she was quite capable of looking after the baby for an hour or two.

'I looked after you and yur sister, didn't I? I'm not bloody stupid, you know.'

When she jiggled the handlebars of the pram a little too rigorously, the blue eyes of the little girl opened wide with alarm.

'Not so rough, Aunt Rose,' said Lucy, taking charge of the handlebars and reassuring the alarmed-looking Polly.

'I do know 'ow to look after a baby, you know.'

'You've already said that.'

Lucy gritted her teeth and pretended not to notice that the teacup her aunt was sipping from contained dandelion and burdock wine which was brewed a little way out of town by the same farmer who made strong cider.

Mentioning it would only spark a row and although she loved Polly she was overdue for a night of fun and laughter. Besides, Brian of the lush lips and languorous features awaited her.

'Ma Skittings shouldn't be too long,' Lucy pronounced. 'Mr Painter is dead.'

'I was told in Bumbles.'

Percy Bumble ran the hardware shop which was sandwiched between the hairdresser and the sweet shop.

'Amazing how quickly the news spreads.'

'Gossip,' exclaimed Aunt Rose. 'Gossip! Believe me, you get more news in a high street shop than you ever get from the *Somerset Herald*.'

Lucy didn't entirely think that possible. The fact was that Aunt Rose rarely read a newspaper so wouldn't know what was in it.

Settled in her favourite armchair, Aunt Rose repeated the news of the day picked up in a variety of shops all along the high street and in The Rose and Crown.

'Mrs Bumble's got a bad belly. Women's trouble, he said. She intended going to see your lady doctor, but Mr Bumble said he was told that the best doctors were men and women were only good enough to be nurses. Said it was all to do with their emotions. They've got too many emotions.'

Lucy grimaced. 'Is that so.' It was all rubbish but explaining why would be wasted on Aunt Rose.

'And that they can't bear pain and blood like men can,' she added.

'Despite spending hours in pain and bleeding profusely when they give birth?'

Aunt Rose took another sip from her cup and her face creased with amusement. 'We all laughed and told him that. Her who cooks for the vicar pointed out that it takes a woman to know a woman so if 'is wife's got belly problems – women's problems – it makes sense for her to go to a woman doctor 'cos she's as like had some of the same.' Aunt Rose took on a girlish and almost shy expression. 'It's a matter of modesty and a man doctor not seeing the secret bits of Mrs Bumble. That sight should only be for Mr Bumble.'

Seeing the deterioration of her aunt, Lucy resolved that if she had to, she would get a message to Brian telling him she couldn't come.

Aunt Rose's head lolled onto her chest.

'You might as well get yurself ready, Lucy. I'm looking forward to seeing you done up to the nines.'

Lucy glanced at the time on the glass-cased wall clock. Its brass pendulum moved from side to side and its tick was slow and sonorous.

Might as well, she thought. Still loath to leave the baby with Aunt Rose she decided that at least she'd be ready to go if Ma Skittings did turn up.

Her dress was blue and made from a length of cloth she'd purchased at the Saturday market some weeks before. The buttons sparkled like diamonds. Nobody would ever guess that she'd cut them off a stiff-necked blouse dating from the last century, part of a clear-out sale up at the manor house. *Who knows*, she thought, *it might once have been worn by Lady Compton-Dixon herself – or perhaps one of her ancestors.*

After double-checking her hair, she picked up a pale mauve reticule trimmed with jet beads.

She longed to go but the child's grandmother had not arrived and she was still wary of leaving Aunt Rose with the baby who had begun to stir and would shortly want feeding and changing. She would much prefer if Ma Skittings was here.

Aunt Rose seemed unaware that Lucy was biding her time before leaving. Another sip from the cup and she was waxing forth with wisdom she didn't own.

'Now don't you go letting that young man yur going out with take advantage of you. Don't you go bringing sin and disgrace to my house. 'Ave you got that, my girl?'

Boiling with indignation, Lucy would have retorted that she couldn't bring any more disgrace than Rose sat there boozing most of the day, but she held her tongue.

Just when she'd decided that she couldn't possibly leave the baby with her aunt, a loud 'yoohoo' sounded from the back kitchen, where the rear door led out to a long garden and the back lane.

A breathless Ma Skittings breezed into the room, slammed down a tapestry bag with sturdy wooden handles, smiled down at Polly, who gurgled at the sight of her, then plonked her broad backside into the armchair immediately opposite the one Rose was seated.

'Good day to you, Rose. And to Lucy. Sorry about that, love, but Mrs Painter's a broken woman. Can't stop blubbering she can't. Couldn't leave her there weeping away at the chapel of rest all by 'erself. Once she 'ad a brandy or two inside 'er she was all right. So here I am. And how's my little princess been?'

'As good as ever,' exclaimed Lucy, hardly able to contain her relief. 'I'll be off now if that's all right with you.'

'You go and enjoy yurself. I'm here now.'

Aunt Rose reached for a flagon of dandelion wine. 'Care for a drink, Bertha?'

Ma Skittings looked pointedly at Rose's teacup. 'Only if it's tea.'

Rose giggled. ''Course it's not tea.'

'Then I don't want one.' Turning to Lucy, she said, 'I'll take Polly round to my place. I won't take her to Ned. He needs to convalesce.'

Despite her shoes having heels of nearly three inches, Lucy skipped ahead of Ma Skittings down the garden path to the front gate which was hanging precariously on one hinge.

Ma caught up with her and began telling her all about the fracas surrounding the demise of Harald Painter. 'I didn't know he had a bit of land next to the quarry over at Penallt Junction. Apparently it was left to 'im by his grandfather, though nobody seems to know for sure who his grandfather was. Well, you know 'ow it is. Back then, Norton Dene was only a handful of houses and three pubs. Just think. Three pubs for a small place like that. If my reckoning's up to the mark, I reckon it worked out at thirty 'ouses for every pub! Mind you, they did like a drink. Helped get rid of the dust in their throats. Same for the miners. Men get dry doing jobs like that.'

Lucy was only half listening. She was sorry old man Painter had popped his clogs but was looking forward to a night out with Brian. She'd had her cap set at him for some time, though he'd been stepping out with Meg Reynolds up until six months ago. Meg was a bubbly, curvy girl with a mass of reddish blonde curls and laughing eyes. She'd turned many a young man's head with her vivacious ways and infectious laugh.

Their relationship had ended abruptly a month or so ago when the family had moved to the coast. Gossip had it that her father intended throwing in his lot with his brother as a fisherman and that they'd bought a boat. Questions were asked about their knowledge of fishing. Nothing at all according to some, but others wished them success in their new venture. Not that she cared about the Reynolds family in general. Brian Faulkland had turned his attention to her and that was all that mattered.

'Have a good time,' Ma Skittings called after her as she pattered away.

By the time she got to the Miners' Institute, she was only about five minutes late and she hoped he wouldn't mind.

Her heart began pounding nineteen to the dozen when her gaze fell on the rangy figure leaning nonchalantly against the wall of the institute.

'Sorry I'm late.'

She blushed at the way he looked into her eyes, touched her hair and gently kissed the tip of her nose.

'You look good. You smell good. You feel good. You, Lucy Daniels, are something worth waiting for.'

* * *

Back in her own house, Ma Skittings thought about Lucy and Brian Faulkland. Did she know the truth about Meg's family going away? Somehow she doubted it, but then Meg Reynolds wasn't the first girl to give in to a young fella and fall for a baby.

She recalled Meg seeking her advice as to what she should do.

Ma had agreed that there were herbs that could help bring on a miscarriage. She had also pointed out the other options. In the end, it was her parents who couldn't stand the thought of gossip. Neither had they liked Brian Faulkland and she for one wouldn't trust him as far as she could throw him. Lucy, my girl, be careful.

Tonight, she thought, *he'll treat her like a princess and tell her that he loves her. But tomorrow? Ah. That was another matter.*

25

Frances was coming to realise that the women of Norton Deane were as tough as old boots, not because they were unfeeling but because responsibility lay heavy in their day-to-day lives.

Three days ago, a woman named Mrs Thirsk had been brought into the hospital with a possible breached birth. Being told not to push, but to take things slowly, first one foot had appeared, then another close behind it. All had gone well.

Despite it being suggested that she stay in hospital for at least a week, Mrs Thirsk insisted on going home.

'I've got a family to look after. I'm all right. 'Course I am. And so's the new lad,' she added with a sideways nod at the baby.

Frances recognised Mrs Thirsk as one of those tough women who regarded childbirth as a fact of life, the pain swiftly forgotten once the baby had arrived.

'Does your husband have transport to take you home?' Frances asked.

'Only a bicycle,' answered Mrs Thirsk.

'Well, we can't have you sitting on the crossbar,' Frances laughed. 'We'll see what can be arranged.'

Back in her office, she phoned Mr MacDonald, who informed her he was booked for a funeral today in the village of Holt, some miles away. 'I won't be free until late evening.'

'Then it's me and Matron Molly,' sighed Frances once the call had disconnected.

Gladys Thirsk was chuffed to bits at the thought of arriving home in a motorcar at the opposite end of Waterloo Terrace from where Lucy Daniels lived.

With Mrs Thirsk and her newborn in the back of the car Frances made her way across the town square and down the winding cobbled streets to Waterloo Terrace.

'Lucy Daniels lives at the other end of the street,' Mrs Thirsk remarked.

'So I understand.'

'It's time she was married.'

'She might not want to get married.'

'I 'ear she's going on a date with Brian Faulkland?' Mrs Thirsk tutted in a disapproving manner. 'My eldest Aileen fancies 'im too, as do half the young girls in this town. Wants to make his mind up 'e does. Plays the field. And there's rumours that one young girl...' She stopped herself. 'I'm saying too much. It's none of my business, but there'll be more red-haired babes in this town by the time he makes up his mind and jumps the broomstick. His dad had red hair. It didn't come out so much on 'im but the next generation will get it.'

Frances asked her what it meant to jump the broomstick.

'It was instead of getting married in church. There was a lot of that in Norton Dene and roundabout years ago. Especially if there was a bun in the oven.'

'I didn't know that.'

'You wouldn't. That was before Norton Dene became a town. Back then, it weren't much more than a village.'

'Really?'

'Oh yes. Do you fancy coming in for a cup of tea?'

'No. I'm sorry. I must get back.'

'Are you sure? The family would love to meet you.'

Mrs Thirsk's hurt expression made her relent. 'Perhaps just for a minute.'

On entering the two-bed terraced house, her immediate impression was that she must be mistaken. That the house had to have more than two bedrooms to accommodate such a large family. Each chair and sofa was taken up with children. Older children looked after younger ones, doing their best to wipe the dried jam and other sticky items from their faces. Most of them wore no shoes and the youngest of the children were bare-legged and occasionally a bare backside flashed into view.

The arrival of Mr Thirsk gave Frances enough of an excuse not to linger.

'Pleased to meet you, Mr Thirsk.' He looked surprised when she shook his hand.

The children clambered around him and although he must be worked half to death keeping them fed, he had a cheery expression. His amiability was obvious when he tickled the new baby's chin and winked at his wife.

'Well, who'd have guessed she got this from the hospital. And there was me thinking she went in just for a rest.'

Gladys slapped his arm. 'Cheeky sod.'

* * *

Having dinner with the vicar was becoming a habit and she told him so.

'A nice habit I hope,' he said, his eyes twinkling with merriment.

'You're incorrigible.'

'Yes, but you have to admit that I'm a very good cook.'

'You cooked this yourself?'

He looked suitably proud. 'I did.'

'I thought Mrs Cross cooked all your meals.'

'I bought a cookery book. All she had to do was show me how to make sure the oven and gas hobs were at the right temperature. Anyway,' he said, his eyes full of mischief. 'We wouldn't want her telling everyone that she was always preparing meals for two people rather than just one. That's how gossip starts.'

'I wanted to ask you something.'

'Ask away.'

'I need to explain something first.'

His smile was undiminished. 'Explain away.'

'It's about Matron Molly, my car. Would it be possible to keep her in the coach house – the part behind the double doors?'

His eyebrows rose. 'A home for a motor car? Well I don't see why not seeing as it used to house a predecessor to the horseless carriage!'

'I'm very grateful.'

'Grateful enough to explain why you want her to hide her away?'

Frances flinched. 'I didn't say I was hiding her away.'

'Are you lying to me?' He said it with humour but it still made her feel guilty.

On seeing the look on her face his smile lessened. 'What is it, Frances? Why the worried look?'

She started with Izzy taking her out of a workhouse and giving her a good education and a good life. 'The car was a present from her for passing my final exams.'

'I see.'

She went on to tell him about Izzy dying and her family turning her out of the house that had been her home all her life.

'And then I had a letter demanding I hand over the car.' Frances slammed her hand down on the table. 'It was a present and all I have left of her. I won't let them take it.'

'That's settled then,' said Gregory, his broader hand making more noise when that too thudded on the table.

The next morning whilst sitting at the bureau in the coach house living room she smiled at the thought of him. Every time she thought of him she couldn't help smiling and it had been hard to tie him down to his thoughts on the improvements she wished to make at the hospital.

'I will peruse at leisure and vote accordingly at the meeting on Wednesday.'

Her concentration was disturbed when a glossy black Bentley pulled up in the narrow street beyond the garden.

A chauffeur got out from the front driver's door of the vehicle and opened the rear door. A silver-tipped walking stick appeared first before the imposing figure of Brigadier Grainger.

Frances went to the door and let him in.

'Doctor Brakespeare.'

'Brigadier.' Frances swallowed her surprise 'This is a surprise. Is there something I can do for you?'

'Yes. I want you to examine my chest. No shilly-shallying. And don't spare the horses. Tell me the truth. If I'm off to meet my maker, then I need to make plans.'

'You've taken my breath away.'

A terse smile appeared and swiftly disappeared beneath the hedge of pure white moustache. 'It's been a long time since I had that effect on a woman.'

So, the brigadier had a sense of humour.

She invited him to sit on the green leather couch she'd had the good luck to buy second-hand from Mrs Walker without the good lady telling her husband.

'If you could remove your jacket and shirt please.'

For a man of his age, he was still in pretty good condition. Although his chest was bad, it lacked the concave look beneath the ribcage, common amongst quarrymen and miners and all those whose diet made worse the effects of hard labour.

The crackling sound from the brigadier's chest came as no great surprise. He sat perfectly still as she listened to his chest before proceeding to his back.

'You're not coughing so badly as you were when we first met.'

'I've given up smoking.'

'I'm glad to hear it.'

She suspected he had something else to say when the profuse thatch of hair on his upper lip moved hesitantly, then more profoundly.

'I don't get so breathless.'

'Good.'

'I can smell the fresh air.'

'Even better.'

He regarded her with a look she could only describe as bordering on reverence.

'I was always told that smoking was good for the lungs.'

'Lungs run on oxygen and so does your body. Coughing up phlegm is not a natural occurrence. Something must get in there first to invade your lungs and need coughing up.'

There was shrewd appraisal in the way he looked at her. 'That seems perfectly logical.'

'I wish others would heed the laws of logic,' she said with a smile.

When he laughed, she fancied it was the first time for a while.

As he buttoned up his shirt, he cast his eyes around the room, the fireplace, the comfortable chairs, the green leather sofa.

'This is your living room. Do you still see patients here?'

'Not any longer. I will have the new surgery at the hospital. I'm just moving the last items in and then I will be very happy indeed.'

'Would it be just for private patients?'

'No. Everyone is welcome. Medicine should be free to those who cannot afford to pay.'

'Ah. Yes. Your fee,' he said once he was dressed. He placed a five-pound note on the green couch he'd just climbed off.

'My fee is not...'

She was about to say that five pounds was too much, but Brigadier Grainger held up a hand, palm facing her, an order to desist.

'I owe you at least that. So do other people in this town. Have you made a list for the committee meeting?'

'Yes. I have. Setting up an evening surgery is one of them, plus a clinic for expectant mothers during the day. It will be long hours but I can't expect men and women who work all day to leave their employment when they're sick. I need to facilitate something that suits them.'

'A first-rate plan.' The brigadier had a loud voice, one that could carry to the ears of subordinates, but principally due to wartime proximity to artillery fire. With an air of finality, he picked up his stick and put on his hat. At the door, he turned to her and said, 'Leave it with me. I'll make sure your suggestions are given thoughtful consideration by the committee. You deserve to be respected in this town and I for one will see that you are.'

26

Edith Harrison was determined to have a word with Lady Compton-Dixon before the Wednesday committee meeting. She stood fidgeting before pulling the cast iron bell pull at the side of the door, grinding her teeth when she heard its sonorous note ringing through the interior of the house.

Inside the manor her ladyship sighed when Grimes announced her arrival before wearily inclining her head and asking Grimes to show her in.

She came in wearing a teal-coloured dress in a style that would better suit a younger woman, the ruched side seams falling into flounces at mid-calf.

'Miss Harrison. What can I do for you?'

For a brief instant, annoyance tightened her lips.

Calling her 'Miss' rather than the professional 'Sister'.

Her ladyship was good at weighing people up. She knew who she liked, who she didn't like and who she thought was ostensibly out for their own ends. Edith Harrison was about to present facts that might or might not be true but were viewed from one perspective only – her own. Disinclined to be lectured and wanting to keep their meeting to the bare minimum, she did not offer her visitor either refreshment or a chair.

Edith Harrison fiddled with the clasp on her handbag. 'I wanted to speak to you prior to the committee meeting.'

Copies of the proposals had been circulated to the hospital committee prior to the meeting. As far as Araminta was concerned everything suggested seemed advantageous to the hospital.

Simon Grainger had sent her a note suggesting that the hospital was fine as it was. His father, however, had phoned her ladyship and stated in his loud and deep baritone that it was all quite capital. Good plan. Let's press ahead.

However, Sister Edith Harrison was determined to have her say.

'Unlike many in this town I will not bestow sainthood on Doctor Brakespeare. She is a capable doctor but not perfect – as none of us are.'

Questioning eyebrows rose above her ladyship's unblinking eyes.

'Pray tell me what you mean, Sister Harrison.'

'I feel that the nurses at the hospital should be under my supervision and mine alone.'

'And your reason for this?'

'I object to the use of quack medicine.'

Her ladyship's eyebrows rose higher.

'To what are you referring, Sister Harrison?'

The little head on the rounded body rose a bit higher. 'A short while back, I discovered Nurse Skittings smearing her husband's wound with some honey quackery supplied by her mother-in-law.'

Lady Araminta Compton-Dixon nodded sagely as she evaluated both the incident and the woman standing in front of her. Sister Harrison was a nurse of longstanding and she appeared to be totally committed to her job but being of an observant disposition, her ladyship suspected that she was sometimes a bit of a bully.

Like a judge about to pass sentence, her ladyship tucked in her chin and fixed her eyes on the woman standing in front of her.

'I understand that Mr Skittings, her husband, is home now.'

'Yes.'

'I know something of this matter. According to Doctor Brakespeare the concoction prepared by Mrs Skittings did do some good in the absence of the modern medicine Doctor Brakespeare required. There was none in the dispensary, in fact she confided to me that a lot of standard items were not stocked.'

'The nurses must have shifted things.'

Her ladyship also knew a lie or excuse when she heard one.

'I understand the nurses did not have access to the dispensary storage facilities because you, Sister Harrison had sole access to the keys.'

'That is no longer the case.'

'So I understand,' said Lady Araminta with a slow nod, an all-consuming look in her eyes. 'Is there anything else you wish to mention?'

Sister Harrison passed her handbag from one arm to the other and went on to suggest that the hospital do as others nationwide and not employ married nurses.

'I presume you mean Nurse Skittings. Am I right?'

'Yes. And now she has a child.'

'Has it not occurred to you that she needs the money? Doubly so at present following her husband sustaining an injury.'

'With respect, my lady, she doesn't need to work. Mr Grainger has offered her husband more money if he agrees to work at the quarry at Monkswell.'

'Monkswell?'

'Yes. It's on the other side of the River Severn in Monmouthshire.'

'I know very well where it is,' snapped Araminta. 'But why? The Skittings family have lived here for generations.'

'Ned is a valued employee. He's been paying him extra money since the accident.'

'Your praise for him is admirable, but I myself suspect there is more to this than meets the eye.' Her ladyship frowned. 'The lease of the quarry is due to be renewed in six months. I fully admit my family's wealth depends on the quarries and mines around here. However, that doesn't mean shirking one's moral obligations.'

'His intentions are good. There's even a cottage...' She was almost shrieking now a sure sign that Sister Edith Harrison was alarmed, though not for herself, but for Simon Grainger.

'She'd be living among strangers,' her ladyship snapped. 'Nancy has lived here all her life. Think of that.'

'Of course,' said Edith with a simpering smile. Her ladyship perceived her attempt at warmth as somewhat tepid. 'But the quarry at Monkswell is working flat out and can accommodate extra wages more easily than this one.'

She fixed Sister Harrison with a look so sharp she flinched. 'Are you here as a champion of the hospital or on behalf of Simon Grainger?'

Usually unflustered and cool as a cucumber, Sister Harrison flushed bright red. 'Of course not.'

Her ladyship thought otherwise and suspected she'd worked out what was going on here. 'So you're saying that this quarry doesn't have the money to compensate for Ned's injuries, but the one in Monmouthshire does. A little tweak to the Skittings income – i.e. reducing Nurse Skittings wages – would put pressure on Mr Skittings...'

'But she's married. A married nurse. It wouldn't be allowed

elsewhere. Them moving would settle everything and suit everybody.'

Her ladyship rang the small brass bell she kept close to summon Grimes.

'Well I don't think so,' she said in icy tones. 'Good day to you, Sister Harrison. Your comments have been noted but are not supported by me. I suspect the committee will feel the same way – except for Simon Grainger perhaps.'

After Sister Harrison had left Lady Araminta Compton-Dixon weighed up all she had heard and came to an iron-clad conclusion. There was something disquieting about his offer to send Ned and his family away to a cottage in Wales and she didn't trust Simon Grainger one little bit. It could not be refuted that it was a sound financial plan. However, Araminta was not the kind to take anything at face value. She respected the brigadier, not so his son. In recent years, the brigadier had left the running of the quarry to his son. It crossed her mind that he might not be fully aware of all that was going on. She intended to make enquiries.

27

Prior to the Great War and for some time during it, the rooms above the stables at the Grainger residence had been occupied by the coachman and his wife. Horses had been kept in the stables beneath where Simon Grainger now kept two cars – a low sporty type and a Bugatti that he intended racing at Brooklands, the circuit close to Weybridge in Surrey. If he could have done, he would have kept at least one more motorcar, possibly two, but, unfortunately, his father's Bentley took up the only available space. He secretly looked forward to the time when both were gone and he had more space and more sway in the business.

The coachman had been given a reference and let go a few years ago. Nobody knew where he'd gone, but the reference should have got him something. Not that anyone gave it a second thought. It was up to him if he secured another job. Earning a bit driving horses and drawing on the 'Lloyd George', the new pension arrangement brought in by the former prime minister, should keep him in the manner to which he was accustomed – that is, enough to keep him and his wife fed. The children were old enough by now to go out to work. Never mind school for the likes of them. Likely as not if they had stayed local they'd be down the mines by now – or in one of the factories producing rubber or engineering items.

Edith crept around the main house to arrive at the coach house which was round the back looking flushed and wearing a pale cream frock and a hat that looked to be no more than a bunch of feathers.

With breathless anticipation, her arms reached for him and he automatically ran his hands down her body – more so from habit than desire.

'Simon! I've been waiting all day for this.'

He couldn't bring himself to say that he too had been looking forward to their regular meet-up. It would be only a half-truth.

The silky dress fell to the floor. There she stood in her camisole and lace-trimmed petticoat. Her stockings were a pinkish colour and slightly wrinkled at the knees and ankles. A bit like her really.

Their affair had begun when she was a lot younger. Back then, her body had been firm and he'd been easily aroused. Not so much now.

He made an excuse. 'I'm a bit tired. I've been trudging around the Frome quarry most of the afternoon. A lot of walking and a lot of driving.'

'Oh dear. You poor thing.'

'But I believe I can rise to the occasion,' he added, as though he was doing her a great favour. It reassured him to see her doting smile. He badly wanted to ask her about her meeting with her ladyship but was mindful of keeping her on side. First things first.

To her, it was as if they were melting into each other. For him, it was steeling himself to something he had to do to make her pliable and open to discussing what was said.

Close your eyes and think of England. That's what he told himself.

Edith purred like a kitten once he'd finished.

Simon lay on his back smoking and impatient.

'So what did she say?'

She snuggled up under his arm, her head heavy on his shoulder.

'Like you suggested, I mentioned the forthcoming committee meeting to put her off her guard. After that I went on to outline your offer and how generous it was and that it meant Nancy wouldn't need to work.'

Simon smiled. 'It's the least I could do.'

Edith snuggled closer. 'You're a wonderful man.'

He smiled at that, thrilled at Edith's naivety. Unknown to her, there was a very important reason he wanted Ned as far away as possible.

The normal procedure when one of a series of holes failed to explode was to give it a prod with a long wooden pole.

Ned standing immobile closest to the hole had stirred Simon up no end. He'd staggered over the rubble-strewn ground and frequent boulders in handmade leather shoes spitting expletives all the way.

'What are you waiting for, man?'

At some distance, other employees had wiped the dust from their faces and turned away to spit it from their mouths. Someone had passed around a jug of cider weakened with water, a necessary evil to ease their dry mouths as they prepared to move the stone from the holes that had exploded.

Out of earshot, Ned had explained that there were no wooden staves except for broken ones that were too short and wouldn't reach.

Simon had spotted another long pole. In his haste to gain the lode from that last hole, he hadn't noticed that it was not one used to 'tickle' an explosion. This was of the kind with a metal spike at one end used to split boulders too big to be crushed with the aid of a lump hammer.

His eyes sore and dust-filled, Ned never noticed the spike but took the pole.

Simon had pushed him forward with a hefty slap on the shoulder.

'Go on, man! Get on with it.'

Owning and running a quarry was one thing. Getting involved in the more dangerous events was something he'd always avoided. He was the boss. He paid others to take risks.

With quick but careful steps, he had retreated to a place of safety behind a roadmender's cart.

Ned should have been able to use the stick to flick the detonator out of the top of the explosive which is what he did. Unfortunately, the metal spike completed the circuit. Up it went! Three men had lain injured, Ned the worst of them. Simon had stared at him in disbelief. The spike at the end of the pole was nowhere to be seen. Not until the doctor turned up did Simon track it down. The pole was evidence of negligence and had to be hidden. Luckily, none of the other men there had been close enough to see the metal tip of the wooden pole and he'd made sure to dispose of it once he'd realised the reason for the explosion.

Whatever happened, he had to get Ned out of the way before her ladyship discovered the details and the lease came up for renewal. If they lost control of this quarry, he was the one who would be sent over to Monkswell, the one sent to the back of beyond to repair his reputation and wait until his father had simmered down – or died.

He kissed Edith goodnight and declined when she asked him to walk her home.

Though she didn't know it, their relationship was in its death throes. He would allow it to linger on until he'd transferred Ned and his family to the other quarry.

Getting even with Ma Skittings for pouring scalding water over his neck was priority.

Marian, her ladyship's maid and his latest female interest, had done as he'd asked and stolen a little morphine from the medicines taken by Devlin Compton-Dixon. His intention was to mix the drug with the bottle of tonic he'd stolen from Jim Forester's coat pocket. His clerk had thought he'd mislaid it, that it had dropped from his pocket on the way home. He was so keen to get home to that beloved wife of his that he hadn't been thinking straight. If he had, then he would have noticed. After adding the morphine to the bottle, Simon had given it back to him.

'Don't want your little lady going without, do we.'

No. Of course we didn't.

It was some days later that he saw Forester's distraught expression and of course asked if anything was wrong.

'My youngest is unwell. She's had teething problems. My wife rubbed some of her tonic onto her gums and now we've had trouble waking her up.'

The colour had drained from Simon's face. His aim had been that Mrs Forester should become ill. A child falling sick had not been his intention.

'I'm so sorry, old chap.'

James Forester had looked devastated.

Simon Grainger's surge of sympathy had given way to self-survival.

'Have you been to a doctor about it?'

James had shaken his head. 'No. My wife poured it down the sink and swore she would never purchase anything from Mrs Skittings ever again.'

Simon had immediately rallied, patting James on the shoulder and assuring him he'd done the right thing. 'Stick to modern medicine. You know it makes sense. It's our duty to tell everyone in Norton Dene that the woman manufactures poison. It shouldn't be allowed. Tell everyone.'

James Forester nodded but said nothing. He had no intention falling in with Simon Grainger's plans. He didn't trust him.

Alone in his office, Simon congratulated himself that although he'd had a narrow escape, he had triumphed. If Mrs Forester was like most women, she would tell her friends what had happened. In turn, they would tell their friends. His only regret was that he had suggested sticking to modern medicine – in which case that meant patronising Doctor Brakespeare – but still, even his father had gone in that direction.

All he had to do now was to persuade Ned and his family to accept his offer to move on. It wouldn't be easy and, as before, Doctor Brakespeare was at the heart of the matter. If he could persuade her that it was in Ned's best interests, he might yet achieve his goal.

First things first, he would be all sweetness and light at the committee meeting. He hadn't bothered to read the papers his father had circulated. This forthcoming meeting would be quite enjoyable. He would, as his father had decreed, agree with whatever Doctor Brakespeare had in mind. At the end of it all, he would mention Mrs Skittings and the fact that some day she might kill someone, or at least make them very sick.

28

After presenting her list of suggested improvements to the committee, Frances had been called away to tend to a miner who'd been unlucky enough to have a pit prop fall on his head at the same time as a pit pony trod on his toe. For that reason she couldn't stay to the end but asked her ladyship to let her know the result of the meeting.

Frances was going through the hospital accounts when her ladyship entered her office unexpectedly and closed the door behind her.

She immediately got to her feet and offered Lady Araminta a chair.

'I wasn't expecting you.'

'I bring news. As a result of the committee meeting, I've sent a personal letter to all general practitioners in the area declaring my absolute faith in your capabilities and outlining the proposed improvements at the hospital. I think they'll be very impressed.'

Frances sat back in her chair. 'That's very good of you.'

'Yes. It is. Now all you must do is live up to my faith in you.'

The statement was delivered with an uplifted chin verging on pomposity, though not quite. A twinkle of amusement glinted like chips of diamonds in her ladyship's eyes.

'I will endeavour to do that. I'm glad the committee approved my suggestions.'

'Of course they did, because they made sense. Too many people around here rest on their laurels – some simply because the status quo suits them. No change means no effort on their part.'

'Even Simon Grainger?'

Amusement fled the twinkling eyes. 'He did, though I see through his smarmy façade. God help us when the brigadier passes away. I wouldn't trust his son as far as I can throw him.'

Frances found herself agreeing.

'There's something else, Doctor. I've decided to take you on as my family doctor. I used to go into Bath, but like many others, he's not keeping up with modern developments.' She leaned forward, her eyes locking on those of Frances. 'If you'll have me, that is.'

Frances stopped her jaw from dropping but managed to say, 'I'm very flattered.'

First Brigadier Grainger and now Lady Compton-Dixon. She was doing well.

Her ladyship nodded curtly. 'Thank you. But I'm not engaging you purely for your own sake. I'm not one for scattering favours without expecting something in return. To that end, I want you to come out to Orchard Manor.'

'Of course. Might I ask what ails you?'

'Nothing ails me.' The response was as curt as the stiff-necked nodding of her head. 'I want you to meet my son. Afterwards, I would like to discuss how best to treat him.'

'So you want me to examine him...'

'No! I want you to meet him.'

'But you said...'

'Meeting and examining him are two very different things.'

Frances narrowed her eyes. Those born into privilege were apt to be demanding, but that didn't mean to say she had to conform with her ladyship's wishes. 'I'm sorry, but I do have genuine patients...'

'Let's not mince words. I have no hesitation in giving you my total support. Please do me the honour of returning that favour.'

As Frances considered the rather cryptic statement, an expression crept over the strong features that held both pleading and sorrow.

'How soon do you want me to... make his acquaintance?'

Her ladyship was already rising from the chair, her kid-gloved hand firmly clasping the ebony handle of her old-fashioned parasol. 'Tomorrow afternoon, at a time to suit you.'

'I do need to speak to my nurses before I leave – just to make sure that they will have something to do.'

'I take it you mean the Daniels' girls. How do you find them?'

'Good nurses both.'

Her ladyship eyed her quizzically. 'And Sister Harrison? What do you make of her?'

'Faultless professionally, though a tad bit overbearing – even with me.'

'Me too,' muttered her ladyship.

'There seems to be a barrier between us – even between her and the other nurses. I do wonder if she has any friends or if her mother keeps her that close, she can't find time for anything else.'

'A woman of secrets rather than depth.'

'Perhaps. I find everyone else easy enough to get on with and do my best to ensure that their work fits in with their lives.'

'We're back to the Daniels sisters. I understand you're responsible for keeping them occupied.'

'If by that you mean I employ them to help me at the coach house, yes if they've nothing else to do, though it seems I am no longer persona non grata. The number of patients attending the hospital has increased.'

'Sister Harrison still feels that married nurses should not be employed. How do you feel about that?'

'I believe so long as the children don't suffer it's perfectly fine. I recall female conductresses being pulled off the trams after the war finished, protesters shouting that the jobs should go to the men now they were back. It didn't seem to occur to them that some of these women were widows working to supplement their meagre war widows' pension in order to put food on the table and a roof over their children's heads.'

Her ladyship shook her head sorrowfully. 'Men can be so stupid at times but then some of those protesters were women. Sometimes I wonder what we were fighting for, not in the war but fighting for the vote. Will our efforts be appreciated in the years to come?' She shook her head again. 'I just don't know.'

'We can only hope,' said Frances.

Her ladyship got to her feet. 'Now, if you'll excuse me. I will see you at some time tomorrow. I have a plan that might help him cope better and the sooner it is implemented, the happier I will be.'

'What is that?'

'I will speak to you about it tomorrow. Something to ease the pain of his altered life. I'll send a car.'

'I have my own.' Though she would have to get it out of the garage.

'My chauffeur will pick you up.'

It was all a big vague but Frances contented herself that the chauffeur wouldn't appear until after she'd finished at the hospital.

'Very well. I'll be ready.'

29

Lucy was over the moon. She was on another date with her heart-throb, Brian Faulkland and couldn't wait to get there. It was just another dance at the Miners' Institute, but tonight there would be no Nancy arriving at the hospital with the baby in the wickerwork pushchair and no Mr Painter needing to be laid out by Ma Skittings.

The Miners' Institute was the only venue in town for dances, was always looked forward to and always crowded.

He was waiting for her outside, his tawny eyes narrowing against a pall of cigarette smoke. The hint of a smile played around his mouth. He looked so sure of himself that part of her wanted to turn him down.

Two girls she knew, one of whom worked in the haberdashery in the high street, the other in service at Orchard Manor, lingered close by, giggling and batting their eyelids in Brian's direction.

Brian straightened and offered her his arm. Lucy threw a look of triumph at the two girls as she gained her prize and laced her arm into his.

'Thought you weren't coming,' he said to her as he guided her through the double doors.

'Well, I'm here now.'

A blast of warmth and noise hit them full on.

'Fancy a drink?'

He guided her to a three-legged table grouped around the dance floor.

'Won't be a minute.'

Although she knew a lot of people there, him leaving her and heading for the bar made her feel slightly abandoned.

The band was playing a foxtrot. Men danced with women and some women danced with women. With a pang of regret, Lucy knew this was because there simply weren't enough men to go round. The Great War had seen to that, three-quarters of a million men gone forever.

'Who you here with then?'

The question was asked by Betty Knight who worked at the bottling plant where Somerset cider was transferred from vats to bottles. The faint smell of apples came with her, sweet and sickly though not entirely unpleasant.

'Brian Faulkland,' Lucy responded and couldn't help looking pleased with herself. She would be dancing with a man and, what was more, that man was Brian Faulkland. Nobody could help but be envious, though what Betty said next dented that premise.

'Oh yes. His old girlfriend left town months ago.'

'I know,' said Lucy with a toss of her head, though piqued to be reminded. 'Her father's bought a fishing boat.'

Betty chortled and pulled a wry expression. 'If you believe that, you'll believe anything.'

Lucy turned accusing eyes on her. 'What do you mean by that?'

Betty leaned in close. 'I heard that the reason they went away was to do with Meg being in the family way – thanks to Brian Faulkland.'

Lucy rounded quickly. 'Wash your mouth out, Betty Knight!'

Brian had come back with the drinks.

With a brief glance at Betty, he dragged out a chair, slamming it against her hip so she had no recourse but to step away.

'Right. Drink up. I've got some wages to spend.'

He said it jovially and although Betty continued to linger, he totally ignored her.

Betty, however, was not going quietly. 'You want to watch 'im,' she shouted. 'Wouldn't trust 'im as far as I could throw 'im – which ain't far.'

Brian glared sourly before his badge of confidence returned and he said, 'Noisy cow, ain't she?'

He said it laughingly. Lucy managed a tight smile and said, 'The band's good.'

'Let's dance.'

Brian dragged her up from her chair.

She went willingly. For a start, her feet were tapping to the music and the band weren't doing a bad job. She also wanted to get away from Betty who was still glowering in their direction, her look as sharp as daggers and aimed straight for Brian Faulkland.

'She a friend of yours?' Brian asked her as they glided around the floor.

'Not really. I know her if that's what you mean. Just like we all know people in this town. Some better than others.'

'Well, I know' er,' he said scathingly. 'Believe you me, you want to take anything she says with a pinch of salt. Right troublemaker, she is.'

His smile felt as though it was for her alone, that she was the only girl in the room. It instantly melted any doubts Betty had placed in her mind.

'You mean she's a bit of a gossip,' Lucy said laughingly, and felt reassured by him, by herself by the fun feel of the evening. 'Mind you, there's plenty of them in this town. A car runs on petrol like this town runs on gossip.'

'Witches the lot of 'em. Bloody women.'

'Not only women,' returned Lucy somewhat affronted. 'Once a clique forms, men get nasty too.'

Brian picked up on her dark look. 'What men's that then?'

She found herself telling him about some people who couldn't accept a woman doctor, Doctor Brakespeare.

'She's a lovely person but also she's got a modern view on medicine.'

'But she's a woman.'

'That's just it,' Lucy responded hotly. 'She was an auxiliary nurse during the war. Did a good bit more than the doctors that stayed home. It's despicable. Not right at all.'

She was speaking louder than she meant to, causing heads to turn in their direction which seemed to make Brian discomfited.

'Keep yur voice down, darling,' Brian said, good-humouredly nodding acknowledgement to those whose eyes met his. 'Don't need to broadcast it all like they do on the wireless.'

'I don't mean to embarrass you.'

'You're not. Some blokes are like dogs. Once they're in a pack they're looking for someone to tear apart.' He tickled her chin with his finger. 'Your doctor's right up their street. Not tied to the kitchen sink. She's doing stuff.'

Lucy pondered on whether she should say more. She decided she would.

'I hate the way men think they know more than women and that women can't do the same job as a man.'

'I take your point, though wouldn't want to see a woman down the mine or working in a quarry. But a doctor? I don't see the problem.'

Lucy smiled her appreciation.

'And now let's 'ave another drink, shall we? This dancing's thirsty work.'

Lucy threw her energy and thoughts into enjoying herself. Brian gave her all his attention. He even whispered into her ear that from now on she was his girl.

'I've always wanted to go out with a nurse, especially you. I should 'ave asked you before.'

'Why didn't you?'

'Well. When we was at school I always thought you'd do better than me.' He whispered into her ear, 'And I love a girl in uniform.' He grinned before saying, 'I think I'd look good in a uniform.'

'Not a nurse's uniform,' she said in a bubble of laughter.

He frowned. ''Course not. I ain't a cissy, you know. A soldier's uniform. Or a sailor.' A faraway look came to his eyes. 'Yeah. I fancy meself as a soldier.'

Brian Faulkland was one of those local young men who'd been too young to join the battle back in 1914–18. Despite the terrible fatalities of the Great War, some young men still retained a sense of having missed something glorious.

'Don't you think I'd look good in a uniform?' he asked her.

'Very good.'

The look in his eyes took some time to fade. It might have been the drink and the excitement of the evening. She hoped it was, though suspected in his mind he was seeing some far-off battlefield and the chance to prove himself a warrior.

He was still mulling over the possibilities when the dance ended.

'Since you approve of me in a uniform – even if you ain't seen me in one – yet – I'll walk you 'ome.'

By the time they were traversing the high street, a light rain had begun to fall and gradually got heavier. The heads of roses drooped over garden walls and rivulets of water gurgled along the gutter.

His arm snaked around her, pulling her in close to his side. At first, it felt protective until his grip grew tighter. 'You're getting wet. Let's get in here for a minute.'

Before she could protest, she was dragged into an empty doorway and his body was pressing against hers. Words of appreciation spoken on boozy breath filtered into her hair.

'I've always fancied you, Lucy.'

She began to relax, until he said, 'You can give me a bed bath any time.'

She pushed him away. 'You can stop that talk.'

His amiable expression that she'd liked up until now hardened. 'No need to be prudish. Not you. A nurse. Everyone knows nurses know everything about a bloke's body. Come on. Give us a kiss.'

Fleshy lips slick with cider clamped on hers and made a sucking sound as she pushed him away with clenched fists.

'Oh come on...'

'No. I want to go home. I'm working tomorrow.'

Strong, blunt fingers clenched around her wrists.

'Let me go!'

He let her go and spread his arms. 'Sorry. I'm full of the apple juice. Sorry again ten times over. You're my dream, Lucy Daniels.'

'Your dream?'

'Yes. I've had my eye on you for ages. Never thought I'd be in with a chance. I've seen you with blokes. Peter Venables for a start. Works in an office, so I hear.'

'An insurance office.'

'There you are then. The likes of 'im got far more to offer than a working bloke like me with rough 'ands and rough manners.'

He plunged his hands into his pockets and with his eyes down-cast looked thoroughly dejected.

Lucy couldn't help feeling sorry for him. No, he was not comparable to Peter Venables or the young doctor she'd met when in training at Stoke Park. Neither of those romances had come to anything, though for a while it had seemed likely that they would. Peter had lost interest in her following promotion and earned enough to purchase a Morris motorcar. She'd seen him since driving merrily along, a sleek blonde in the passenger seat beside him. The last she'd heard of the doctor she'd dated he'd married the daughter of a surgeon at a London hospital.

On her last date with Peter, his behaviour hadn't been that different from Brian's – though more forceful. Blouse torn and tears streaking her face, the only reason he'd backed off was because, on hearing the muffled shrieks, a woman out walking her dog had stopped and asked what was going on.

'Nothing,' Peter had called back. 'My girlfriend was feeling a bit faint.'

Lucy had taken the opportunity to button her blouse and tidy herself up a bit.

The woman had walked on but slowly.

'You're frigid. That's what's the matter with you!'

His comment had hurt more than the bruises he'd left on her arms and wrists. Brian hadn't said she was frigid, but she couldn't help but get the impression that he was thinking the same.

He sauntered to the front of the doorway, where he lit yet another cigarette and stayed leaning against the shop window, eyeing the falling rain in the light from the streetlamps.

Was he waiting for her to reach out and touch him, tell him that everything was all right and if he wanted to...

Her hand reached out, but something inside her stopped it

from covering the full distance between them. Her fingers curled into her palm.

'I'd better be getting home.'

Without saying a word, he moved aside so she could pass. The rain had intensified, falling onto wet pavements, droplets landing like broken pennies.

Boyfriends past and present bobbed around in her mind like the raindrops bouncing on the pavements.

Her mouth was dry. She'd been so looking forward to going out with Brian, but her vision of a handsome prince had shattered.

'Do you want to go out with me again?'

The tip of the cigarette glowed red as he inhaled.

'That depends.'

She wasn't sure how she felt. Earlier today, she would have been ecstatic, but now... her thoughts went back to what Betty Knight had said about his former girlfriend. They'd been together a long time and now she'd moved and rumours as to the reason why abounded. This, she'd thought, had been her opportunity to fill the other girl's place and perhaps refusing Brian's advances would earn his respect.

'I'm working tomorrow night but free the night after – if you're free.'

Did she sound too forward? She hoped not.

Heart fluttering, she eyed him questioningly as he craned his neck and blew a cloud of smoke out into the night.

'I'll see you in the Plough.'

She wasn't keen on pubs. She had hoped he might offer to take her to the pictures. On reflection, at least the pub was well lit, whereas the picture house was dark. She didn't want to be with him in the dark where he might again make advances.

'All right. What time?' Her mouth was dry. Her palms slightly sticky with sweat.

'About eight o'clock.'

It seemed a bit late to meet up. Seven would have been preferable. But still...

'That should be all right.'

She found it difficult to read anything into the funny look he gave her.

'Right.'

He turned his coat collar up around his jaw.

'It's raining. Better get home.'

They set out in the same direction along the street without saying much – except about the rain. Funny how people talked about the weather when they couldn't think of anything else.

She let him kiss her. This time, he didn't grab her and although his lips were less slippery than before, she didn't feel any great enthusiasm, just a sense that there was some format she had to delight in but couldn't quite work out what it was.

'Goodnight. See you tomorrow.'

They parted at the end of the road, Brian turning along Rownham Terrace towards the railway line that linked the quarries to London. She turned in the other direction towards Briar Way and the row of cottages in Waterloo Terrace.

By the time she got home, her stockings were soaked, her shoes waterlogged and the sodden hem of her dress stuck to her knees. She'd felt like a princess when she'd gone out this evening but now knew she resembled a drowned rat, drenched from head to toe.

Her spirit had taken a bit of a bashing, but she told herself that next time it would be different.

30

———————

The regimental band was playing something French and although Frances strained to hear the guns, they were strangely absent. She had the impression that they were not far from Cambrai, where men were training their rifles on the enemy trench just a hundred yards away and Ralph was with them – his last battle. His very last.

The sound of the band was replaced by the cawing of crows who were so numerous they became a black cloud that obscured the sun. She could hear the flapping of wings close behind her as she ran through meadows that became mud until she entered the broken remnants of a farmhouse. Breathless and afraid, she closed the door behind her and prayed she'd be safe. The crows that pecked at the battlefield dead were attacking the house, their black wings flapping, their beaks, open and cruel as they flung themselves against the window.

She woke quickly. The room was dark, her body hot, sweat trickling down between her breasts.

There was that sound again, as though the crows had followed her out of her dream into reality.

As she came awake, she realised that the sound was not due to crows. Stones were being thrown at her bedroom window and a voice was calling her from outside.

'Doctor Brakespeare.'

In a matter of minutes, she went from sleep to full wakefulness, threw back the bedclothes and in three strides had flung open one half of the casement window.

Dawn had come upon her too quickly this morning and so had her ladyship's chauffeur, who stood there looking up at her slightly bemused.

'Rise and shine,' he shouted up. 'No rest for the wicked.'

She wanted to snarl back that she could do without brisk platitudes at that time of the morning.

'I expected you later. Not at the crack of dawn.'

'Her ladyship insists you join her for breakfast.'

Breakfast!

'I'll wait whilst you get dressed, Doctor.'

Damn him, she thought. *He'll have to wait.*

It took half an hour before she was ready to head downstairs with the silver framed photograph under her arm.

There was no time to pin a hat in place but just enough to gather up a selection of medicines she thought she might need and slide Ralph's photograph into the bag. As ready as she was ever likely to be given such short notice and the time of day, she headed outside.

The chauffeur had come round from the back of the coach house and was waiting for her by the gate, his buttons polished, the leather straps of his spats binding his calves at equal distance from each other. It made her wonder if he'd measured each one to the inch so that the highest standards of presentation were observed.

Feeling just a tinge exasperated, she settled herself in the back of the car and off they went.

A veil of mist shrouded the park and skirted the house.

Grimes, her ladyship's butler, met Frances at the door of Orchard Manor. She noted that his back was slightly stooped and his hair more prominent at the rear of his head than it was at the front. He had to be at least seventy years of age. His voice creaked almost as much as the door had when he'd opened it.

'Her ladyship sends her compliments. She suggests you see Mr Devlin first before joining her for breakfast. Will you come this way, please?'

'Lead on.'

Inside the house Frances took in the banisters of turned wood, their smell and feel testifying to frequent applications of beeswax polish and the elbow grease of diligent and badly paid housemaids. The stair carpet of rich reds and blues were held in place with brass stair rods that looked as though they had been recently polished – perhaps that very morning.

Grimes, his steps a little ponderous, turned left, to where a marble and sparsely clothed goddess gazed stonily down at their progress.

Brash daylight bombarded the passageway and helped alleviate the frowning gloom thrown by linen presses, cabinets decorated in what was termed chinoiserie, a European interpretation of what Chinese scenes might look like.

A muted growl from her stomach reminded Frances that breakfast had been promised. She hoped she wouldn't have to wait too long.

Grimes rapped at a pair of double doors in a no-nonsense manner, and although no permission sounded from within, he turned a gleaming brass handle and pushed open one half.

The room was bright despite the heavily patterned wallpaper. The windows stretched from ceiling to floor and were the source of the great flood of light from outside.

A man stood with his back to her silhouetted against the morning light flooding in from the window. Everything about him was average, apart from his absolute stillness. In fact, it was easy to believe that he had been hewn from the same marble as the Greek goddess they'd passed.

Obviously he heard her for he turned from the window and lifted his head.

The uniform of an army officer hung spare and unfaded from his frame. The Sam Brown crossing diagonally from waist to shoulder looked supple and the brass buttons and officer insignia gleamed.

'Mother?'

Before she could make comment, he sniffed the air and answered his own question.

'No. Not my mother. Who are you?'

'Doctor Frances Brakespeare.'

'A doctor and a woman.' He sounded surprised before saying, 'You smell like a woman.'

'Not like a doctor?'

'You don't smell of carbolic and any of those other horrible smells associated with male doctors. But then neither did Doctor Walker. Motorcycle oil. That's what he smelt of. I told my mother I couldn't stand the smell. It brought back nightmares, so she replaced him with Doctor Dando from Bath. He had bad breath, though I didn't mention that to her. Smells matter a lot to me. It's the first thing I notice about people before they speak and even more so when they do.'

'So you have experience of more than one doctor?'

His expression was rueful, contemptuous even. 'A whole army of doctors. Some were more positive than others, but not many. I am what I am. What happened happened. There's no going back.'

She saw the blankness in his eyes. There was no great scar

across his face. He looked as if he could see but accepted he could not. From what she'd learned when training – and before that in the fields of northern France – she guessed he'd sustained some kind of trauma to the optic nerve. A blow perhaps when in the proximity of an explosion or he might have inhaled poisonous gas, which had then spread through his nasal, audio and optic nerves.

'I'm nothing like Doctor Walker.' She said it with humour.

He responded in the same manner. 'No. Not at all. You're a woman, but not like my mother. For a start, you don't smell like her. My mother wears lavender water or gardenia. The latter is extremely overpowering. She considers anything else unsuitable for a woman of her age. My father didn't approve of her being too flamboyant. He'd probably have horsewhipped her if she'd dared defy him. He did me enough times, but then, not surprising. He enjoyed it, I think.'

She stood there still and silent as she considered the likelihood that he would allow her to examine him.

'Your mother asked me to look in on you.'

An overall uplifting of his face ensued and tipped into amusement. 'My mother wants to know if I am mad.'

'Are you?'

His eyebrows arched. 'Isn't that your job to find out?'

'Only if you want me to.'

'Only if I want to?'

He was staring straight at her, lured by the sound of her breathing and looking surprised that the decision to be treated by her was entirely down to him.

One corner of his mouth turned upwards in a permanent smile and she wondered if she'd been wrong about a facial scar. On reflection, she realised the look was sardonic, Captain Compton-Dixon's contempt for the world.

She decided to digress. 'I've never entered this house before. It's rather beautiful. Quite a history, I shouldn't wonder.'

She set down her bag and wandered the room. Although the sound of her footsteps was absorbed in the thick Turkish rugs, Devlin, his hearing going some way to compensating for his lack of sight, heard her. His head moved as his ears followed her progress around the room.

'I try not to wonder what went before. History is best forgotten.'

'I think forgetting history can be a mistake.'

'Not if you've lived it.'

A sneer pulled at the flexible corner of his mouth whilst the other remained in its rictus smile. His tone was bitter and not surprising under the circumstances.

She felt compelled to agree with him. 'We are all part of history.'

'Ah yes. I heard you were a VAD or something in France.'

'I was.'

'Most commendable of you.'

She fancied a hint of sarcasm in his voice.

'I felt it my duty.'

'Most women thought it their duty to keep the home fires burning. You didn't have to go.'

She swallowed the words she could have said, ones that provoked old and painful memories.

'I felt it my duty,' she repeated resolutely, determined the subject was finished and that she would not mention Ralph, her real reason for going. Like the old English folk song, 'Sweet Polly Oliver'.

> *As Sweet Polly Oliver lay musing in bed,*
> *A sudden strange fancy came into her head.*
> *Nor father nor mother shall make me false prove.*

I'll list for a soldier and follow my love.

He grunted. Somehow she suspected he knew her real reason but would not lead him into the truth.

She stopped at a glass-fronted cupboard, each shelf displaying colourful lead soldiers from different periods of history.

'I played with them as a child.'

It amazed her that he'd known where she'd stopped and where she was looking.

'Do you play with them now?'

'No. I'm attempting to write my memoirs. Memories of what lingers in my mind.'

She didn't press him for further details but stopped at a large desk set in a dark corner. An A4-size sheet of paper flopped over the carriage of a black metal Imperial typewriter.

'Touch typists brag about their speedy proficiency. There's really nothing to it, you know. A few lessons guiding my fingers to the keys, someone to look over my shoulder until I could find my way – that's all it took.'

She fingered the pen and pad placed on the blotting pad. The residual outlines of written words from a ripped-away page showed faintly.

'But sometimes you write.' That's what she presumed.

'No. I get other people to read what I type, make corrections and write notes that they read out loud.'

'It sounds quite idyllic in this beautiful room.'

'It is. Hidden away. Out of sight. That's how I like it.'

'That's a beautiful window.'

'Is it?'

She felt stupid pointing out. After all he couldn't see it. 'I'm sorry.'

'Oh yes. I remember. Despite the lovely window, I suppose it's rather dark in here for a sighted person. Wait a moment and I'll...'

He moved sideways from the window so that the light fell upon the room and on his face. He felt for the switch on a table lamp that sat close to the wall on a table beside him. 'We have electricity. Did you know that?'

She didn't comment that the dawn light was plenty enough to see by. 'Shall I draw the curtains back?'

'It matters little to me.'

She pulled them back anyway, although they did not really pose any impediment. The day was bright.

He tilted his head to one side and held out his hand. 'Can I touch your face? It might help me learn what you look like.'

'You may.'

She stood close to him, so close that she could smell the faded wool from which his uniform was made. A uniform from back then and although demobbed he was still wearing it. Clinging on to the past or wearing that uniform as a shield against the present? Or the future?

His fingers gently followed the outline of her jaw, her cheek-bones, her nose and the arch of her eyebrows. He gasped, like a man taking a deep breath, when he ran his hands through her hair and felt the silken tresses falling through his fingers.

'Lovely hair. And no hat. A woman's hair is a fitting crown. A hat is unnecessary.'

The comments seemed only for himself.

'Can you get me a drink? It's over there on the table.' He jerked his head to the right. 'Gin,' he said. 'I want gin. Pour in a good measure, then add water. Not too much, mind. Then a drop of that stuff from the small glass medicine bottle. It helps ease the pain – in my body, if not in my head.'

Despite what he'd told her, she fingered the bottle, reading the label before pulling out the stopper and adding the tiniest drop of laudanum to the gin. She initially considered warning him of the dangers of daily doses of laudanum, but what right did she have to deny him relief from pain?

His fingers brushed hers when she handed him the glass, then lingered.

'Your hands are so soft. Healing hands.' He took a small sip of his drink before tipping the lot down his throat. 'Another one. Might as well drown myself in the stuff. That way, I won't notice much as I'm carted away and locked up. That's why you're here, isn't it? They want you to sign whatever it is you sign, to have me committed. The madhouse: that's where they think I belong. The bloody madhouse!'

'That's not the reason I'm here. Your mother suggested I should meet you, not examine you.'

'Really?' He sounded surprised. 'Never mind. I don't need an excuse to drink. I'll have another.' He held out his glass.

'No. I won't get you another drink – not laudanum anyway. It's very addictive.'

'Very addictive,' he mocked. 'Then perhaps the doctor will pour me the less injurious medicine. Gin if you please.'

She found his attitude irritating and was half inclined not to fetch him a drink at all. She relented, though added more water before giving him the glass.

'Piss!'

He flung the glass in her direction. She stepped sideways so that it missed her. Then she turned on her heel. As far as she was concerned, she'd fulfilled her ladyship's request. Breakfast no longer such an attractive option, though she doubted she would be allowed to leave until she'd had the promised words with her ladyship.

'I'll leave you with your self-pity for company,' she called over her shoulder.

'Come back!'

'I will not. Throw glasses at someone else. Not me.'

'Come back here. I insist you come back here.'

He was still shouting.

'Please!' he called suddenly. 'Doctor. Please. I need to talk to you.'

She heard the plaintive pleading and although still annoyed with him she stalled, her hand clinging onto the door handle, in two minds whether to go or stay.

'I know you're by the door. If you were wearing a silk dress, I would hear you better,' he said.

'I was asked by your mother to pay you a visit. I've done that. I have patients to attend who are more grateful for my services than you are.'

Finally, she closed the doors and found her way back to the reception hall, where Grimes awaited her at the bottom of the stairs.

'Breakfast is served.'

Grimes stretched out his arm, indicating a pair of double doors with brass finger plates and handles.

Despite his bowed legs and slow movement, he opened both before she could get there – or before she could change direction and head for home – even if she had to walk there.

Lady Compton-Dixon was sitting at the table reading the newspaper, a pair of wire-rimmed spectacles perched halfway down her nose. She raised her eyes as Frances entered and indicated for a maid to pour coffee.

'Rose will get you some eggs and bacon. Plus toast.'

'I'm not really...'

'Yes you are hungry, especially after visiting my son. He saps one's energy, including my own. Do you know he was engaged to be married?'

Frances watched as the maid placed a plate, a cup of hot black coffee and a rack of toast in front of her. The sight and smell were irresistible.

'No. I did not.'

She didn't ask why he hadn't married because she thought she already knew the answer. The war had marred relationships and planned marriages as well as bodies.

Her ladyship sat back in her chair, took the spectacles from her nose and smiled at whatever memory she was currently entertaining in her mind.

'My son was a great one for the ladies. He loved them and they loved him. Grace would have made him a wonderful wife, but...' Her face fell as the latter-day truth took hold. 'He still loves women – would love them physically too if given half the chance. But...' She leaned closer to Frances and there was no doubting the twinkle in her eyes. 'You two have so much in common. The war, your age, your experiences and...'

Guessing where this was going, and having lost her appetite Frances pushed her plate away and got to her feet. 'Look, your ladyship...'

'Minty. Call me Minty. That's what my friends call me.'

Frances saw the hope in her face but steeled herself.

'Minty. Thank you, but the man I loved dearly died in the war. For both me and in honour of his memory I have committed my life to medicine.'

Realising she'd made a terrible faux pas, her ladyship's face crumpled. 'I'm sorry. I had it in mind that some of the son I once knew would return if he had female company. I didn't mean any disrespect... please... just an old lady clutching at straws.'

Frances regarded the distraught and apologetic expression of the older woman. In all honesty, she couldn't really condemn her. Everyone tried to do what one could for their children, especially for those who had been through so much. Lady Compton-Dixon came across as a strong, indeed formidable woman. It seemed she hid her pain and sadness very well.

'I really must go,' said Frances.

Her ladyship breathed a regretful sigh of acknowledgement. 'Grimes will get the car round.'

'Thank you.'

'You will call again?'

'As his doctor, yes. If that's what you wish.'

'I do wish and I think you'll be good for him – as his doctor,' her ladyship added swiftly on seeing the rebuke building in Frances's eyes.

'Very well. As you wish.'

Her ladyship frowned as another thought took hold. 'There is another thing I wanted to ask you about. Grimes acts as Devlin's valet and general companion. He helps him dress, rubs liniment into his muscles and administers his medicine.' Her brow furrowed. 'Like me, he's getting too old to continue, so I wondered if it were possible to have a nurse attend – on a part-time basis – Grimes couldn't bear to be completely displaced. I wondered if it might be possible for one of the nurses from the hospital to provide an element of respite for poor old Grimes. Do you think that would be possible?'

Frances understood immediately that if she didn't succumb to her ladyship's request, then someone else would. More important than that she recognised the need for Devlin Compton-Dixon to move forward – his mother too.

'I'll see what I can arrange. Can I also make a suggestion?'

'Of course.'

'Get him out of that uniform and burn it.'

* * *

In the back of the car on the way home she wondered at how calmly her ladyship had taken her advice. Others of her ilk might have thrown her out of the house and told her she was impertinent. There had been no sign of fierce rebuke in her eyes but instead a moment of reflection before she'd sighed, her straight backed posture suddenly diminished.

Frances had no doubt that her ladyship's gardener would shortly be overseeing the smoking remnants of that uniform on a garden bonfire.

The car dropped her off at the entrance of the hospital where Sister Harrison was waiting for her with a full list of patients some of whom were new arrivals.

So, she thought, the brigadier's and her ladyship's endorsements had yielded results. With more speed than anticipated she was being accepted.

A poster advertising the new services at the hospital had been placed outside the post office where most of the townspeople could see it.

A Mother and Baby Clinic was top of the list and in second place was an hour-long session dedicated to children's health where they would be seen by a nurse with a large spoon dispensing cod liver oil. She would also be looking for nits with a fine comb and sheets of newspaper – one sheet for each child.

The day proved long but fruitful – one aspect being her informing Nurse Daniels that she wished her to come back full time at the hospital.

'We're getting busier by the day and I'm hoping the two new clinics are going to prove popular.'

She said this in front of Sister Harrison who although being told earlier had pursed her lips before agreeing. 'At least she's single and has no children,' she said pointedly.

It was obvious to Frances that the snide aside was aimed at Nancy who Frances had informed would remain employed by the hospital on a part-time basis for however long it suited her.

Sister Harrison was less enthused when told about Lucy's sister being retained part-time.

'She manages very well,' Frances pointed out to her. 'As long as she does that neither I nor you can have any objection – unless there's something else relevant to the matter?'

There was a moment when Sister Harrison's stiffness looked likely to snap her in two. It was as if Nancy's coming or going was upsetting an internal plan she was not prepared to expose. Not that Frances needed her to declare her support for Simon Grainger. The woman was in love with him. Pity her, she thought. Even though a newcomer to Norton Dene Frances had heard the rumours.

She worked it out that Simon Grainger wanted Ned Skittings to take the job at Monkswell so that he was out of the way of serious enquiry into the accident. If Ned refused it was not beyond the bounds of possibility that Simon would threaten to sack him, but at least the little family would still have Nancy's small but useful income. They could survive. BUT without that income they would be sunk.

It wasn't for Frances to challenge her about it but she could put obstacles in Simon's way. Nancy was such an obstacle.

Just for this once she walked home, the chauffeur having dropped her off at the hospital and her car hidden behind the coach house doors.

The sun peered out in a blaze of red and orange from behind a lattice of pearl grey cloud.

She'd barely got halfway up the garden path when Gregory's voice called out to her. He was waving what looked like a letter.

'I took delivery for you.'

He smiled down at her as he handed her the letter, his smile diminishing on seeing the look on her face when she read the postmark.

'It's from London.'

'You still have friends there.'

'Yes, but this letter isn't from a friend. It's typewritten.'

'Ah. Something more official?'

She nodded, her soft grey eyes still pondering the envelope.

'Do you want me to come in and help you open it?'

It was a daft, funny thing to say, brought a weak smile to her face and persuaded her that his company would make her feel better.

'It's from the solicitors. I'm guessing they want to send someone to take my car.'

'In that case I'll pop back to the vicarage and fetch a bottle of elderberry wine.'

'Not parsnip,' she countered with a slightly braver smile.

'No. This one's quite special. I've been saving it for our next supper together.'

* * *

Warmed by the wine, she perused the letter whilst he sat watching her. From the very first time he'd seen her he'd been spellbound and in the most gruesome of places. That was when he'd heard her doing her best to console a dying man. He felt he'd fallen in love with her then though had never expected to see her again. Until he'd found the locket in the tunic of a dead man. And since then, he'd been dumbfounded when she'd turned up in Norton Den

Both God and the fates moved in mysterious ways. Or someone had engineered this and he had a shrewd suspicion of who that might be.

He saw her downcast look. 'It's about the car?'

'Yes.'

She let the letter flop onto the table. 'I need to find something that proves it was a gift and did not belong to Izzy.'

'Do you have anything?'

Frances frowned. For the first time in a long while she contemplated the contents of the box of letters, notebooks and other bits and pieces. Without bothering to check she'd tipped the lot into the box. She explained it to Gregory.

'What with so much happening here I've never checked what's in there.'

He poured her another glass of elderberry wine. 'Then perhaps it's time you did. Shall we drink to that?'

31

Dear Deborah,

I thought I should write to you to say that Doctor Brakespeare is doing very well though that is no more than we expected. I am truly glad that you wrote to me. I doubt whether her letter in response to the classified advertisement would have got anywhere if you hadn't. We are both aware that despite our fight for the vote the world of men still exerts immense power over the world of women.

I only wish Isabelle was still here to share our joy in what is to all intents and purposes a triumph for the rights of women everywhere.

Sincerely yours, Minty Compton-Dixon

Deborah whooped with joy on receiving the letter. She'd always been overly exuberant each time a small hurdle was cleared regarding the rights of women. Both Izzy and Minty had told her she was.

'United we stand and shall overcome everything,' she was fond of proclaiming. 'One day we might even have another queen on the throne and even a woman prime minister.'

They'd all laughed at that and said it was a bit far-fetched, but Deborah had remained adamant. Once they'd got the right to vote on a par with men they began to dream that one day it might come true.

One thing they also knew was that she was useless at keeping secrets yet there was one she'd kept for a very long time, one entrusted to her by Izzy a while back. So far she'd kept her promise though how long that was likely to last she couldn't say. The fact was that they were all getting older and it made sense to share or tell that secret. Thanks to the murmur in her heart and her doctor's prognosis that time was growing near. Soon, very soon, she would have to face her own mortality and refused to let the secret die with her.

Lucy was tired. She'd been on duty since early morning and Sister Harrison appearing on the ward had been a sight for sore eyes. A bonus was Nurse Bennett turning up. The two of them had a lot in common. Both were spinsters and lived with their mothers and nattered to high heaven when they were on duty together. It turned out that Nurse Bennett's brother had insisted their mother come to live with him in Brighton.

'And it's not out of the kindness of his heart,' Nurse Bennett laughed. 'He thinks she's got money to leave. Little does he know.'

Just before she said goodbye to her shift and the two older nursing staff, a message arrived that Aunt Rose was down at the Plough drunk as a lord and in no fit state to get home by herself. She needed help.

She recognised the dirty-faced scamp who brought the letter as one of the Shawbrook family who lived in Trafalgar Close which went off at an angle at the far end of Waterloo Terrace, its houses set on an embankment above the railway line.

'Pouring cats and dogs,' she muttered as she headed home with enough time to pull on an old sou'wester hat and cape that had once belonged to her uncle. It was far too big for her and almost reached her ankles. Back out into the night it wasn't long before water dripped from the elliptical brim of the hat, whilst the hem of the cape flapped in the wind like the sails of a ship. Anyone seeing her pass wouldn't have guessed that there was a slip of a girl inside that expansive outfit.

There was little traffic, although every so often, the wheels of a bus or coalman's lorry splashed water all over her. Gas lights flickered through the rods of rain and people hurried past huddled into their clothes with the brims of their hats pulled down over their faces.

Brian Faulkland didn't notice her, but then he was sheltering in a shop doorway, his body clamped against that of a woman. The sight of the huddled pair brought her up short. Thrusting together as one, a rhythmic movement coupled with groans of ecstasy and the rustling of displaced clothing.

Lucy felt sick. Not upset. Not tearful. Just sick.

For a moment, it seemed Brian looked her way but saw only the oversized garment she wore, not the person within, not Lucy Daniels. She rushed on but shed no tears. All she felt was anger and a deep regret for having had feelings for a man who just wasn't worth it.

The Plough loomed up in the driving rain, which contributed to the humidity of the pub interior. Damp clothes, damp people, the windows misted with condensation, water trickling down onto windowsills.

Aunt Rose was being supported by two other women of her age

and one man who was holding on to her as though about to take her for a spin around the dance floor.

The landlord was shouting from behind the bar. 'Aunt Rose. Come on. Off home with you.'

She'd never expected getting Aunt Rose home would be easy. The old lady could be a contrary old cuss once the cider was inside her.

'You're pinching me,' she cried as Lucy manhandled her out of the pub and into the damp darkness. On the way, she tried not to look into the doorway, where Brian and whoever it was were still in the throes of unfettered and grubby passion.

* * *

Having heard about Aunt Rose, Nancy came round to check that everything was all right.

'I've put her to bed. Do you want to stay and share a pot of tea?'

There was something about the sheepish way that Nancy agreed that made Lucy ask her sister if something was wrong.

'You look like the cat that's got the cream.'

A secretive smile came to Nancy's face. She patted her stomach to give extra meaning. 'It's time I was leaving. I'm lucky to have my mother-in-law to look after one baby, but I can't expect her to cope with two.'

'Nance!' They laughed together, Lucy remarking that it hadn't taken Ned too long to recover from his ordeal.

As they sipped tea the conversation got round to the future and when she would leave her job and how she and Ned would manage without her wage.

Nancy's happy countenance was replaced by one of concern.

'Mr Grainger mentioned to Ned that he'd be laying some men

off and there was a chance he'd be one of them. He's given Ned an
ultimatum. No job or take the one at Monkswell.'

Lucy frowned. 'He's very intent on getting you over there.'

'Ned challenged him.'

'Good for Ned. What did he say?'

Nancy perched on the arm of the chair, folded her arms and
recited what Ned had said. 'He was telling me that he's pretty sure
that Mr Grainger gave him the wrong rod. Not a wooden one but
one with a metal spike on the end.'

'Is that significant?'

'Apparently so.' Nancy's frown deepened. 'The wires connect
each hole. If one doesn't go off, someone can give the dud a poke
with a wooden pole. That's what Ned was doing.'

'And that set off the explosion? But don't they do that all the
time?'

'Yes. A plain wooden pole. Mr Grainger passed him the pole
and told him to get on with it. Ned wonders whether he passed
him one of the steel-tipped poles used to break boulders apart.'

Lucy's eyebrows rose. 'Is he sure?'

'Not sure. Not exactly unsure. He's just questioning.'

Lucy thought about it. She was no expert, but if the wrong pole
had been used, then Grainger might have contravened safety at the
quarry. And wasn't the quarry leased from the Compton-Dixon
estate? Lady Compton-Dixon was very top drawer, but a lady in
every sense of the word. She was a stickler for fair play and if
Simon Grainger had contravened safety she would be far from
amused.

The sudden opening of the front door heralded the arrival of
Nancy's mother-in-law.

'Heard about Rose. Anything I can do?'

'She's sleeping it off.'

Ma Skittings helped herself to a cup of tea. Lucy mentioned

that it had been brewing a while and might need some more water added to the leaves.

'I likes it strong.' Ma sat down in one of the armchairs, poured a portion of tea into a saucer and slurped it back.

Their sullen faces were suddenly noticed. Ma asked them what the matter was.

'Simon Grainger's had a word with Ned today. He told him that some men would be laid off and he would likely be one of them. If he still wanted to earn a living wage, he'd have to take the job offered at Monkswell.'

'Did he now? And when was that?'

A slight chuckle ran through Ma's tone.

Nancy looked at her. Something was going on here.

'This morning.'

Ma chuckled more loudly now. 'Well, you can forget that Nancy my girl. The old man surprised young Grainger this morning. Told him he knew how Ned got injured and that if Simon didn't pull his socks up, he'd be the one out on his ear. In fact, the old man told him that he was going to transfer him to one of the lesser quarries down in Somerset. Something small that didn't jeopardise the renewal of the lease. The land belongs to her ladyship and she's a stickler for doing things right by the people whose labour makes the business profitable. The brigadier stated categorically that her ladyship had made it plain. Principles mattered if the Graingers wanted to keep the lease.'

The sisters eyed Ma Skittings with gaping mouths.

'How do you know all this?'

Ma took another sip of the treacle-coloured brew in her saucer.

'I've got inside information. Mr Forester, the wages clerk, is an upright man.' She tapped the side of her nose with a work worn finger. 'Keep it quiet, but he tells me what's happening. Reckons he owes me for saving his wife's life and what with that nonsense with

Simon trying to blacken my reputation. Mr Forester is a clever man
with insights, insights no less. So not a word to anyone – including
Ned.'

'We wouldn't dare,' Lucy declared with disbelief.

'And you won't be going anywhere, Nance. Not if the brigadier
is in charge.'

As Ma Skittings poured herself another cuppa, Nancy held a
finger to her lips, a sure sign that only Lucy knew her sister was
pregnant. 'I think it's only right I tell Doctor Brakespeare before
anyone else. I don't want her to hear it from anyone else before she
knows.'

Feeling warm inside and totally in agreement Lucy smiled. She
would support her sister through hell and high water. So too it
seemed would Ned's mother.

32

Nancy insisted on going along herself to tell Frances that she would be easing off on her nursing duties. She also told her the reason why.

Frances leapt from her chair in the neatly appointed surgery that was now situated in the hospital rather than the cosy but cramped coach house.

'Congratulations!'

Nancy looked taken aback. 'You're not mad at me for letting you down?'

'Of course not. How are you feeling?'

'Sick in the mornings but all right otherwise.'

'I can get someone else to cover for you whenever you feel sick. A district nurse who's just moved into the area contacted me the other day to ask if we could make use of her. As it happens she's exactly what we need. Someone to visit those who do not need to be hospitalised in their homes. It should work very well, so don't worry about anything Nancy. Take care of yourself and the baby. In the meantime if Lucy would like to expand her duties to oversee patient records and such like until we can get someone who knows their way around a filing cabinet. Someone has approached me, a Miss Margaret Beck... It's a big ask but if she could cover until then...'

'She'd love to.'

* * *

Lucy arrived bright and early the following morning wearing her uniform but ready to tackle anything that needed her attention.

Besides looking ready for action in her smart uniform, Lucy had also brought a notepad and sharp pencil.

'I see you've come prepared,' Frances exclaimed.

'Nancy told me what to expect and what to bring.'

Together they covered Nancy's procedure for keeping patient records up to date and ensuring that nobody attending surgery jumped the queue.

'Some people are very pedantic about their place in the queue. Not that they're likely to be overlooked, but it pays to keep patient emotions under control. I'll leave that to you.'

Things went swimmingly until the recently installed telephone, sitting like a small wooden lighthouse on the corner of her desk, chose that moment to ring.

Concentration broken, Frances sighed and reached for the stick. The dial sat at its base, the hearing piece at the end of a fabric-coated wire.

'My goodness. That thing ringing makes me jump every time,' she said as she covered the mouthpiece before pulling the hearing end of the device close to her ear. 'Good morning. Doctor Brakespeare here.'

She smiled at the mouthpiece as though the person calling could actually see her.

The voice on the other end was unmistakable.

'Doctor. It's Grimes up at the manor. Her ladyship asks if you've found a nurse for Mr Devlin.' His voice was as loud as ever.

My, thought Frances. *Does the woman have no patience?* She decided not.

'Mr Grimes. I am about to see patients in my morning surgery. Is a nurse required there immediately?'

She fixed her gaze on Lucy whose head was bent over a folder, picking papers out and putting them in order.

Her attention went back to what Grimes was saying.

'Her ladyship suggests that the person concerned should meet with Mr Devlin before being allotted the position on a more permanent basis.'

Frances gripped the phone just that bit more tightly. In normal circumstances, she would have suggested that a little more patience was needed. But she understood how hard it must have been for her ladyship to watch her son live a half-life for years. She understood, too, how difficult it was for a man who had been whole to fall so low. A part of her was with him and she could certainly empathise. There but for the grace of God – Ralph might have returned in the same state. Instead he hadn't returned at all. It was hard to know which was worse.

'Her ladyship is very anxious for something to be arranged as quickly as possible.' What could she do at such short notice?

Her eyes caught the movement of Lucy's hand hovering over the open drawer of the wooden filing cabinet. At the present time, there would only be mornings available for Lucy at the surgery, although that could increase once there was a new facility at the hospital. There were more patients than there had been thanks to Lady Compton-Dixon and Brigadier Grainger spreading their recommendations.

'Mr Grimes. What exactly does her ladyship have in mind for this preliminary meeting between Mr Devlin and the nurse?'

'She suggested tea.'

'Tea?' She had to smile. Her last visit had included breakfast.

'Mr Devlin likes to have tea at half past four precisely. Her lady ship suggests the new person attend then.'

'I'll see what I can do.'

'Her ladyship is insistent.'

'I repeat again, I will see what I can do.'

Deep in thought she sat tapping her fingers on the desk Things were going well. Two new clinics and the likely involve ment of a district nurse. In the meantime she would start the bal rolling. The prospective district nurse had not yet been taken on but Lucy was here and Nurse Daniels was perfectly capable o carrying out more widespread duties. Her first would be to pay a visit on Devlin Compton-Dixon.

* * *

Lucy looked amazed when Frances asked how she would fee about having tea with her ladyship's son.

'You do know he was badly injured in the war.'

'Yes. Everyone does, though nobody's seen much of him. They say he doesn't like to be seen.'

'Are you willing to consider being a regular nurse to him? Just a couple of hours two or three times a week. My aim is for him to regain the confidence to mix with people. Of course your primary aim will be to administer to his medical needs, overseeing the administration of his medicine for example.'

Lucy looked unsure. 'That depends. I wouldn't want to live in or anything. I still want to work at the hospital – and here – if I can.'

Frances carefully considered how to portray what she though was needed for her reclusive patient.

'He's war torn. Some of the medical and military profession will still not accept that the mind is injured in war as well as the body. Horrific memories are not easily buried and are likely to affect a man for the rest of his life. My aim is to minimise the damage as much as possible. He's had Grimes, the old retainer, looking after him ever since he came home. After all this time I think he needs a lighter touch. Please take your time to consider this. I won't force you.'

Frances had been prepared for Lucy to look uncertain as she did now.

'Think carefully, Lucy.'

'Well...' Lucy sighed and her dark eyes were full of contemplation. 'As long as it is only occasionally. I should be able to manage.'

She didn't divulge that she'd never been inside the manor house. The closest she'd was a party on the lawn along with other needy kids from the town.

'I appreciate that and I'm sure her ladyship will too. The district nurse can take it on once she's settled in. And anyway you're a young woman and deserve a social life. Do you have a sweetheart?'

Lucy's open and hopeful expression was replaced with something a little glum.

'No. I thought I did, but it turned out he was still on the market.'

'Ah!' She fixed Lucy with a questioning look. 'So can I inform her ladyship that you will be there for tea?'

Lucy sucked in her lips as she considered what she was letting herself in for.

At last, looking a little nervous but slightly excited, she said, 'Yes. I will. I can bicycle out there. It won't be a problem.'

'Not tomorrow,' said Frances, the smile on her lips also in her eyes. 'Her ladyship is sending a car. You're going to arrive in style.'

33

It was late afternoon when Frances saw Lucy into the car that had been sent for her. Looking just a shade apprehensive, Lucy Daniels looked out at her from the back seat. She raised her hand in what was less than a wave, more an entreaty to wish her luck. Frances wished her all that in buckets. She was on her way to Orchard Manor.

Frances continued to look at the spot where the car had disappeared. Meeting Devlin had brought waves of melancholy washing over her. Memories came flooding back of men who had valued contact by way of letters that as a member of the Voluntary Aid Detachment she had read out to them when they were unable to do so themselves. Briefly their eyes had sparkled as she'd read the news from home until finally, drawing their last breath, they had clutched those letters to their breasts.

She could still see them now, their frightened faces, the smell of death all around them.

Her chest felt tight. She needed fresh air and to be away from the hospital. Although it didn't mean she could wholly escape the memories, it helped her cope.

Her feet found their way to the churchyard, where the smell of mown grass lay pungently edible on the air. Before meandering around the graveyard, Frances headed for the entrance to the church itself. The oak door was set into an eighteenth-century version of a Norman arch. The wood felt warm beneath her fingertips and when she pushed one half of it, both doors opened inwards. The familiar smell of warm wood, fresh flowers and damp plaster came out to meet her.

It was gloomier inside and even the arched window behind the altar failed to capture what sunlight dared pierce the clouds.

There were shadows and chasms of blackness falling between the windows, like slabs of granite hewn from a cliff face. In between, caught in the light, dust motes whirled and danced, somehow irreligious in their movement amongst such great silence.

A rood screen divided the front of the church, the more ornate pews and greater comforts intended for the Compton-Dixon family and divided from the plainer, narrower pews reserved for the servants and lesser mortals.

She headed straight for the altar, the sound of her footsteps echoing to the rafters. Joined with her footsteps, a sound like fluttering wings disturbed the silence.

A cawing suddenly sounded from the elm trees outside. Rooks or crows? She couldn't tell the difference but feared one might have got in. Her heart raced. She looked for a weapon. Her fingers grasped a copy of the Common Book of Prayer. It could deal the wicked bird a mighty blow should it come too close. Strange how the worst of old memories came back as nightmares. Black flocks of crows had dominated the battlefield and plucked at the dead. She would never forget those scenes as long as she lived.

Suddenly a pigeon fluttered its wings and flew from one rafter to another. Disturbed by the movement, the dust motes whirled upwards.

'Calm yourself, Frances,' she whispered, relieved to see that her fears had been for nothing.

Bowing her head, she said a short prayer before heading back along the stone tiled aisle into daylight.

Her steps took her to a massive mausoleum that looked out of place in a small-town churchyard. She went right up to the heavy iron braced door and tried the bronze doorknob.

Polished and oiled by whoever looked after this place, it turned easily.

'My God,' she whispered and waited for her heartbeat to stop racing before she pushed it open. She'd once entered such a place in France to find it full of life, people trusting in its thick walls to keep them safe from artillery shells. Here, inside, it was silent.

A shaft of light fell through the open door onto scrubbed grey flagstones. Stone sarcophagi ranged along both walls, some resting on the ground, others shelved on ledges at a higher level.

Engraved in the grey stone were the names of the occupants. Her heart began to race again as she trailed her fingers over each one and read the names. Perhaps, just perhaps, Ralph had been buried in here and that was why his name was on the war memorial.

She repeated the process, getting more frantic as the daylight outside faded and the stone structures turned to graphite.

She had to get out of here.

Once outside and gulping fresh air, she leaned against the stone and tears began to fill her eyes. All she had left of Ralph was a name engraved on the war memorial. There was no sign of him ever having been here.

A lone figure in black stalled beneath the lychgate before putting one foot in front of the other and heading her way.

He looked at her and then at the open half of the mausoleum door.

'It's not supposed to be left open. I'll have a word with the verger about that.' Gripping the bronze knob, Gregory pulled it to, the door shutting with a heavy thud. He turned the knob. 'That will have to do. I can't lock it and the verger has the only key. I'll get him to lock it in the morning. It should be fine for one night.'

He kept his face turned away from her, almost as though he was the guilty party who had left the tomb unlocked – and regretted it.

Ralph. She wanted to talk about Ralph. The open stone structure had opened something up in her mind.

'You may recall me telling you about Captain Ralph Porter,' she proclaimed. 'His name is engraved on the war memorial.'

'Please correct me if I'm wrong, but your fiancé was not a resident of Norton Dene.'

'No. He was from Suffolk.'

She fancied he winced, that there was something he wasn't telling her, and in that moment she was angry.

'Why do I get the impression that you know something about his name being on the war memorial? Why does your manner change when I mention it?'

'You're imagining things...'

It wasn't like him to say something like that without a trace of humour. Gregory was a natural for raising anyone's spirits.

'No I'm not.'

His condescending comment had only served to anger her more.

'Her ladyship was on the committee who arranged for the war memorial to be built, but even she cannot explain why Ralph's name is on there. Can you?'

The loudness of her voice disturbed the starlings roosting

along the church parapet, wings fluttering until reassured the
returned to their slumbers.

She had no reason to suppose that Gregory knew any mor
than her ladyship but she couldn't help herself.

Gregory displayed no smile when he faced her and for the ver
first time she saw no mischievous amusement dancing in his eye
His chin jutted. His Adam's apple faltered as his eyes wandered t
the perimeter wall of the graveyard to where the leaves of a silve
birch tree rustled and rattled.

Finally, he said, 'I have some explaining to do.'

Sensing he'd been holding back, Frances folded her arms an
her expression was one of anger, but her voice had becom
subdued. 'I think you do.'

She couldn't bring herself to be angry because her rage ha
subsided. Anger had turned to heart-rending anguish as though al
the years that had passed were piling on top of her.

A few raindrops fell, spattering like sequins over her hair.

Gregory nodded towards the church. 'Explaining might tak
some time. There's no point us getting soaked. Let's go inside.'

They stood at the back of the church. Gregory with his hand
in his pockets, head bowed, though not in reverence but as thoug
he was churning over deep thoughts in his mind.

'This is difficult. Worse than writing or giving a sermon.'

The expression verging on amusement revived for a second
then vanished again.

'Still, being honest is my job. It must be done.'

She wondered at the reason for such a comment. Guilt
Regret?

'Do you ever regret becoming a vicar?' Her question came ou
of the blue.

He shook his head. 'No.'

Expecting him to say more she waited.

'Do you ever regret coming here to Norton Dene?'

He shook his head. She was about to ask him where he'd been before, when she suddenly remembered and was astounded at something mentioned a while ago over supper and overlooked.

'Suffolk! Your family came from Suffolk.'

'Yes.'

'So did Ralph.' Her voice was breathless. 'You knew him. Did you?'

She sensed hesitance, not that of someone in the least bit embarrassed but more like an angst of warring factions within.

He looked down at his entangled fingers. 'Yes. I was born in Suffolk, but I didn't know him, at least not when either of us lived there.'

His answer confused her. 'Then where?'

He sighed as though something heavy had landed on his shoulders and was hammering him into the ground.

His clear blue eyes met hers. Was that apology she was reading in his eyes.

'May God forgive me. I am breaking an oath, but it is something I can no longer avoid.'

He'd been a friend from the moment she'd moved here and she suddenly regretted sounding so harsh.

'I'm sorry for shouting.'

Her hand landed on his and she felt the fine golden hairs his knuckles and sinews rise warm and soft in her palm.

He shook his head dolefully. 'You have a right to.'

'Gregory. Whatever it is, I want to know.'

Eyes full of regret and promise met hers and sensing he was going to say something quite profound her pulse quickened.

'I love you more than God I think.'

This was not the profound comment she'd expected. She was taken aback.

'You can't really mean that. You hardly know me.'

Their looks locked. He didn't need to answer in words. The truth resided in his eyes.

'Let's make ourselves comfortable whilst I tell you my story.'

He led her to a pew, where they sat side by side, only the smallest of spaces between them.

Once she'd taken her hand away, he rested his elbows on his knees and his head into his palms.

'Where do I start?'

'At the beginning is always a good place.'

His smile returned and for a moment seemed no different than it usually was. However, she perceived he'd decided about what needed to be said.

'I would like you to come to London with me.'

She drew in her chin. This was not at all what she'd expected.

'Is there a special reason for that?'

'Yes. There is. It would explain a lot. I'm not sure otherwise how I can find the words and I so want you to understand.'

'I need to know more.'

His smile was guarded, almost as though he had no business smiling at all. 'Let's just say that if you say yes, you could learn something to your advantage – and make me feel better about betraying an oath.'

Confusion, puzzlement and intrigue ran like a train through her mind. Only he wasn't talking northbound. He was talking in an easterly direction towards London and she wanted to know why.

They both turned their heads when the light from one of the candelabra on the altar, the only light piercing the interior gloom, was disrupted by two moths circling the guttering flame.

Frances came to a decision.

'I have no idea about your oath, only that you must have given it for a momentous reason.'

'Come to London and I will show you that tremendous reason.'

'If it tells me something about Ralph's last resting place, then yes, I will come.'

He assured her that he would make all the arrangements.

They eased themselves out of the plain oak pews and once out of there he was heading towards the altar, where he bowed his head before the nineteenth-century crucifix and genuflected as a Catholic priest might do.

'First, in order for you to understand why I want you to go to London with me, I need to confess.'

He said it without turning round, his face upturned to the golden cross.

'Do you want me to leave?'

Thanks to the candle flames, his tawny hair gleamed like gold as he shook his head.

'No. It's to you I need to confess.'

He came back to her, took hold of her hand and led her to one of the ornate pews on the other side of the rood screen, waited for her to sit down, then sat beside her and took both of her hands in his.

'I need something to hold on to,' he said laughingly when he thought she might withdraw her hands from his clutch. He needed those hands. He needed to see and feel them. His head downcast, he fixed his gaze downwards, his voice barely above a whisper.

'The war. It all goes back to the war. The last resting place of many men was never found your fiancé included. Some that carried no identity and could not be returned to their families were interred without names in communal graves – a terrible thing in my view that there were no bodies for the families to grieve over. All they could do was wonder and say prayers for their loved ones without any focus for those prayers. Plans were made for a special memorial, one that could be visited by those who would never know the whereabouts of their son, brother, father, cousin. Then someone came up with the idea of providing a place to grieve, a tomb of an unknown warrior who might or might not be their relative but would be a focus for their grief. It was for them that the plan was put into practice.'

A cold shiver ran down Frances's spine. 'Are you telling me that's where Ralph is buried?'

He shook his head. 'Not quite.'

She sat numbly, feeling as though the blood had flowed downwards and left her face as pale as the stone angels and saints looking down on them.

'The choice of unknown soldier who would become that warrior had to be kept secret. Plans were made for six unidentified bodies to be exhumed. A commanding officer was commissioned to choose the unknown warrior from the six unidentified soldiers. Whoever he was, his name would never be known. Once that was done, plans were made for reburial of those who were not chosen. I hadn't been a padre when I was serving in the army. I was a humble lieutenant. In the aftermath of war I turned to God, partly to cope with my demons, and partly to seek the reason men killed their fellow men. So I entered the clergy, which was one reason why I was chosen to bless each of the corpses and arrange for reburial. The war had changed me but not taken my life.'

Frances kept her eyes on him, trying to read what he would say next and how relevant it was to her. She asked him outright.

'His name on the war memorial. You did it?'

He nodded. 'My father was a stonemason. He taught me his craft, though the war intervened and I never followed it. I found a silver locket on one of those soldiers. I saw recognised your photograph. I should have handed it over but I didn't. The chosen soldiers were supposed to be unidentifiable but Ralph wasn't. I saw the engraving on the back. Saw your photograph.'

She frowned. 'But how did you know it was me? You said you saw my likeness – a photograph. We'd never met.'

That sad smile again. She found herself wishing for the bemused one with which he'd first greeted her on her arrival at Norton Dene.

'I was a lowly lieutenant and injured. I was lying in bed along with hundreds of others in the medical field station. I saw you and heard you sing a lullaby to a dying boy. Touched to my soul, I asked a nurse for your name and never forgot you. You looked like an angel amid such hellish scenes that I can never forget – neither you nor those scenes.

'I kept my promise to the high command not to divulge anything about what had happened, though I did arrange for Ralph to be interred in secret as I was ordered to do, but somehow I could not bear to forget his name – or yours. So I dug up my old skills and engraved it myself. I'm a dab hand with a hammer and chisel. A very small hammer and chisel,' he added with a smile.

Frances had listened patiently. 'So where was he buried?'

He shook his head. 'I don't know. A military cemetery somewhere. That part I did keep secret just as I was supposed to. But his name... I wanted it remembered.'

'Why did you take so long telling me?'

'I had to come to terms with my own part in the exercise, my guilt. I needed some distance from events. On the first sight I had of you, I was moved. On the second, the photograph in your fiancé's person a little more so. Then you turn up here. The more I saw of you the more you stirred me.'

The silence and dust motes eddied around them as they sat engrossed in their own thoughts.

It was Gregory who broke the silence. 'So you'll come to London?'

She didn't hesitate. 'Yes. I will.'

34

'Two hours a day. That is all I require. At least for now.'

Lady Araminta Compton-Dixon was very specific. She adde
that Grimes insisted on doing all the 'gentlemanly things' mo
suited to a valet.

All the while she thought it through Lucy adopted a respectf
pose, slightly daunted to be in her ladyship's presence as sh
reflected on her duties.

'If that's what you wish, though I have given men a bed bat
and shave before now. As a nurse, it's one of the first things we'
trained to do. Besides which...'

Lucy reflected on whether it would be too cheeky to point o
that it didn't leave her much else to do, then decided she would.

'Might I ask exactly what you want me to do?'

'Whatever he wants. Fuss over him. Act as a worthy compa
ion. Read to him. Administer his tonic. Bathe his face and ey
Grimes will do the rest.'

The moment Lucy had entered the reception hall, she'd had
great desire to explore the house further and at some point ma
up her mind to ask her ladyship if she could.

For now, she had to settle for Mr Devlin Compton-Dixon's suite of rooms, where the curtains at the open French doors undulated in the draught from outside.

The young parlourmaid, who she'd seen on Brian's arm and vaguely recalled her name was Vera, showed her in and said abruptly, 'The nurse is here.'

Biting back the slight she wanted to throw at that triumphant grin, Lucy ordered her to leave.

Doctor Brakespeare had already outlined her patient's injuries and voiced the hope that Lucy would not be horrified at his disfigurement.

Lucy had pointed out that he was hardly the first Great War veteran she'd looked after.

Although the French doors were open, the curtains were closed and no lamps were lit so it was difficult to clearly see his features.

He had his back to her, arm resting on the mantelpiece, head bowed and looking down at the empty fire grate.

'I'm Nurse Daniels.' Now what? Here she was in a darkened room with a patient she did not know.

Whether he knew it or not he'd steeled her spine. She would not bow to his superior attitude and, to that end, commented, 'It's very dark in here.'

'It suits me.'

His abrupt response was meant to put her in her place, but Lucy was having none of it.

'Well. We can't have that. I need to see you and need to see what I'm doing.'

Slipping her cloak from her shoulders and her hat from her head, she went to the double doors that looked over the terrace and garden and pulled back the curtains. The billowing curtains were replaced by welcome fresh air.

He didn't move.

Lucy sensed he would not compromise any aspect of his behaviour. Her task would not be easy if she allowed it.

She came up behind him so there was barely twelve inches between them and said chirpily, 'It's a good job there's no fire in that grate. You wouldn't make a very good fireguard.'

He turned round quickly, his unseeing eyes glaring in her direction without seeing her.

'How dare you!'

Lucy sighed. 'Look. I've been summoned here to be of service. I won't be servile. So if you don't want me here, just say so and I'll go. It matters not to me one way or the other.'

'How often will you be calling?'

'When Grimes is not attending to your needs, you've got me. I know you can tell the difference between us. He's the one with the deep voice and slow footsteps. I'm the one with a higher pitched voice, treads lightly and likes to go dancing.'

Devlin's sight was impaired and his hearing enhanced.

In the process of mulling it over he was slow responding until finally, 'And you live in Norton Dene and we've seen each other from a distance.'

'Yes.'

He raised his head and his face became a blurred reflection in the overmantel mirror. 'I believe my mother did mention you but I wasn't really listening.'

He sounded glumly unimpressed. Had he wanted her to come? It was hard to tell.

He was the one who took a deep breath. 'My mother insisted I wear civvies now you've arrived. I used to wear my old uniform every day.'

'For what reason?'

'It stopped me from forgetting.'

'You prefer to remember?'

'A uniform is like a shield. It protects the wearer, stops them falling to pieces.'

She eyed what remained of the young boy who'd stared at the playing children who in turn had stared defiantly back.

He asked something she hadn't expected. 'How many of your friends died in the war?'

The question was painful. 'Too many.' It was all she could say.

'I'm sorry.'

'Right. And we're still alive. Now let's get down to brass tacks. Would you like me to read to you?'

Wordlessly, he pointed to a book lying on the table.

'*Last of the Mohicans* by James Fenimore Cooper.' He added, 'War was far simpler back then.'

He remained standing whilst she sat and read. After half an hour, he told her to stop.

'I'll have my medicine now.'

There were no medicines to treat either his injuries or his melancholy. Tonic wine or rose hip syrup mixed with a tot of brandy. Her ladyship had told her all this beforehand.

Once that was done, she asked him if he'd like her to read to him again.

Feeling his way across the room, he sat down in a brown leather chair where the draught from the open doors ruffled his hair.

'No. I want you to sit down and tell me about yourself, Nurse Daniels. Tell me how it was when you were a child, when you played games in the town square and watched a privileged child drive past.'

* * *

For many days after that, the procedure was much the same. The main difference was that the curtains were no longer closed when she arrived and he was facing her from what seemed his favourite place in front of the mantelpiece. There was also a decent fire in the grate, the flames flickering in the draught from the wide-open doors.

She asked him why he kept the doors open – even on rainy days.

'It soothes the fevered brow,' he said. 'Rain is refreshing. Wet trees, wet bushes, wet grass... touch it. Wash your face in it – or your feet, come to that. I'd like you to give me a shave. Grimes didn't do too close a job this morning.' He ran his hand over his lower face. 'Have you ever shaved a man before?'

Lucy chuckled. 'And women.'

He turned his head so he was facing her. 'Women?'

He sounded intrigued.

'I shave Aunt Rose. She's got bristles on her top lip and her chin.' She didn't mention about women having their nether regions shaved prior to birth – if there was time that is.

'I thought the bearded woman was of a kind only seen at the circus. Good grief!'

His chuckle turned into laughter, not a belly laugh but light as though it hadn't erupted from his throat for years.

Lucy laughed with him, not that it was that funny, but because this was the first time she'd heard him laugh.

It was customary after each visit for her to report on Devlin's progress to her ladyship. She reported their conversations, how much reading she'd done, how many times he'd used his gramophone and listened to music.

'How often do you wind up the gramophone?'

Lucy had replied that she rarely did. 'Mr Devlin prefers to operate the gramophone himself.'

Her ladyship had nodded approvingly. 'He always enjoyed reading, but, of course, that's beyond him now. The gramophone has been his lifeline.'

Her ladyship generously stated that she felt considerable progress had been made. Her son was beginning to rejoin the life he'd stepped back from on coming back from the war.

That might have been the pinnacle of Lucy's achievements until she told her ladyship that today, for the very first time since she'd come here, Devlin had laughed.

Her ladyship's face seemed to freeze. Her eyes were wide with amazement.

'He laughed,' she said softly.

Lucy nodded. 'Yes. He did.'

A vein in her ladyship's aged neck pulsed against the starched frill of her blouse.

'I want you to tell me every time he laughs. Every time. Do you hear me?'

'Yes. I hear you.'

* * *

The wind whipped at Devlin's hair and in his mind's eye he saw the sheet lightning scalding the sky with electric whiteness. Just as when he'd been a child growing up here and in Imperial India, he counted the seconds until the thunder rolled across the sky.

In India, where his father had traded cotton and silk, the air had been humid, sometimes too heavy to draw breath. Here, in England, the humidity turned rapidly fresher just before the downpour.

Some compared thunder to the volley of artillery fire, this mostly from people who had never experienced the real thing.

The French doors that rattled in inclement weather opened

directly onto his own private terrace, where for his convenience two teak chairs were placed either side of a matching table. His mother had told him that she'd ordered chalk marks made around the furniture legs so that they were always returned to the exact same place after the terrace had been swept. That way he could never bump into them.

The hour was close to midnight and he had no need to sit down. He stood at the edge of the terrace facing the wind and the incoming storm.

Within minutes his hair, his face and his clothes were soaking wet.

Out of habit more than necessity, he closed his eyes and behind them a whole battalion of men washed their faces in the down pour, welcoming the freshness that wiped dried mud from their skin and the lice from their hair.

In time, they'd been up to their ankles in water as the deluge rose over the duckboard flooring of the trenches, turning the surface from encrusted mud to a thick slime.

The rain had been healing. Cool and healing and he still relished it.

With only the night for company, he thought about Nurse Daniels. Though their paths had never crossed socially, he recalled her as a girl, one of a group of children who'd stopped to stare at the family vehicle – whether carriage or car – as it glided by.

The shabbily dressed children had stared with otherworldly curiosity at the shiny vehicle and the clean little boy who stared back at them.

Except for her. Lucy Daniels. She'd held her head high and merry smile had danced around ash pink lips. There was defiance in her look and her brazen curls bounced as she laughed and returned to the game she'd been playing as though the likes of him didn't matter at all.

He'd never seen lips that compared to hers until he'd gone with his parents to India. Ashar had been the daughter of a young lieutenant and a household ayah, a children's nurse. He'd been just eighteen years old when he'd confessed to his parents that he loved her and she loved him. His mother was sympathetic but failed to overrule his father's reaction. He was shipped back to England and Sandhurst. They followed on not long after and took great pains for him to meet debutantes they regarded as fitting wife material. That was how he'd met Grace.

He wasn't sure that he'd loved her, but he did like her. Love, he'd decided, would very likely come later and anyway he'd had the pick of the bunch. He was a 'good catch', as they liked to say. He was fond of saying that nowadays they would throw him back in. Although Grace wrote, he'd never written back but left that to his mother. He'd resolved to live his life in seclusion rather than try to regain whatever it was that he'd had but the smell, the soft movements of Nurse Daniels had altered something. At first reluctant about the arrangement he now looked forward to her visits.

The rain cooled his fevered brow, ran over his face, down his nose and dripped off his chin. All around him, the rainwater made a low chuckling sound as it ran along gutters and down drainpipes.

'Mr Devlin. You'll catch your death of cold.'

Grimes was calling him from the open doors, which the wind had caught and was banging each against the walls on either side of the opening.

'I shan't mind.'

He felt a blanket being placed around his shoulders.

'Please, sir. Come inside – for my sake, if not for your own. Your mother would get very cross with me and put me out on my ear.'

'My mother would never let you go, Grimes. Not now. There's nobody else to take your place.'

Once inside, Grimes fussing around him, he wound up the gramophone and placed the needle on the worn groove.

'*Roses are flowering in Picardy...*'

35

A queue of sobbing women, heads bowed and dressed in black had formed at Westminster Abbey.

Frances convinced herself that it was the vastness of the old building that made her shiver. It was too far-fetched to say it was something else, that the remains buried in the tomb of the unknown warrior was Ralph reaching out to her. As Gregory had said, Ralph had been reburied in a military cemetery. Like the unknown man lying here in the ancient abbey of Edward the Confessor there would be no name on his last resting place, he would be known only to God.

'And we'll never know for sure who this man was,' she said softly as she looked down at the eternal memorial, a tombstone set into the abbey floor.

'That was the whole point. These remains, this unknown warrior, was meant to represent those who were never identified,' Gregory whispered softly so none of the grieving wives, mothers, sisters and other relatives would hear him.

She'd been angry at first when he'd admitted his part in the exhumation of those six unidentified bodies, principally in that of

Ralph, the only one to have carried some form of identification. He'd recently passed her the locket. 'It was yours and should be with you.'

She was wearing it now, and reminded of its presence, stroked it beneath her blouse.

'Am I forgiven?' he asked. 'For not telling you sooner?'

She swallowed a threatening sob and blew her nose rather than swiping at the moistness likely to spill from her eyes.

'You kept the secret.'

'And obeyed orders. Even though I was no longer an army padre, the habit of obeying lingers on. But my conscience... well... that was another matter.'

As the afternoon diminished into twilight, candles interspersed by newly fitted electric lights vied to illuminate the nave and front porch.

Overcome by the moment, Frances stumbled. Her elbow was caught by Gregory and his arm was around her waist, where it remained as they left the abbey and navigated the evening crowds.

Trams and buses rattled past. A yellow fog was beginning to descend over the river and from some way further towards the East India docks, a ship's foghorn sounded. Gregory remarked that it was a lonely sound.

'It's only a ship. It's sadder when a person moans in anguish.' She hesitated before saying, 'I find it quite amazing how you stopped being a soldier and became a priest. You might not have followed that path if it hadn't been for the war.'

A lock of dark blond hair fell over his eyes when he shook his head. 'I think I would have become one anyway. The war taught me to look into myself. Some of the men raged at God and denied there could be one if he allowed such things to happen. I suppose I went the other way. Or perhaps I merely wanted to live in a nice town in a large vicarage,' he said on a lighter note. 'And, of course there was that moment when I heard an exhausted nurse who still cared enough to sing a young soldier out of this world.'

They exchanged sad smiles. The vision of her, Frances, in uniform was as fresh in his head as when he'd first seen her. So was her singing. He'd told her about how he'd come to Norton Dene and knew she'd been earmarked for her position at the cottage hospital even if she didn't. The knowledge made him smile to himself. The reach of the suffragette movement was as strong as ever. Lady Araminta Compton-Dixon had been a standard bearer in that movement. It only took a cry for help and those who had fought for women were there to support and assist.

'Your calling seems to suit you.'

'It's a happy calling – except perhaps for funerals that is.'

'On the plus side you get invited to a lot of weddings.'

'I do. And the receptions afterwards, where there is always cake. I do love cake. The trouble is too much of it and I'll look like Humpty Dumpty. But I'll be brave and take the consequences!'

'A slim waistline is a healthy waistline.'

'Good Lord. You sound terribly professional.'

'I'm telling you as a friend not as a doctor.'

'I appreciate your advice, though prefer the former description to the latter. A good friend who will hopefully become a very good friend.'

She felt the warmth in the sidelong look he gave her. It might have been pure imagination, but she fancied he gripped her arm closer to his side.

By the time they reached Paddington Station, they had discussed everyone they knew at Norton Dene and found their opinions were similar.

'Will you always live there?' she asked him.

'I hope so. The parish is used to having long-term incumbents at St Michael's. They prefer them to be married and thus become a more ingrained part of the community. It's accepted that vicars' wives are tremendously supportive of their husbands. My parishioners live in hope that I will live up to what is expected of me.'

'Jumble sales, church cleaning and flower decorations, garden tea parties?'

She laughed as she said it until she saw the look on his face and realised that Gregory took those things very seriously.

'I'm sorry. I didn't mean to be rude.'

They walked in silence, immersed in their own thoughts, yet at the same time apprehensive of what the other was thinking.

'I should have expected it. You're not the sort to become a vicar's wife.'

'You're not the sort to end up with that sort of wife.'

'You're right. I'm not. First and foremost, I would prefer a companion, someone who would listen to my bleating.'

'You don't bleat. I've never heard you bleat.'

'You haven't?'

He sounded genuinely surprised. Only after a few minutes did she realise that he was joking.

'You don't mean it.'

'No. I was just pulling your leg.'

He saw her wince. Seeming to come to an instant decision he stopped in his tracks, took hold of her shoulders and turned her to face him.

'That was crass of me. It's because my mind was elsewhere. I was thinking of you as a vicar's wife... My wife.'

'Not too carefully by the sound of it.' She took a big intake of breath. She wasn't letting him off the hook that easily.

'On the contrary, I've been thinking very carefully. Not quite sure of you running the jumble sale, but everything else...'

She'd thought of it as a joke but now saw his expression and knew he was deadly serious.

'Gregory... I'm a doctor. I love what I do.'

'I'm a vicar. So do I.'

Her thoughts whirled around her mind like painted horses on a spinning carousel.

'You mean it.' There was disbelief but something else too.

'Of course I mean it. I think we would make a good pair. For better or worse.'

Memories of Ralph had weighed heavily on her mind in those years when she hadn't known where he'd fallen, his whereabouts unknown. He didn't seem so forgotten now. The tomb at the entrance to Westminster Abbey was testimony to that. The Unknown Warrior represented all those like Ralph, missing in action. So too did the memorial at Norton Dene. He was there and she was grateful to Gregory for making it happen. A resting place, his name never forgotten and somewhere to grieve.

'I will think about your proposal. But please give me time.'

'Can I give you a hug in the meantime?'

'I think so.'

People walking along the pavement parted around them as they hugged, looking into each other's eyes with childish fascination.

A costermonger wheeled his cart around them and in no uncertain terms suggested they get out of the way.

'All that canoodling don't last forever, you know,' said the brusque man in a strong Cockney accent. The wheels rattled over the cobbles. A black and white terrier followed on behind.

Frances laughed and leaned in closer to Gregory. 'I was hoping it would.'

Gregory winked. 'So was I.'

36

Brian Faulkland couldn't help being what he was. The pretty child with platinum curls had become a handsome man. Being admired and desired, he considered his by right.

Every woman was fair game, so when he snapped his fingers, he expected them to come running.

He'd told himself that he'd lost interest in Lucy Daniels, but that didn't mean he wasn't in need of her admiration. If he should show interest, he expected her to come running and persuaded himself that she wouldn't resist.

Sometime soon he would put his beliefs to the test but for now he had another distraction with whom to dally away his leisure time.

The long grass along the boundary wall of the churchyard was ideal for seduction and Marian Murray, a maid at Orchard Manor was ripe for it.

Stiff nipples rose beneath his fingers from soft white breasts. He'd had no trouble getting them out and Marian was mewing like a pussy cat.

Tonight's the night, he thought, but when his hand wandered too far above her knee, she stopped him.

'Oh no, Brian Faulkland. You ain't getting me up the spout like you've done others.'

'Who told you that?' he asked, feigning shocked disbelief. 'It ain't true. It ain't bloody true.'

'You're lying. Everyone knows.'

'Who's everyone?'

'Me for a start.'

He'd hoped sounding mortified would have opened the door, so to speak, but Marian was having none of the hand that returned to her knee and fingered its way above her garter. She pushed it away.

Angered by the rebuff he pushed her away quite violently so her head slammed back onto the hard ground. 'You ain't the only fish in the sea.'

'Oh yeah? And who else you got on the hook?'

He grinned and said the first name that came into his head. 'Lucy Daniels for a start.'

To his surprise, Marian burst out laughing. 'You ain't got no chance. Not now she's companion to her ladyship's son.'

Brian frowned. 'Companion? What's that supposed to mean?'

Marian grinned whilst chewing on a piece of grass at the corner of her mouth. 'Could mean anything, couldn't it. Just because he can't see don't mean to say that the important bits don't work.'

Rolling away from Marian, he thought about how he could bring that stuck-up Lucy Daniels down a peg.

It didn't take much effort to find out the days when Lucy was at Orchard Manor and he guessed she rode her bicycle there. He could even guess the route she took.

Well I'll teach her, he thought to himself, *and then some!*

He rethought his strategy when he heard that on rainy days her ladyship's car came to pick her up. Either way he would plan accordingly and it wasn't long before his planning paid off.

His chance came when he saw the shiny black Bentley turn into Thatcher's garage with a flat tyre and heard the ensuing conversation between Lucy and the chauffeur. Despite the rain she had no alternative but to walk.

The road to Orchard Manor wound between streets of terraced houses before it became bordered by fields. The short cut across the fields would lessen the time it took to get there and with a bit of luck she wouldn't get as wet as she might by walking the long way round.

Lucy was unaware she was being followed until she got to the stile and the path across the field leading to the back of Orchard Manor. Back in the streets she'd heard footsteps. Once she'd crossed the stile and followed the footpath there was no sound of footfall, only a feeling that she couldn't overcome.

It could be just a farm labourer, she told herself whilst quickening her steps. He would branch off at the farm and then she'd be alone again.

Her heart fell to her feet when he called out to her.

'Hey, Lucy. Don't you want to know me any more? Got a new boyfriend?'

'None of your business if I did,' she shouted back quickening her steps.

'But you and me was made for each other. I still think that.'

'Well I don't. We had our moment and it's gone,' she called back.

Despite her air of defiance, she couldn't help being scared. The far end of the field seemed so distant, but she had to get there, climb over the gate and reach safety in the grounds of Orchard Manor.

Cow parsley grew over three feet high amongst cornflowers, ox

ye daisies and scarlet poppies. Wild honeysuckle tangled its way
p and around the bushes and trees, profusely colonised by bees
nd butterflies. A rustling sounded from somewhere deep in the
edgerow, possibly a fox, an adder, or a neighbourhood cat. She
oped not a rat.

'I hear that her ladyship's son is an invalid, but that don't mean
hat some bits aren't in good working order. Is that it, Lucy? Has 'e
ot something good that ain't injured?'

Sensing he was gaining on her she began to run. The hard-
acked mud and stone beneath her feet was beginning to become
lick with a film of wetness. Speeding her steps put strain on her
nkles as she negotiated the uneven ground. Her shoes were not
1ade for running and if she tried to go much faster, she would fall
at on her face.

The far end of the path and the field it wound through was
etting closer. Brian's footsteps were thudding along behind her
nd he was getting closer.

'Come yur, you silly bitch!'

A set of strong fingers grabbed her shoulder and pulled her
ackward.

With one last surge of strength, she lunged forward. In doing
o she felt the shoulder seam of her uniform rip. Her legs buckled
eneath her and she fell flat on her face.

'Now let's see...'

His shadow fell over her, but his body that she'd expect to pin
er to the earth did not.

'Take that you, dirty little whippersnapper!'

She heard a clunk of something heavy contact with something
ofter.

Brian fell sideways and shouted every expletive he could think
f when he saw who had landed a thick stick on the side of his
ead.

'Now you better get going, our Lucy, before the rain turns t[...] downpour.'

Ma Skittings still held the broken bough of a tree in one han[...] Over her arm, she carried a garden trug that had seen better da[...] which was full of herbs, plants and flowers. She'd been [...] collecting ingredients for her medicines.

Brian Faulkland was still threatening her with all manner [...] violence. Ma ignored him, but when he got too loud threaten[...] him with another smote of her stick.

'Be off with you, Brian, before I tell yur mother that she spe[...] too much time 'erself in a farmer's field with every bloke in town.

Blood trickled between Brian's fingers from the injury at t[...] side of his head.

'Bloody old witch,' he muttered.

Ma Skittings raised her stick. 'Be off with you before I give y[...] another good bash!'

Brian didn't wait but sloped off, still holding the side of [...] head and throwing a few dark looks before accepting that disc[...] tion was the best part of valour.

Ma helped her to her feet. 'Anything broken?'

Lucy bent down to check her ankle. 'I think my ankle is a [...] sprained but not badly. And my shoes came off. I've snagged bo[...] feet and stockings on the stones here. But I will soldier on.'

Her resolute attitude came as a surprise to herself. Dev[...] needed her. He'd got used to her coming there. It might only be [...] a couple of hours, but he was most definitely coming out of [...] shell.

'I'll walk you down to the gate,' offered Mrs Skittings.

'I'll be all right, Ma.'

'I'm still coming with you to the gate.'

This time Lucy didn't argue.

Devlin was out on the terrace looking towards the trees from where Lucy emerged, dishevelled and limping.

Acute hearing compensating for his lack of eyesight he heard footsteps softly crossing the wet grass and he knew it was her. Lucy had arrived, though later than usual. But at least she was here.

'Lucy?'

'Yes. I'm here.'

He fancied her voice trembled. 'What's happened?'

'The car had a puncture. I had to walk.'

'Is it dark yet?'

'No.'

'Are you all right?'

'I've sprained my ankle and my feet are cut.' She looked down at the ragged feet of her stockings and wiggled her toes. She purposely didn't mention Brian Faulkland. He'd got all that was coming to him and if he ever tried anything again, he would have Ma Skittings to deal with.

'Come inside. Sit down. I'll ring for a bowl of hot water and some towels.'

It was Marian Murray who brought in all that he'd asked for.

'That will be all, Marian.'

The door closed behind her hard eyes and scowling expression.

'How did you know it was Marian?'

He grinned. 'She smells of coal tar soap. Haven't you noticed?'

She laughed. 'Now you come to mention it.'

'On the rare occasions I've been in the vicinity of Simon Grainger I've noticed he smells of it too.' He laughed. 'I dare say there's a few more who don't exactly use it but have a close association with Marian.'

'She spreads her favours quite widely so I hear,' said Lucy and couldn't help smile.

Devlin was being purposeful. 'Right. Let's get to work. First, off with your shoes.'

'They are off. My feet are killing me.'

'I'm not surprised. I recall that the paths around the fields are stony. Now take off your stockings – or would you like me to do it?'

She was about to ask him to look away, but of course there was no need.

With slow deliberation, she took off her garters and rolled each stocking down her legs and off the ends of her feet.

His hands were soft and gentle. She became aware of the sudden racing of her blood and the pinkness in her cheeks. It was the most erotic sensation she'd ever had in her life.

'There. All done.' She tossed the stockings to one side and placed her feet in the water, which felt quite wonderful.

'That feels good?'

'It couldn't feel anything else. It's very kind of you.'

'I'm repaying like with like.'

'Might I remind you that I'm being paid for my services.'

'I would like to think that you would still come here even if you weren't being paid. Are your knees grazed too?'

She lifted the hem of her skirt to take a closer look.

'Yes. They are.'

'Hold still. I have a flannel here and the water is still warm.'

She was about to ask him to hand her the flannel, that she could see her injuries well enough, but instead she found herself looking at the top of his head. His hair was very silky, a dark gold streaked with a lighter hue. The inclination to touch it was very strong.

Absorbed in wondering how it would be, she hardly noticed that he was bathing her knees with the warm flannel and what smelled like antiseptic.

'I'm the one who's supposed to minster to you, not the other way round.'

'We've already discussed that. Besides, your modesty is intact. My eyesight hasn't suddenly improved with my touching you. Now to dry your feet.'

He reached behind him for the towel, held it out and invited her to place her foot in it.

Would it be respectable for her to do so? She decided that it would be.

Gently, he wiped first one foot, then the other.

His face lit up. 'I'm no doctor, but I think it safe to say that I've done quite well. How do they feel?'

'Better.'

She got up, took the towel, flannel and bowl and set it on the washstand.

When she turned round, he was right behind her.

'Can I tell you about India? About the dancers, the snake charmers, the colours and the smell of rich spices and flowery perfumes.'

She smiled. 'You just have.'

'So I have. They danced barefoot, you know, and wore bells around their ankles. I found it terribly exotic. I fell in love with it. I also fell in love with a girl I met there. We used to dance barefoot. I've never danced like that since. I want to do it again.'

Lucy let the words hang in the air between them and something about him and coming here made her feel that this moment was meant to be.

'Would you be so kind as to pour two brandies – one for you and one for me.'

Still barefoot, she did as he asked.

'Add some rosehip.'

Again, she followed his instructions.

'It tastes lovely,' she said as she took a sip.

'A little more brandy in mine,' he said, giving her the glass. 'Whilst I arrange the music.'

She watched as he wound up the gramophone. The brandy had warmed her lips, but not so much as the sight of Devlin looking so pleased with himself.

He began to sing 'Putting On the Ritz' along with the record.

'Brushing off my top hat...'

She laughed. 'You know all the words.'

'Of course. I haven't got through all my recordings yet, but just you wait. I'm not far off reciting the whole of *The Murder of Roger Ackroyd*. I shall be glad when they make recordings of other books.'

Lucy pulled a face. 'Do you prefer me to read to you or would you prefer me to sing, though I would warn you that my voice is resonant rather than tuneful.'

He laughed as he turned to the direction of her voice. 'I'll do better than that. I'll dance with you.' He held out his arms, inviting her to come forward.

She laughed. 'As long as you promise not to step on my toes.'

'Being a gentleman in all things, I promise.'

He smelled of cologne, of clean clothes and oiled hair and she was comforted by the warmth of his body against hers. His arms held her in a gentle cocoon and she felt his breath against her hair and then his lips – gentle as thistledown.

'I so appreciate you walking all the way here.'

His whisper was as soft as his lips and his breath.

'It was my duty to get here.'

'I was hoping it might be more than that.'

He was silent for a moment. The music was quicker than their steps.

'It's been a long time since I held a woman in my arms. I never expected to do so ever again. And then you came along.' He touched her face. 'A little older from when I last saw it, yet I can still see that little girl who held her head higher than any of the children she was with.'

The record finished. With the care of a man who feels his way rather than sees it, he took the record off the gramophone and replaced it with something exotic, a tune she did not recognise.

'The car's not back yet. Let's go out onto the terrace – onto the lawn even.'

'It's getting dark and it's been raining.'

'I won't notice the gathering twilight and I don't mind wet grass. Tell you what, take my shoes off. I wouldn't want to step on your toes.'

His socks were of silk, his shoes of fine leather. His feet were warm. She fancied he held his breath as she carried out this simple task.

Once he too was barefoot, he slid his hand into hers and such was the moment that she cast aside any fears she had for his safety.

In his sightless world, there was no difference between night a day. But smell, touch and taste were enhanced.

Air spiced with early evening and dampness came through t opened door. A narrow path divided the house from the lawn. sliver of moonlight became an orb, appearing like a shiny f from behind a straggle of cloud.

Still holding her hand, he led her out onto the lawn. Her t met the damp grass and caused a sharp intake of breath.

He took hold of her hands and prepared to dance as thou they were in a sumptuous ballroom lit with a hundred chandelie not a wet lawn lit only by the moon.

The record he'd put on finished. He began to hum a roman ballad she thought was far older than they were. 'Wild Mount Thyme'.

Once she had the tune, she joined him and when that song finished, they began another, the moon coming out and shini down on them and Lucy feeling happier than she'd ever felt in I life.

Wrapped up in their closeness, the dancing and the mus they had no idea they were being observed and, for that matt even if they had known, would not have cared.

* * *

Devlin's mother, Lady Araminta Compton-Dixon, watched fro her bedroom window. She'd heard the gramophone, followed the soft patter of feet crossing the terrace.

Hope surged in her ageing breast as she watched the two you people emerge from the artificially lit house and out into t encroaching twilight. Her heart skipped more than one beat they began dancing on the lawn, both barefoot and their singi interspersed with bouts of laughter.

Tears stung her eyes. Devlin had been a long time adjusting to the circumstances wrought by his war injuries. At times during these past years, she'd feared he might do something stupid. By his own admission, his life was empty. Now, Devlin had found a friend, perhaps more than that. The first hurdle had been overcome. Devlin had taken his first step to rejoining the world.

38

The prospect of finding something in Izzy's box of tricks that would prevent Beatrice from taking her car was becoming slimmer.

So far Frances had only got round to emptying one of them and the contents had not yielded anything useful – not as far as holding on to Matron Molly was concerned.

The contents lay piled beside the box and mostly consisted of letters to and from politicians plus many, many more from her to and from her friends.

Some of the letters to politicians were from way back when the struggle for suffrage was a fledgeling movement. Others were from later years when the movement had begun to worry government and cause men to suggest that the world would collapse once the women had their say in how the country should be governed.

There were papers and documents, books and booklets plus hundreds of leaflets from before the war advertising suffragette meetings and rallies designed to upset race meetings, gentlemen's clubs and parliament itself.

The one document that would have proved conclusively that

the car had been a present was in the form of a will or letter of intent. There was nothing in the first box.

The diary in which Izzy had recorded her life right from when she'd been a baby was on top the second box.

Tired of searching for what didn't seem to be there, she took it out, sat in a chair and ran her eyes over words that she expected to record everything that had happened from when Izzy first took her home.

The details were very much as she'd expected; general progress, pretty dresses bought, teething problems, feeding problems and how she could no longer imagine her life without her adopted daughter being in it.

That sentiment plus others further on caused tears to gather at the corners of Frances's eyes. A little respite from reading was in order. During that time she attacked the other tea chest, pulling out bits of silk, a baby's rattle, a rag doll that Frances could not remember owning.

A folder that looked to be made from Spanish leather lay at the bottom of the chest, the very last item to be retrieved.

The contents were not as she'd expected. Her jaw dropped, her heart skipped a beat as she fondled a small bootee, one of a pair threaded through with pink ribbons. A tiny flannelette nightgown, a bonnet so small she could only just about fit her closed fist inside it. Only a newborn infant could possibly wear these items. Her obvious conclusion was that it must have been hers when she'd first been taken from the workhouse.

Tears welled up in her eyes. She found herself imagining herself as an infant wearing these clothes. So small. So helpless cuddled in Izzy's arms.

After blowing her nose and dabbing her eyes she lay all of it to one side, patting it almost reverently as she considered how things must have been.

Izzy had always said that she'd wanted a baby but didn't want a man – husband or otherwise hence she had adopted.

'And before you ask about your natural mother they never gave me that information. Let's presume she was a gentlewoman fallen on hard times.'

Izzy's tone had made it obvious that the conversation was finished. Any more questions would not get answered.

From early on Frances had understood that Izzy had no wish to be reminded of the time she'd picked Frances up like a parcel from the workhouse. It was enough that she was safe, sound and loved.

Sitting back on her haunches she contemplated the leather folder but the baby clothes drew her like a magnet. Happiness had come with the intervention of Isabelle Brakespeare in her life but just occasionally she wondered about the real mother who had abandoned her. Izzy had always said the mother had run away after giving birth. That was the hard part and loving as Izzy was she didn't appreciate just how abandoned Frances had felt. Her mother hadn't wanted her. It was the saddest thing.

Controlling the mix of emotions that whirled inside she turned her attention back to the folder.

The leather was smooth beneath her touch and the clasp looked as though it hadn't been touched for years. Suddenly she became overcome by apprehension though why she didn't know. It was just a feeling perhaps brought on from discovering the baby clothes. She paused and asked herself if she really wanted to go ahead. There was no knowing that she might be opening Pandora's box and she might not want what came flying out.

'Here goes,' she said as a keen sense of resolve got the better of her.

Papers. That was her first impression. Not lots of paper just a few sheets.

There was a heading on the top sheet. *All Saints Workhouse, Whitechapel.*

Her breath caught in her throat. Even before casting her eyes down the ill-formed handwriting she knew what it would say. One baby girl of course. It was more heart-rending to see the sum of money in payment. Five guineas.

Frances sat stunned. Was that all a baby was worth? Was that all she had been worth, just five guineas?

The tightness in her chest did not dissipate until she had read it three more times. Only then could she take it in.

With an air of resignation she set the receipt aside – for receipt was what it was. A receipt for a life.

The rest of the papers seemed like a mountain too big to climb and anyway the most important item was the receipt that had bound her to Izzy. The rest of the papers could be put away for now. She feathered through them disconsolately, her attention constantly drawn by the receipt. Almost by accident she came across a birth certificate. Exactly as she'd expected the space for the name of the father was empty. But her mother. Her natural mother.

Izzy had told her that her mother had been just a poor girl who'd been done wrong. Yet here, in the space for mother was a name she knew very well, one that caused a series of sobs that took her breath away.

Mother. Isabelle Frances Brakespeare.

The year in which she'd been born was noted as 1899 when she'd always thought it to be 1900. Not that it mattered. Izzy had been well respected. Being from a wealthy land-owning family she'd also had power and influence, a life she'd shunned in favour of broadening her mind and treading her own path. Izzy had taken immense satisfaction in launching her adopted daughter into the world, a world where women could be whatever they wanted to be.

To that end she had orchestrated her birth certificate to give her respectability, something necessary if a woman was to progress and reach the heights of her chosen profession. For that and for anything else she loved her dearly.

Her duties at the hospital meant there was no time for dwelling on what she'd discovered. By lunchtime she was exhausted, more so with paperwork than patients.

At lunchtime, in the second post a letter arrived which raised her spirits considerably although at first on seeing the typed envelope she'd jumped to the conclusion – wrong as it turned out – that the solicitors were giving her leeway, or shorter notice, to hand over her beloved car.

She gasped and covered her mouth with her hand when she began reading.

Yes, it was from a solicitor, but a firm of female solicitors, two to be exact.

Dear Doctor Brakespeare,

May we introduce ourselves? We are Miss Charlotte and Miss Caroline Ebony, solicitors. Prior to her death we authenticated and witnessed a will written by your benefactor, Miss Isabelle Frances Brakespeare. In that will you are formally named as Miss Brakespeare's heir and therefore all monies held by the National Lancashire Bank will pass to you.

Miss Deborah Goldsmith, who we have known for many years, informed us that there has been some misunderstanding regarding the car Miss Brakespeare gave you as a present and was paid for from her private funds. This too is clearly outlined in the will. Following information received from Miss Goldsmith we have written to the Brakespeare family and informed them they have no right of lien over the motor car. As yet we have received no response from the other party's solicitors but have no doubt they will henceforth withdraw their claim.

Please feel free to contact us for further clarification should you so wish at 16, Balmoral Chambers, Windsor, Berkshire.

First the receipt from the workhouse and then this from a firm of solicitors nobody knew Izzy had. If she'd ever doubted Izzy's sincerity in rescuing her from the workhouse it had vanished completely.

Matron Molly was officially hers.

The moment she got home she fetched Gregory from the vicarage, told him what had transpired and asked him to help her open the big double doors whilst she drove the car out into the sunshine.

'I know she's a bit of a tartar,' she said happily landing an affectionate pat on the car's roof. 'But we're used to each other.'

Creases of amusement appeared at the corners of his eyes.

'All's well that ends well.'

'It does indeed.'

She knew even before he did it that Gregory would bring round a bottle of wine that evening.

'Time to celebrate,' he said both hands fighting to open the bottle. 'If I can get this cork out.'

'You know,' she said as they sat in the long grass at the back of the coach house. 'Izzy's generosity surprises me.'

'She loved you as though you were a daughter.'

Frances agreed with him before mentioning that she'd found the receipt from the workhouse.

'She paid five guineas.'

'Cheap at half the price,' he said laughingly.

'What do you mean by that?' Frances was laughing too.

'She got a lot for her money. A very nice person, though of course I could be biased.'

'Good. I want you to be biased. It makes staying in Norton Dene worthwhile. Although now I've come into money I could go back to London.'

Gregory leaned over her. 'You belong here in Norton Dene. We both do.'

She smiled up at him. 'Of course I do.'

So long as things go smoothly, she thought. *So long as the sun's shining, the sky's blue and I achieve what I want as well as what Izzy wanted.*

NOTES

There is no town in Somerset named Norton Dene (as far as I am aware), but there is a Midsomer Norton, Norton St Philip, Radstock and Camerton.

Frome is the most famous for quarrying the Mendip Hills. Coal mines in Midsomer Norton, Radstock, Camerton and Kilmersdon were the last ones in the Welsh coal seam.

Cottage hospitals dated way back to the old monkish church hospitals prior to the Restoration. What is now the George Inn at Norton St Philip would have been one of these. It was also the oldest brewery in the country. Such establishments were destroyed along with their monasteries on the orders of King Henry the Eighth.

Cottage hospitals catered for the local area, doctors sending their patients there for treatment unless more intensive care was needed, in which case, in Somerset at least, they were packed off to the larger infirmaries/hospitals, such as the King Edward the Seventh in Bristol.

As regards doctors working in battle zones, the Great War rumbled on from 1914–18 and due to many doctors losing their lives, there was no option but to employ female doctors, though these were few.

It should be noted, however, that female doctors were admitted into medical colleges way back in the middle of the nineteenth century. This included the first Indian female doctors who were needed in some parts of India where purdah prevented men from examining women.

Last but hardly least, the procedure for selecting the remains to be interred in the Tomb of the Unknown Warrior in Westminster Abbey was as described, the idea being that this soldier would represent those unidentified and a focal point for the widows mothers and orphans to grieve for those they'd lost.

ABOUT THE AUTHOR

Lizzie Lane is the author of over 50 books, a number of which have been bestsellers. She was born and bred in Bristol where many of her family worked in the cigarette and cigar factories. This has inspired her new saga series for Boldwood *The Tobacco Girls*.

Sign up to Lizzie Lane's mailing list here for news, competitions and updates on future books.

Follow Lizzie on social media:

 facebook.com/jean.goodhind

 x.com/baywriterallatı

 instagram.com/baywriterallatsea

BB bookbub.com/authors/lizzie-lane

ALSO BY LIZZIE LANE

The Tobacco Girls

The Tobacco Girls

Dark Days for the Tobacco Girls

Fire and Fury for the Tobacco Girls

Heaven and Hell for the Tobacco Girls

Marriage and Mayhem for the Tobacco Girls

A Fond Farewell for the Tobacco Girls

Coronation Close

New Neighbours for Coronation Close

Shameful Secrets on Coronation Close

Dark Shadows Over Coronation Close

The Strong Trilogy

The Sugar Merchant's Wife

Secrets of the Past

Daughter of Destiny

The Sweet Sisters Trilogy

Wartime Sweethearts

War Baby

Home Sweet Home

Wives and Lovers

Sixpence Stories

Introducing Sixpence Stories!

Discover page-turning historical novels from your favourite authors, meet new friends and be transported back in time.

Join our book club Facebook group

https://bit.ly/SixpenceGroup

Sign up to our newsletter

https://bit.ly/SixpenceNews

Boldwood

Boldwood Books is an award-winning fiction publishing company seeking out the best stories from around the world.

Find out more at www.boldwoodbooks.com

Join our reader community for brilliant books, competitions and offers!

Follow us
@BoldwoodBooks
@TheBoldBookClub

Sign up to our weekly deals newsletter

https://bit.ly/BoldwoodBNewsletter

Printed in Great Britain
by Amazon